SUBJECT
TO CHANGE

SUBJECT TO CHANGE

Karen Nesbitt

ORCA BOOK PUBLISHERS

Library and Archives Canada Cataloguing in Publication

Nesbitt, Karen, 1962–, author
Subject to change / Karen Nesbitt.

Issued in print and electronic formats.
ISBN 978-1-4598-1146-1 (paperback).—ISBN 978-1-4598-1147-8 (pdf).—
ISBN 978-1-4598-1148-5 (epub)

I. Title.
PS8627.E765S83 2017   c813'.6   c2016-904483-1
c2016-904484-x

First published in the United States, 2017
Library of Congress Control Number: 2016949051

Summary: In this novel for teens, fifteen-year-old Declan struggles to make
sense of his older brother's delinquency, his father's sexuality and his feelings
for a girl who is way out of his league.

*Orca Book Publishers is dedicated to preserving the environment and has
printed this book on Forest Stewardship Council® certified paper.*

Orca Book Publishers gratefully acknowledges the support for its publishing
programs provided by the following agencies: the Government of Canada through
the Canada Book Fund and the Canada Council for the Arts, and the Province of British
Columbia through the BC Arts Council and the Book Publishing Tax Credit.

Cover image by Getty Images
Author photo by Janice Wilson

ORCA BOOK PUBLISHERS
www.orcabook.com

Printed and bound in Canada.

20 19 18 17 • 4 3 2 1

In memory of Dad and Fabien, who were loving men of quiet fortitude. And for boys who can't ask for help.

ONE

I'm standing outside the rink on a smoke break. An old blue Ford Taurus with mags and no muffler pulls up beside me. I'm wondering what kind of loser thinks that's cool when I realize my brother's sitting in the passenger seat. He cranks the window down.

"Hey, dickhead!" he yells.

I shake my head and butt out my cigarette in the can attached to the side of the building. In two steps I can easily cross the sidewalk to the car, but I take my time. The gravel I just spread on the ice crackles under my boots. The sky is gray, like we're going to get wet snow.

I lean close to Seamus because I can't hear over the motor, but I don't say anything. He's being a jerk. The usual.

"Hey, asshole, you got any cash?"

"Nope." *Not for you.* There's such a cocky look on his face. I recognize the driver of the piece-of-crap car. He goes to my school and isn't old enough to have a license.

Seamus probably told him it would be easy to get me to hand the money over.

Seamus elbows his friend, who's grinning like an eager puppy with its tongue hanging out. "Aw, c'mon! Me 'n' Rob, we were hopin' to score some E, and maybe some chicks!" He elbows him again. "It's Sa'rday night, right, bro?"

My brother and his juvenile-delinquent friend chair dance in the car like they're going to party right here in front of me. Seamus laughs way too loud. I'm embarrassed by them, but I can't help watching. They're such freaks. He pulls a big Evian bottle out of his coat, takes a swig and passes it to Rob. They're drinking something murky and brown.

"Get lost, Seamus." I shove my hands into my jacket pockets and turn my back on them.

"Huh? What did ya say, dickhead? C'mere." His favorite nickname for me is dickhead. He thinks it sounds like Declan.

"Get lost. I gotta go back to work."

"Oooh, didya hear that, Robbie? He tol' me t'get lost!" I look back, slowly, cool. Robbie has an idiotic smile pasted on his face. None of this is sinking into his tiny brain.

"Go home, Seamus. You're hammered." I start back toward the rink.

"You're fuckin' gay, dickhead!"

I spin around with my fist ready to pound the car, but Robbie guns it, and I just catch the back fender as one white-wall sprays me with a grimy mixture of slush, sand and salt.

Fuckin' asshole brother and his puke-faced friends.

Inside, I clean myself off with paper towel before I take down the *Back in 10 Minutes* sign and open the canteen window. I'm just in time for the rush on slushies after a hockey practice. Seven-year-old boys and their parents line up for crushed ice, sugar and enough food coloring to turn their teeth bright blue.

When the rush is over I wonder if I should call 9-1-1. Rat Seamus and Robbie out to the cops.

Then I decide not to.

Why?

I grab a cloth and start to Windex the fridge doors.

Why not call the cops?

Because he's my brother.

Yeah right. He hasn't been a brother for years.

Because they'll put him in jail.

So? It'd be a night of guaranteed peace for the whole neighborhood. He barely sleeps at home these days anyway. Who'd miss him?

It'll upset Mom.

Well, someone has to do something. One of these days he's going to kill himself or someone else. Then what?

Because he'll kill me.

Really?

I'm used to him being bigger and older and meaner than me. But I'm probably taller than him now. I was six foot two when the phys ed teacher measured us in the fall for some national fitness torture program. But I have to be honest. At 145 pounds I make a garden rake look hefty.

Whack!

Stunned, I turn around to see what hit me in the left shoulder. There's a yellow ball, one of those foam things you get at the dollar store, rolling away from my feet. I look across the room at a kid, frozen, with a hockey stick in one hand.

"Hey! The sign says *Absolutely no playing hockey!* Do it again, you're out!" I glare at him for effect. "Get it?" I squeeze the ball in my fist and stick it in my pocket.

He nods and walks over to his dad, puts the stick down on his bag and starts to drink his chocolate milk. He peers at me over the plastic container, and I give him the evil eye again just for good measure.

I actually like kids. You kind of have to if you're going to survive working at the rink. But you have to get tough with little boys right away or they won't respect you. Pretty soon they'll be having food fights in the canteen. Then the parents will take them home, and I'll get stuck cleaning up the mess.

Running the canteen is a pretty good gig. Easy. I get to do my own thing. And I get tips, especially from the moms. When it's not busy, I shoot the shit with Phil, the Zamboni guy.

Things quiet down. Just before the boy with the chocolate milk and his dad leave, I chuck the kid his ball, and I'm by myself again. The only sounds for now are the blast of the coach's whistle from inside the rink and the hum of the big fridge. In fifteen minutes, Phil will get the Zamboni out and do rink two. Just before the next rush.

I finish cleaning the fridge doors. Phil walks into the canteen and motions for me to come outside for a smoke.

I grab a shovel at the door to push away the slush while I'm out there. I hate the in-between weather. Not spring. Not winter. Just god-awful slippery, filthy mess everywhere.

Phil's holding his smoke pack open for me to take one as I walk toward him. I fish my lighter out of the pocket of my big winter jacket and light both our smokes. It takes a few tries because the wind is picking up. There'll probably be a blizzard tonight.

The idea of Seamus and Robbie the Moron driving around drunk in a blizzard bothers me. I don't like Seamus much, but I still don't want him to kill himself. It would destroy Mom. So many kids get in car accidents on the narrow country roads out here. Seems like every year there's a funeral, and there are flowers tied to trees and lampposts all over the place. Last June a kid trying to pass slammed head on into a gravel truck from the quarry. The truck swerved and ended up on its side, dumping sand all over the ditch, and the kid lost his arm because he had it out the window. Freaked everyone out. Must've hurt like hell.

Aw, why do I keep thinking about my asshole brother?

Phil taps his watch, stamps his cigarette out on the ground and kicks the butt onto the street. "Later." He's going in to do the rink.

I pick up the shovel and clear the crap away from in front of the automatic door. Two more cycles like this—break, canteen rush, clean up, Zamboni—and I'll be on my way home.

If Seamus is partying, at least he won't show up there.

TWO

Snow is starting to swirl around me on the road. I put my hood up, switch my cigarette to my other hand, and jam the other one in my jacket pocket.

The sun is almost gone, but I can still see the colors of the houses as I walk along the road home. It's quiet. It's been ten minutes since I left the rink and the thriving metropolis of downtown Rigaud. I haven't seen one car or person. Just me and the road, the trees and the snow.

I don't mind the cold, and walking gives me a chance to come down. After school or a shift at the rink, I like having the time to think. Over the last two years, I've done some of my best thinking on the 138. For instance, it's where I came up with my plan to make money by shoveling walks in town, so I could buy an Xbox. I ended up with about seven clients right in Rigaud, doing their front walks and driveways. It was all I needed. By the end of the season I'd saved enough to buy a console and a couple of games to go with it.

Walking past the rink every day on the way home from school gave me the idea to get a job there. My brother-in-law, Ryan, is a security guard at a medical center in the next town—one of those places with a clinic and X-rays and stuff all in one building. It turns out he knows the guy who runs the Rigaud Arena, and both buildings are managed by the same company. When I told him I was thinking about applying for a job there, he talked to his friend. The guy likes Ryan so much, he hired me as soon as I turned fifteen.

If it was up to me, I'd ditch school and work all the time. I hate school. The rink is my place. I do my job, I get along with everybody, I love being in charge of the canteen. No one gives me a hard time there.

At least, not until now.

Why'd my stupid brother and his moronic friend have to show up? Where does he get off bothering me at work? The only time he talks to me anymore is to ask for money. What if Mr. Bergevin had been there? No boss would want them hanging around. I don't need Seamus causing trouble for me. I wish he'd just piss off.

My parents' divorce didn't turn me and my sister, Kate, into lunatics like Seamus. When he's out, Mom is usually upset because he's supposed to be at home. And when he is home, he makes everyone so miserable we all want him to leave. Where does he go when he's not driving around and getting in my face? Actually, I'd prefer not to know. Two summers ago, he and his band of merry losers burned down a neighbor's shed. The cops couldn't prove it, but everyone knew it was them. Seamus and his friends were having a party in our backyard. The neighbors complained and the cops showed up, shut it down. Three days later, the shed was incinerated. Since then we don't get along with the neighbors too well.

Stop thinking about Seamus!

I smell fireplace smoke through the trees. It makes me want to be home. I wish we had a fireplace. That would be special. I can imagine sitting in front of a fireplace, listening to music or just being quiet or hanging with my friends. I've seen mobile homes with fireplaces and woodburning stoves before. Maybe me and Ryan could put one in someday. That would be cool. Aw, but Seamus would probably burn the place down.

When I was in elementary school, kids called me and my brother trailer trash, and once a boy told my friend Dave that's why he couldn't come to my birthday party. When you're eight, that hurts. After the divorce, when I was ten, money was really tight. We never had things other kids had. The school even gave us coupons for some special program for families who can't send their kids to school with a lunch. The only other kid I knew on the program smelled funny. I hid my coupons and got used to being hungry.

In those days, I was glad our trailer was way back in the trees so no one could see it when we got off the school bus. Now I like it. It feels like we're in the country.

I switch my cigarette to my other hand and check my watch. Mom will still be out with Kate. They took my niece,

Mandy, shopping today, and then they're going for pizza. I should get a couple of hours alone to chill at home, put on my music, play on my Xbox. Hey, I'll finally get to read the comic Dave lent me. I even made myself a burger on the grill before I left the canteen. It's in my pocket, wrapped in foil, keeping my fingers warm.

In between gusts of wind it's so quiet I can actually hear snowflakes landing on my jacket. Through the blowing snow, I can just make out my driveway, across the 138 from the big green sign that says the highway to Montreal is up ahead. I'm almost home. We're less than an hour from Montreal, but it's like the middle of nowhere. I bet there are a lot of people in Rigaud who've never even been to the city. I've only been a few times, for school field trips, concerts. When I was a little kid, Mom and Dad took us to the Santa Claus parade. Apparently I cried when I saw some A&W bear mascot. It's a family story that everybody still laughs at.

There's a little pile of cigarette butts at the end of our driveway. They're all mine. I don't like to throw them on our property, so I leave them on the road. As soon as I turn up the driveway, I see fresh tire tracks in the snow—a dark-colored car is parked about halfway between the highway and the yard. Wanna bet it has mags and whitewalls? What's he doing here? I was counting on him not showing up. He usually steers clear of home when he's partying with his stupid friends. And why'd they park so far from the house? Were they trying to sneak in?

About an inch of snow has settled on the car. As I pass by, I clear off a circle on the window and try to see inside. The bottle they were drinking from is empty on the passenger seat. McDonald's wrappers and smoke butts and a blue box that says *POP POP* are trampled into the floor mats. The steering wheel is wrapped in a fuzzy thing that looks like the Kleenex-box covers old ladies sell at the church craft fair. The driver's window is down a crack, and I smell stale cigarettes and nasty aftershave leaking out. I bet Robbie has a water bed. He's the cheesy water-bed type.

I continue up the driveway, wondering what I'm going to find when I get to the trailer. It's long and low and gleams white in the dusk. Everything's normal outside. Same old broken chair beside the front door. Same old pile of bald tires and cracked toilet on the lawn, starting to peek through the snow that's melting around them.

The door's open. There are two sets of snowy shoes in the mudroom at the entrance to the trailer. I hear voices for a second, but they stop when I open the inside door. Like when we were little kids, afraid of getting caught doing something we weren't supposed to. It makes me wonder what they've been up to.

Seamus appears in the doorway to the kitchen, his side-kick nipping at his heels. I leave my boots in the mudroom, take my foil-wrapped burger out of my pocket and chuck my wallet and keys on the table in the front hall. With the burger still in my hand, I wriggle out of my jacket and hang it up. There isn't room for three people in the front hall. As Seamus brushes past me on the way to his shoes, he purposely pushes me into the table. My hand with the burger in it gets squished between me and the table, which hits the wall. I grab the toppling lamp with my free hand. Mom's travel mug rolls off onto the floor, dribbling creamy coffee behind it.

I turn around. "Why'd ya do that?"

Seamus rolls his eyes.

They're close to me now, and I can smell alcohol on their breath, and that nasty cologne. Robbie the Moron waves bye and says, "*À plus!*"

Later? Really? Not if I can help it. Does he ever lose that brainless grin?

I return the greeting by raising my eyebrows. He's carrying a liter of apple juice. Seamus has the remainder of a block of cheddar cheese, which he's just taken a bite out of. There's a box of soda crackers stuffed under one arm, a bag of Oreos under the other. He's leaning on the doorjamb to balance as he tries to ram his feet into his shoes. He doesn't speak.

Seamus is eighteen, but because of his freckles and curly red hair, he still looks like a little kid. He has wide blue eyes, like our dad's. I catch a glimpse of one of them before it flits away.

I shake my head and hold my hand up in a wave. "Thanks for droppin' by."

He walks out in front of Robbie, who turns around and waves at me again before pulling the door closed. He acts like Seamus's puppy. I wonder if he pees in the backyard or still uses newspaper.

I navigate around wet snow on the carpet to lock the front door behind them and switch on the outside light. They're laughing and talking as they walk back to the piece-of-crap car. I lean against the paneled wall of the mudroom and watch them for a minute through the window

I head to the kitchen to get a Coke and a plate for my burger. I open the wrapper. The burger's not completely mangled. The top of the bun is split, and the tomatoes and pickles are all spilling out. I take the top off, rearrange the stuff and fit it back together like a puzzle. Pop the tab on my Coke.

So they came to raid the refrigerator. Is that all? I open the cupboard above the sink. Mom keeps a jar there with money in case we run out of things during the week.

It's empty.

I go to my wallet and get out a twenty. I take it back to the kitchen, put it in the jar and place the jar back on the shelf.

Finally, I get to my room and connect the iPod Kate and Ryan gave me for Christmas to my portable speaker. I pick a Metallica song, blast it and take out the comic Dave lent me. He found a used copy of the hardcover version of a classic comic from 1988, *Batman: The Killing Joke*. It's supposed to be the one Heath Ledger used to learn how, in one bad day, the Joker became crazy. Some blogs say it drove *him* crazy, trying to get into the Joker's head.

My friend Dave and I started getting obsessed with comics when we were really little. At first we watched the TMNT cartoon series on TV, and then we moved on to the comic books when we could read better. Comics got me through some rough times. One summer I had a stack of about a hundred of them beside my bed—Superman, Batman, Avengers, Titans, Ninja Turtles of course. I even had some Archies. I actually read every single one.

There's supposed to be a new TMNT movie coming out soon. We'll probably go see it for old-times' sake, take our friend Mitch along. But I almost don't want to because it'll probably suck.

It should be a crime to make something about the Ninja Turtles that sucks. We still share other comics, but nothing's ever been as great as those first TMNT comics.

I push my pillows against the wall and lean back with my burger on my chest. The Joker stares at me, propped up against my knees. After a swig of my drink and a good belch, I dig in. I can't help smiling as James Hetfield sings, *"And nothing else matters..."*

THREE

Monday morning. I get my ass into the seat just as the bell rings. Mr. Jamieson is correcting some suck-up's homework, but he takes a break to give me a dirty look, even though I'm on time. There are still kids standing around, talking, and he's giving *me* the evil eye. The girls in the corner are texting. How come they don't get the look? We're not allowed to use cell phones in class. Not that I have one.

From the seat in front of me, Mitch stretches back for a fist bump. I bump back, my eyes still on Jamieson. I'm sure he's got it in for me this morning. I can feel it. You know how you can tell when someone is watching even when they're doing something else? Well, I can tell he's doing that. I slide down in my desk so I can't see him. So he can't see me.

The class gets quiet. Jamieson's standing at the front, getting ready for what we idiots call Bobo math—the one you have to take if you failed math in ninth grade. It's also why Jamieson thinks he can treat us like we're lowlifes.

I look over at Theresa in the desk beside me. She glances at me so I can see she's sulking, which is my usual cue to ask her what's wrong. I pretend not to notice. We've gone out, off and on, since seventh grade. These days we're off. She'd be more into me if I wore vampire clothes or a studded dog collar. I'd be more into her if she didn't.

She always comes back to me when she has a problem with some other guy though. I feel like a fish on that catch-and-release TV program; I'm learning to avoid the hooks.

"Mr. O'Reilly!"

Hiding's not working so well. Jamieson always calls us Mr. or Miss when he's angry. He also likes to throw stuff. Chalk, markers—once he even threw a water bottle. Full! I straighten up.

"Please remove your winter coat and put it in your locker."

I look at him. But I don't say anything. I don't move.

"Now."

"But sir—"

"I said *now*, Mr. O'Reilly. Put your coat in your locker or leave my class and don't come back."

"Sir, I can't—"

He cuts me off again. "You can't remove your coat, or you can't find your locker?"

A few kids snicker.

"Sir, the problem is—"

He's walking toward me now. I get nervous, so I sit up straight as a board. He throws his shoulders back and starts to lift his right arm. I think he's going to chuck the chalk he's holding, so I put my left arm in front of my face. He grabs the sleeve of my jacket and starts to pull it up, like he's going to lift me from my seat. I stand up fast and knock the books off the desk behind me. My legs are all tangled under the chair.

Jamieson guides me around the desks and up the aisle to the door. I'm tripping over my own feet, and I see the faces of the kids we're passing, like their alarms just went off. The girls in the corner are texting like mad. "Don't bother with your jacket or your locker. You can go straight to see Mr. Peters. Perhaps he'll care about your problems."

I turn around to look at him when we get to the door. He's serious. I can see Mitch over his shoulder, a stupid grin on his face, waving bye-bye. Jamieson opens the door and launches me into the hall. The door bangs behind me. I wait for it: *Clack!* Chalk hits the back of the door.

I'm alone.

I stay put for a minute, trying to figure out what just happened and what to do. I decide I better go find the VP before he finds me. What I really want to do is take off, but either way I'll end up in Mr. Peters's office eventually. I keep my head down, hands in my pockets. I could sneak out for a smoke and then go see the VP. Better not. Jamieson probably already called him on the intercom to say I was on my way.

I pass a class with the door open. The lights are off and there's a French movie on. Kids are sleeping sitting up with their arms crossed, bracing themselves so they won't fall out of their chairs. The teacher is playing solitaire on her computer. Her screen glows in the dark. Why couldn't this be my class?

Two gym teachers in track jackets and shorts are talking outside the weight room. It's March—too cold for shorts. One of them used to do landscaping with my dad. His eyes meet mine as I pass, and he waves. I pull up my shoulders to hide my face in my jacket.

Finally I get to the main office. The secretary says Mr. Peters will be with me in a moment and to take a seat. Just like I thought. He's expecting me. I can see him behind his desk, talking on the phone. When he sees me, he swivels around so I can't hear what he's saying.

On the wall beside me there's a big map of the school. It says *Harwood Senior High Catchment Region* at the top and shows all the little towns around it where the kids who come here live. Harwood is right in Hudson, the town in the center. Hudson's right next to Rigaud, but they're completely different. Hudson's a posh place with mansions on the lake and people living on golf courses. Who actually lives on a golf course? The other towns near Hudson are your basic suburbs. The country kids and trailer trash like me live in Rigaud and in tiny places farther from Hudson, like Coteau-du-Lac, where my dad lives. I have a pencil stub in my pocket. When I'm sure the secretary's busy behind her big reception desk, I draw a penis on the map where my friend Dave's house is.

Just as I'm putting my pencil back in my pocket, Mr. Peters calls me into his office. I sit in one of the chairs across from him. His computer is on the side of his desk, and the screen is swiveled toward me. The screen saver flashes a picture of him standing with a bunch of suck-ups. His desk is super neat, like everything fits into an invisible grid: one square for the stapler, one for his coffee cup, one for the pile of papers, one for the metal thing that holds his phone messages, one for his cell phone. Everything's even facing the same direction. Seems kind of anal.

"Declan, Declan, Declan."

Three Declans? "Sir." I push my hair back so he can make eye contact with me. Adults like it better when you make eye contact with me. They're nicer.

"So Declan." *That's four.* "Mr. Jamieson says you refused to take off your jacket in class."

"No, sir. I just didn't..." I realize I don't know what to say. I can't tell him I don't have a locker because I lost it in a bet with a stoner. I think the guy uses it to stash stuff he's selling. "Yes, sir."

"Well, is it yes or no? I see you still have it on, so is it yes?"

"Yes, I mean, no. I still have it on, but I didn't refuse. He didn't give me a chance. He just pulled me out. I was trying to explain."

"To explain what?"

"I would have been late for class if I'd gone to my locker. So I kept it on. I figured it was more important not to be late."

"Hmmm. You shouldn't be late or have your jacket on. You're not allowed your jacket in class. I think you know that."

"Yes, sir." Maybe if I agree and look guilty enough he'll just give me a detention and get this over with.

"This is not the first time we've had this conversation about your jacket."

"Yes, sir."

"What is it about this jacket? It looks pretty expensive. Maybe you're afraid to take it off, afraid someone will steal it, eh?"

Expensive? Huh? "No, sir, I mean, I wouldn't want someone to take it, because I need it. But my mom got it for me—" I was going to say *secondhand*, but I don't want to tell him that. Mom found it for me at the church thrift shop. We get a lot of stuff there. I don't exactly go around telling people. I love my jacket because it doesn't look like it came from a church basement. It's normal. Like the other kids wear.

"In fact, how many times has that jacket gotten you a detention?"

"Um…I don't know. A couple?"

He swivels the screen away from me, turns to his keyboard and types something in. "Actually, seven. Seven for the jacket." He scrolls down, following along with his pen.

Seven? Really? I guess I lost track. I hope he doesn't go poking around to find out about my locker. If I get the guy who has it in trouble, I won't have to worry about any more detentions.

He taps the screen with his pen. "Three for smoking on school property, one for just 'being there' while your pals passed around a joint, and eleven for being late to class."

Twenty-one. Twenty-one detentions." He's boring a hole through me over his glasses.

How could there be twenty-one detentions? It's only March. There must be some mistake. My face starts getting hot—I'm sure I'm turning red. I remember a detention here or there, but mostly, nobody bothers about me at school. I like it that way. Twenty-one? I guess twenty-one detentions means people are starting to notice.

I hold my hands in my lap and tap my thumbs together. My brother skipped so much school he eventually got kicked out. Of course, Seamus may have done a few other things. Like set fires in garbage cans, snap the mini wipers off some teacher's headlights, come to school drunk...things like that.

Mr. Peters leans back in his chair with his arms crossed and stares some more at the computer, tapping the end of his pen on his teeth. *Tick, tick, tick.* He must be going over my impressive report card. I was real excited to show that one to Mom. Finally, he stops tapping and motions to me with the pen, straight out of his mouth, still looking at his screen. "I saw you last night."

I look right at him. He's totally changed the subject. Now I'm afraid he's a creepy stalker, like one of those pedophiles that prey on teenage boys. Why would he pick someone as big as me? I'm, like, a head taller than he is.

"I saw you walking on the 138, near Rigaud. On the highway in the dark." He says the last part peering at me over his glasses again, with his eyebrows up, like I'm supposed to know it means something.

"I live there."

His raised eyebrows change positions, squinch in the middle of his forehead.

I explain. "Not on the highway, in Rigaud. I was walking home from work." It's not even a highway—it's a country road. What a city boy.

"Where do you work?"

"At the rink. Old-timers play really late sometimes, to get the ice."

Why was he driving on the 138 at eleven anyway? Once, when he was supervising DT and trying to look cool by comparing biceps with one of the guys (which, come to think of it, was also kind of creepy), he told us that he works out at a gym in Montreal. I'm sure he doesn't live near me.

"Any other kind of work you're doing out there?"

"Huh?"

"There's quite a bit of alternative commerce in Rigaud these days, or so I hear." He puts the words *alternative commerce* in air quotes.

Alternative commerce? What the hell does that mean? Then I realize what he's talking about. "You mean drugs?"

"I don't know. What do you think?"

He thinks *I'm* selling drugs? I clue in and start shaking my head. I can't believe it. He's accusing me of selling drugs, hiding stuff in my jacket. "I don't know anything about that, sir. I have a job at the rink to help my mom out, and I can't always be asking for a lift, so I walk. That's why my mom got me this jacket—so I wouldn't be cold. I would never sell drugs.

She'd kill me. You can search me if you want." I start pulling the lining out of my pockets. Nothing but smokes, keys, some change and that pencil stub.

He motions for me to put my stuff back, "No, it's okay. I understand. You have to work to help out your mom. It's tough with divorced parents, isn't it? You working many hours?"

"Couple times during the week, and on the weekend. I guess about twenty hours."

"That's a lot. You're only in tenth grade."

"I can handle it. Like I said, it's so I can help out." I really don't see why we're talking about this. My family life is none of his business.

He nods, like he gets it. I can tell by his nice clothes that he doesn't. I'm sure I've never seen him wear the same shirt twice. What would he know about not having any cash? "You can't have much time for homework."

We just look at each other. I'm pretty sure we both know I don't do any. What's the point? I'm basically putting in time till I can leave this place.

"You know, if you ever need to talk, I'm here. I've told you before, high school's important. It's going to help you get a good job, leave money problems behind. Besides"—he gets all serious and looks me in the eye—"I know something about being a stressed-out kid and about having a single mom."

If he isn't a creepy pedo, he sure acts like one. Does he really think I'm going to spill my guts to him? Why doesn't he just get off my ass? I realize my eyebrows have risen to my hairline, so I straighten out my face and nod.

"So, about Mr. Jamieson and your jacket…"

Back to my jacket. He looks at me, waiting for me to add something. I take a deep breath to calm down.

"Sir, it won't happen again. What's the problem anyway? It's just a jacket."

"Declan, Declan, Declan." *Wow, three more. He really likes to say my name.* "We've already been over this. It's against school rules to keep it on in the building."

"I understand, sir. I was late. I should've taken off my jacket before I went to class. It won't happen again. I'll make sure to leave it…in my locker."

"Okay, okay. You have no books or school supplies with you?"

I decide not to pull out the pencil stub. "They're in my locker." *Yeah, sure. They're in there with my homework.*

Of course he knows I'm lying. No school supplies. No binders. The school year's half over. Twenty-one detentions. What does that say about a person?

"You have a job. Can't you get yourself some school supplies?"

"Yes, sir."

He nods a few times, puts his pen down in its square and starts to straighten things on his desk, even though everything's already perfectly in place. "Well, Declan, clearly detention isn't doing anything for you. You're late almost every day, and we can't seem to get you to take off that jacket. I see no point in assigning another one."

Yes! "Thanks, sir."

"Thanks for what? I said detentions aren't working. We need something that will."

I'm afraid to ask. "What?"

"I haven't decided. When I do, I'll let you know."

The bell rings. Classroom doors open, and the hall starts to fill with kids. Students and teachers make their way into the office. I look at Mr. Peters for permission to leave. It's recess. Time for a smoke.

As I'm pushing myself out of the chair, he says, "Hold on. You need to put away that jacket before you go to your next class."

"I know, sir. I will. It's just…"

He's waiting for me to finish.

"…I'm going out first, for a smoke. I *will* put it away though."

He shakes his head and looks at the papers on his desk. "Declan, Declan, Declan."

If I counted right, that makes eleven.

FOUR

There are kids everywhere, talking, smoking, horsing around, outside for recess because it feels like spring. It's so warm I can feel the sun on my legs through my jeans.

Mitch lights my smoke with a lighter he fishes out of his military-issue parka. He and his dad got their coats from an army surplus store. His dad's this ancient hippie. They do stuff like that.

"So what the hell happened with you and the VP?" he asks.

I shake my head. "Man, I didn't think I was ever going to get out of there!"

"I almost pissed myself when Jamieson hauled you out. You were, like, arms and legs everywhere!" Mitch imitates Jamieson dragging me out by my jacket, waving his arms and legs around. He's even doing Jamieson's squinched-up face. Pretty entertaining. Other kids are watching him and laughing too, reliving the moment.

Dave stops talking to the drama teacher and comes over to the smokers' area. He fist-bumps us both. Dave's the jock in our group. He doesn't smoke. He plays lacrosse, and he's like a friggin' acrobat. He does these random backflips all over the place, has done since we were in elementary school. I remember one summer he even went to circus camp.

We start to tell Dave about what happened in math. Dave doesn't take Bobo math. He's in the kind of math you take so you can go to college, so you can take a whole bunch more math and then go to university and take even more. He's with all the math brainiacs, but he's already heard about me and Jamieson. Mitch isn't the only one talking about how funny Mr. J looked dragging me to the door. In Dave's version of the story, I towered over Jamieson and gave him the evil eye, and, after telling him he had problems, shut the door just in time to escape being hit in the head with *Testical Math* (that's what we call our technical math text).

Way more interesting than what really happened, but I kind of hope Peters doesn't hear it.

"So didja get another DT?" Dave asks.

"No. Apparently, I've already had twenty-one. He's finding something *better*." I make air quotes with my cigarette in one hand.

"Ooh, something special just for you." Dave makes it sound creepy, like Peters is going to ask me to give him a blow job or something. Sometimes Dave has no filter.

Mitch slaps me on the back. "Twenty-one! That's probably some kind of a record. I'm proud of you, little buddy." He pretends to wipe away a tear.

"Thanks, guys. Real supportive." I decide not to tell them about Mr. Peters stalking me at night on the 138. They'll bug me about my "special relationship" with him for the rest of my life. I also don't want Mitch to know he was asking about drugs. It'll freak him out. Mitch has weed on him most of the time.

We goof around with the other smokers for a while. I spy Robbie the Moron standing with a group of hard-core stoners. He's looking at the guy who has my locker with those same clueless, puppy-dog eyes he uses with Seamus. It makes my skin crawl. I turn my back on them.

A couple of kids come over to talk to Dave, and he wanders away with them. Something about the variety show. He gets roped into things like that because of his acrobatic skills and because he's such a show-off. He's also really smart. I'm sure his IQ is higher than Mitch's and mine combined. We do what we can to keep him humble though. Like the time we ran out of the changing room with his jeans and gym shorts after gym class and put them in the lost and found. He showed up in the main office looking for them with a hoodie tied around his backside, like it was no big deal. But there's something about a guy in briefs and running shoes that you just can't forget.

If Dave is the jock with brains in our group, then Mitch is the stoner. In addition to carrying it around, he'll share with anyone, not just me and Dave. His dad grows it. Once Mitch showed us the plants in his basement, with grow lights and a watering system and everything. Cool operation. Then he swore us to secrecy. Kids hang around him because he always has weed. It's bullshit. It reminds me of a joke about the mom who ties a pork chop around her kid's neck so the dog will play with him. Mitch is just this easygoing guy people take advantage of. So Dave and I watch his back.

Dave and I have been friends since elementary school. We met Mitch last year because they made him repeat ninth grade. But it feels like the three of us have been friends forever.

A woman in a tracksuit jogs by with her dog on a leash, a little white, fluffy thing wearing a red-and-white sweater with the Montreal Canadiens logo on it. The dog poops on the school lawn, and the woman just keeps going. She doesn't even scoop it up. I want to call her on it, but it's too much hassle, and besides, I don't want to look like a Goody-Two-Shoes with everybody standing around. I watch them continue down St. Charles.

"When will you find out?" Mitch flicks ash onto the glistening pavement. The snow is melting so fast you can hear it crackling underneath the piles made by the snow plow on the front lawn.

"Good question. I guess it's going to be a surprise." I act excited, like it's a birthday present. But I do wonder what it'll be. Twenty-one detentions. I bet that's even more than Seamus had.

I elbow Mitch. "What beats twenty-one detentions?"

"I dunno. Twenty-two?"

"No, asshole. Peters says detentions aren't good enough anymore. What if he expels me?"

"Isn't it more of a punishment if he makes you stay?"

Mitch hates school even more than I do. One of the good things about living in Quebec is that high school only goes up to eleventh grade.

A fire engine screams around the corner from Main Road a block away and heads toward the school. You can feel every kid praying for it to stop here so there'll be no third period or at least an extended recess. But the school alarm isn't even ringing. As the fire truck passes us, the guys in the cab wave out the open window, and the truck continues down the road until we can't hear it anymore.

Theresa walks up to us, still sulking, still trying to get me to ask her what's wrong. Someone probably said something mean about her online. Her mascara is smudged so everybody can tell she's been crying. She's wearing a beanie, and the ends of her hair are dyed blue. Cute for a train wreck.

"Hi, Declan."

Mitch rolls his eyes. He can't stand her.

"Hi, Theresa."

She stays with us for a couple of minutes but leaves when she realizes I'm not going to take the bait. She actually flicks her cigarette butt at my feet as she's walking away.

"Oh my god, what a bitch." Mitch shakes his head.

I nod and butt out my own cigarette on the side of the *Ville de Hudson* garbage container, put there for the smokers. But I throw it on the ground. Something about fires in garbage cans. It makes me nervous.

The bell rings. Everyone who's been standing outside bottlenecks at the entrance. I see Robbie the Moron again as we're shuffling toward the door. He looks at me with that stupid grin. I turn my head away and pretend I didn't notice.

"Hey, Mitch, remind me to leave my jacket in your locker, or I'll end up back in Peters's office."

"Leave your jacket in my locker."

Idiot. I smack him in the head.

If Dave is the smart jock in our group, and Mitch is the stoner, what am I? I love comic books and screaming-guitar rock, but I'm not really known for anything. I walk so much my sister calls me *the hobo*. My mom makes the best lasagna in the world. Does that count? On the flip side, my brother is a juvenile delinquent, and my dad? I don't even want to go there.

Having twenty-one detentions is pretty special.

I guess that's me. Mr. DT.

FiVE

Miss Fraser, the guidance counselor, sticks her head out the door of her office to see if I've bolted yet. "You can come in now, Declan." For some reason, she's called me out of art class. It's one of the only two classes I like. Why couldn't she have chosen French or history?

I put down the *Smoking Kills* brochure I've been hiding behind and get up from my chair. I check to see if anybody notices I'm here. This is so *not* cool. Inside her office, the walls are covered with posters. My favorite is for the kids' help phone—the one with the telephone cord coming out of the bathroom stall like some kid's calling and taking a crap at the same time—*Please help me. It's not coming out! What do I do?*

She motions for me to sit, and I collapse into a chair with *prick* carved into the arm. Somebody's idea of badass. I slide down to try and be inconspicuous, and peer at her over my crossed legs. She swivels in her office chair to face me.

"Thanks for coming down, Declan. Do you have any idea why I called you here?"

Why is she asking me? I just look at her, trying as hard as I can to give her a blank stare. I have no clue why she called me here, so I settle on a shrug, which is pretty effective in my big jacket.

"Mr. Peters suggested this appointment. He says you may have things you need to discuss."

I roll my eyes. So this is what he decided on instead of detention. Sneaky. He thinks I have problems, so he sent me to the guidance counselor for an *intervention*, like on that TV show where they ambush people and send them to rehab. What does he know about my problems? I'd like to give him some problems!

"Well, Declan? Do you know why you're here?"

Now I'm getting angry, and I feel like yelling at her. But that wouldn't be smart. So I sit up and lean forward in my chair. "Yeah, Miss. He thinks there's something going on because he saw me walking on the highway at night. But he doesn't know anything about me! I'll tell you what—he needs to get a life. Yesterday in his office, he's all like, *Oooh, Declan, your parents' divorce must have been so hard for you. I guess having a single mom is tough, Declan. Declan, Declan, Declan!* Fuck!" I realize I've gotten carried away and stop dead.

She looks amused and waves for me to continue. I try to calm down. "Sorry, Miss, but Mr. Peters is always on my case. He thinks I *am* a case, like he's some kind of social worker. I don't need a social worker. It's none of his business why I'm walking home at night. Is he following me? 'Cause it seems like he is. It's creepy!"

That felt good. I don't need some stupid intervention. Maybe now she'll back off.

She doesn't look like she's going to back off though. I can't tell what she's thinking because her blank stare is really good, but I can tell she's about to say something. "Why were you in his office?"

That's it?

I settle back in my chair and lean on the arm. "Mr. Jamieson freaked out because I had my jacket on in class."

"You wouldn't take off your jacket?" She checks a notebook on her desk, which makes me realize she already knew why I was there.

I snort. "Yeah."

"Your jacket's big, Declan. You know that the no-jacket rule is for safety. Students have been known to hide things in their jackets."

"I know, I know, Miss. But I can't afford a gun, and I don't deal drugs. I wish Mr. Peters would just get off my back."

"It's not Mr. Peters, Declan. It's just a rule. It's for everybody. Can't you see it'll be easier for you if you just leave your jacket in your locker?"

I love it when adults say, *It'll be easier for you*. Like I'm wearing my jacket because I haven't figured out how to simplify my life. Yup, that's me, always trying to make things more difficult for myself. Actually, I'm lucky. I have other people to do that for me. I'll tell you what would simplify my life: if everyone would just lay off!

I hit the arm of the chair with my hand. "I don't have a locker." I hit it again. "I'm not in a gang or anything." I hit both chair arms with both hands. "I live in Rigaud, in the middle of nowhere, and I sure as hell don't have a car. Walking on country roads in the winter, it's cold. It's nobody's business about my jacket." I keep hitting the arms of the chair as I speak. "Or how much it cost. Or where my mom got it. Mr. Peters thinks he knows about me. Well, he doesn't! Why can't everyone just leave me alone about my jacket?"

"You want everyone to leave you alone?"

I've been to see Miss Fraser before. At the beginning of the year there was some special-needs meeting about me, and she tried to convince me to do a test for ADD. I know she plays these guidance-counselor games, answering everything I say with questions to keep me talking. It bugs me, so I turn away and take a few deep breaths. But I don't answer her. My eyes land on another poster: *For information on gay, lesbian and transgender issues visit www.lgb—*

"Your mom bought you the jacket?"

I resist the temptation to answer her with another question. If I said, *I don't know, what do you think?* we'd probably go around in circles all day, and I'd really like to get out of here. I decide to simplify my life and answer her. "Yeah."

I look at her and chew my fingernail. She's expecting me to say more. "She's really busy," I add. "She has a life."

Unlike Mr. Peters. I'd love to see him do what Mom does. I chuckle at the idea of Mr. Peters, with his dress shirts and nice shoes and manicured fingernails, working in the animal-testing lab.

"What does your mom do?"

I sigh. "She was an office manager. Now she takes care of research animals for a drug company. Cleans cages and stuff. It's a shit job, but she lost her other one."

I stop myself from telling her the whole story.

"Oh?"

I can tell *she* still wants me to talk about Mom losing her job, but instead I say, "Yeah. Last night she told me about a rabbit. A furry little bunny rabbit, like the one my brother-in-law got my niece for a pet. That thing craps all over the place. But it's cute! What the drug company did to that rabbit... *Man!*" I shake my head.

"So are you going to tell me what they did?"

I shrug and continue. "She said they do a test where they drip chemicals into the rabbit's eyes. Can you believe that? She told me rabbits don't have tears—that's why they use them. That's torture! And there are no painkillers allowed. It's cruel, man. No one should have to see that. I mean, why is that okay?" I pause. I'm thinking about why Mom had to leave my grandpa's landscaping company, and all the crap that happened when Mom and Dad split. I slide down in my chair again.

She's still watching me. Her eyebrows are a little raised now. "How does that make you feel?"

"What? You mean the rabbits? Obviously, it's disgusting. Anyways, my mom takes care of the animals. Feeds them, cleans their cages and shit like that. It's not easy." Not like sitting in an office, organizing your desk and giving out detentions.

"Once she saw one having a fit. A *seizure*, she said. It went all stiff, and shook..." I stretch out every inch of my long skinny body so there are no bends in my arms and legs and start to kick. I even add gagging noises and hang out my tongue.

Now she's pushing herself back in her chair, and her eyes are open wide. I stop, straighten up and blow a big puff of air out through my lips. *Calm yourself, dickhead.*

I shake my head. "Anyway, things aren't easy for my mom, you know, me and my crazy brother still living at home. It's hard for her. She has a pretty shitty life."

"Your brother?"

"Yeah, my brother. He's the scary one. He can lose it, man." I punch my fist into my palm, and she flinches. "He threw a chair at my head when I was ten. I got stitches, and now there's a place above my left ear..."

I pull some long blond strings of hair aside so she can see my scar. I had twelve stitches! I'm pretty proud of it. Chicks are all, *Eeewwww. That's awesome!* Miss Fraser, on the other hand, doesn't react at all. "Anyway, he's a total dick. My hair doesn't grow there anymore." I let my hair fall into place, lean back in my chair.

She raises her eyebrows. "I think I remember your brother. Seamus?"

"Yeah."

She nods and makes a squinty face, but she's smiling. She's thinking about Seamus, and she's smiling. Weird. Most people cringe when they find out who my brother is. Teachers try to hide it, but I can tell they're relieved to find out I'm not like him. He's one of those people who are busy *un*simplifying my life.

"How is Seamus? How old is he now?"

"He's eighteen. He's fine, Miss." He'll never be fine. Fucked up is what he is. Makes me look like the good kid.

She's staring out the window, probably lost in thought about Seamus. I wonder if he got sent here too before he got kicked out.

Seamus wasn't always fucked up. When I was little, he was just a regular big brother. We fought sometimes, but just about normal stuff like toys and TV. And he always took my side when our big sister flipped out on me.

Before my dad left, Seamus did a lot of fun shit with him. Dad taught him how to drive the snowmobile, and they'd go up Rigaud Mountain, into the trees, and explore. I thought he was so lucky. Once they even went winter camping. Then everything changed. It's like when Dad left, Seamus left too.

Miss Fraser's waving to get my attention. Her face is concerned. "Declan? What are you thinking about?"

"Nothing." I want to tell her it's none of her damn business, but I don't. I don't even feel that angry anymore. Just kind of droopy. I look down at the arm of the chair and start scraping the gooey varnish off with my fingernail.

I wonder if I could change the letters of *prick* to make it say *dickhead*.

"Declan?"

My eyes wander up to her face, but my thoughts are still on my brother. The last time I was here, I never talked about my family. I didn't think she even knew I had a brother. I nod my head to show I heard her, but I don't say anything. She leaves me alone, and I go back to scraping varnish.

Seamus was two grades ahead of me. In elementary it was fun having my big brother in the same school. He looked out for me and didn't set fires in garbage cans. By the time I got to junior high, Seamus already had a rep. I got nervous before every class, just waiting for my teachers to say something embarrassing in front of everyone about his latest stunt. He got kicked out when he was in tenth grade. I was relieved.

"Miss, can I ask *you* a question?"

"Of course, Declan."

"Can somebody *change* because of something that happened to them? I mean, turn out different than they were going to be?"

"What do you mean, Declan?"

"Never mind." I've got to stop thinking about my stupid brother. I check my watch. I've only been here for fifteen minutes, but it feels like forever.

My eyes are back on that poster. "What does *transgender* actually mean, Miss?"

"Pardon me?" She doesn't get that I changed the subject.

I point to the poster.

"Oh." She looks at the poster, then up at the ceiling tiles for a moment. "It means someone whose gender is different from the one they were assigned at birth. They feel it's not who they really are."

I nod like I get it, but I really don't. I'm just sure I'm not supposed to say that. A lot of kids talk about whether they're gay or bi or whatever. Theresa does. I don't really get into it.

"Anyway, Miss, can I go now?" I reach into my pocket and put my hand around my cigarettes. I'm ready to leave.

"That all depends on whether I feel you understand about your jacket, and about the rules."

"Yeah yeah, I understand. I won't wear it anymore in class. Otherwise Mr. Peters will send me here again, and no offense, Miss, but…"

"I know you don't want to be here, Declan. But there are still a few little things I want to talk to you about before you leave."

I sigh and settle back down in my chair. Let go of my smokes.

"First, we're going to make sure you have a locker. Second, I would like to set you up with a senior peer tutor, someone who can help you with history. I think you can graduate, Declan. But you'll need some help catching up."

She can't be serious. I don't want a tutor! I can't wait to hear what she's saving for number three.

"Also, I think it would be a good idea to have you tested by the school psychologist to see if you have an attention problem."

"No, Miss, I'm not getting tested like some crazy nutcase. Forget it!"

"I don't think you're crazy, Declan."

I try to speak more calmly. "Please. I'm not doing that."

"Then you'll work with a tutor?"

"Aw, c'mon, Miss!"

"Tutoring or testing? Your choice. I'd like you to do both, but I'll settle for one."

"Miss, that's blackmail!"

"No, it's called helping."

"I can take care of myself."

"Of course you can, Declan. But you have a lot on your plate. We—Mr. Peters and I—just want to help. So what's it going to be?"

I want to laugh. School? Help? No way will she understand why this is so funny. I try to keep a straight face, but I feel strange, like I'm getting the giggles. "I mean, thanks and everything, but you can't make me see a tutor, can you?"

"Maybe not. But Mr. Peters can. I'd rather leave him out of this though."

I lean back in my chair and put my hand over my eyes. Man, I want a smoke. "Miss, can't I just have a detention?"

"I don't give detentions. That's Mr. Peters' job."

No matter what, it's back to Mr. Peters. *So, dickhead, what'll it be? Testing to see if you're a moron or tutoring to prove it?* Then I think about the rabbits in my mom's lab. No one's doing any testing on me.

"Fine. Tutoring."

SIX

Surprisingly, Miss Fraser doesn't ask any questions about why I don't have a locker anymore. She just talks to someone in the office and gets me a new one and—bonus—a new lock to go with it. She says the school will pay for my lock, which makes me feel like I'm in the lunch program again. I'm glad I didn't have to tell her what happened to my locker, because for sure she'd try to get me to say how it made me *feel* when the guy took it, like she did about the lab rabbits.

I check the pockets of my jacket. Smokes? Wallet? Keys? Pencil stub? I put my wallet and the pencil stub in my pants, take off my jacket and hang it on one of the hooks. It looks pretty empty in there. The sleeve is sticking out, so I pat it into place. I check my watch. Mr. Peters will be patrolling the halls any minute. I don't want to give him another excuse to be on my case. *Get going, dickhead.* I close the door. *Slam!* Fasten the lock. *Click!*

I stick the little piece of paper with the combination in my pocket, then make sure my fly is done up and my plaid shirt isn't tucked into my jeans. I don't want to look like a dork. I check the number of my new locker one last time. Then I turn on my heel, and my feet start running before my head gets all the way around.

I don't even see her.

She's coming around the corner full tilt and doesn't see me either—a girl with a whole stack of books and stuff piled up in her arms. When we smash into each other, it's epic. Books and papers go flying everywhere.

I get the corner of a math text right in the ribs. It hurts, but I don't say anything. I think her name is Leah, one of the popular kids in eleventh grade. A real Little Miss Perfect who's always doing volunteer work and organizing dumb events at school. She's staring at me like she thinks I'm going to say something. I stare back because I'm not. I bend down and start picking up her stuff while she stands there and watches. She's irritated. I can feel her eyes searing the back of my neck.

When I'm finished, I hold the pile of papers and books out to her. Then I try to step around her and head to my class, but she doesn't actually take her stuff, so I have to stop. Why is she just standing there? I guess she hasn't checked the instruction manual for how to talk to lowlifes like me.

I muster up the most brilliant low-life thing I can think of to say. "Uhhh."

"Thanks. I mean, I'm sorry. You were going kinda fast." She's perky. I hate perky.

"Yeah, whatever." *It would be supercool if you'd take your stuff, lame-o.*

She flips her long hair over her shoulder. "You shouldn't be running in the hallway."

I feel my eyes get big. Who is this bossy chick? *"You* ran into *me!* I was barely moving!"

"You were running and not even looking where you were going."

"How could I have been running? My locker's right there." I point at some random locker with my elbow because my hands are still full of her stuff.

She's looking up at me with annoyed big brown eyes. Her arms are crossed over her chest. Guys are weird. Even though this perfect little pain in the ass is totally yanking my chain, I catch myself checking her out. She's wearing those stretchy black pants that all the girls say make their asses look good. They do.

"Whatever. Here, can you take your things? I've gotta go to class. I'm late. Sorry." But I'm not that sorry. She's being a bitch. She finally reaches for her stuff.

I'm about to make my getaway, only Miss Fraser sails around the same corner right into our little crash site. A long purple sweater and the smell of her perfume float in with her. Shit.

"Declan, Leah, what are you doing still in the hallway?"

"Actually, I was just trying to get to cl—"

"Hi, Miss Fraser. We were both rushing, I guess." Little Miss Perfect's all smiles now. "Bumped right into each other." She chuckles.

Yeah. It was hilarious. I feel like she's all nice now because Miss Fraser is here.

"Ah." She pauses and nods her head. "Well, seeing you together has given me a great idea."

I can hardly wait. I love her ideas.

"Can the two of you spare a couple of minutes?"

I start to protest, and she puts up her hand. "I'll give you both admit slips to get into class."

Right, 'cause that's what I'm most worried about.

Little Miss Perfect chirps, "Sure!"

I sigh.

I can tell by the way Miss Fraser looks at Little Miss Perfect that they know each other. "Leah, Declan could use some help, some tutoring. Right, Declan? For history."

I roll my eyes. Miss Fraser frowns and wrinkles her forehead at me so her eyebrows almost meet in the middle.

"Yeah, history." Out of habit, I start to pat for my smokes in my jacket pocket, which of course is not there because my jacket's in my new locker. This is going to take some getting used to. I shift my weight from one foot to the other and start scanning the lockers along the wall, trying to figure out which one's mine. Until I realize it's on the other side.

Miss Fraser has a goofy smile on her face, waiting for me to say something. I haven't been listening, but the word *tutor* registers in my brain. "Wait, you want *her*—Leah—to be my tutor?"

"Leah's a very good tutor."

I'm sure she is. But not for me.

Leah slides a snotty stare in my direction. She hasn't exactly fallen in love with me either.

How's this supposed to work exactly? Would she have to come to my house? What if my crazy brother shows up? Or, worse, am I going to have to stay after school? Any longer in this place and I'll probably hang myself.

Miss Fraser is tapping her foot. "Declan?"

"Yeah. I'm just thinking."

"Maybe you two could meet later to make the arrangements. Perhaps at recess?"

Sure. Why not? Who needs recess? I'd probably just waste it hanging around with the only people I can stand in this place. I open my mouth, hoping some fantastic excuse will find its way out, but Little Miss Perfect beats me to it. "Actually, it would be better for me if we could just figure that out now. I'm pretty busy all day."

Of course, because you're a ninja-level suck-up, saving the world from loser lowlifes like me.

Miss Fraser asks us to take out our agendas. I haven't seen my agenda since about September. I'm sure it's helping some other kid simplify his life. "I'll keep it in my head, Miss."

She raises her eyebrows, but I've never missed an appointment with her or Mr. Peters or anyone else, for that matter. My problem isn't my memory.

"After school Tuesdays is really good for me. Or Saturday?" says Leah, like it's the coolest idea ever.

Are you kidding? There's no way I'm giving up part of my Saturday for her. "Okay. Tuesday it is." I take a step in the direction of my class and do a little wave with my hand. I'm finished here. Surprisingly, I'd rather be in French.

"Declan?"

I turn around as Miss Fraser says my name. "Yeah?"

"Where are you going to meet Leah on Tuesday?"

"I assumed at school. Don't people do tutoring in the library?"

"Actually, I have to go home after school to stay with my bubby," Leah says. "But you could take the bus with me and come to my house."

Bubby? What's a bubby? I must look clued out, because she says, "My grandma is eighty-three."

Her house? Eighty-three-year-old grandma? What the hell do I want with tutoring anyway? I suck at everything at school, except maybe art and science. I even failed phys ed, and all you have to be able to do is dress yourself. Let's just say I do pass history. What good is it going to do? I haven't passed math since about third grade. Or French. I don't need a tutor. I need a surgical brain implant.

Leah's standing with her hip stuck out and her arms crossed in front of her, over her books. I'm starting to feel like I'm wasting everyone's time.

"I get it. I need help. I really appreciate all this. I'm sure your grandma doesn't want me in her house. And I'm not sure about Tuesday."

"You can't make it Tuesday, Declan?" says Miss Fraser, again with the raised eyebrows. She knows I'm not going to say I can't make it. She also knows I just don't want to.

"Fine."

"Good. You can speak to Mr. Peters, Declan, and he'll give you a permission slip to get on Leah's bus with her. And before I forget…" She takes a pen out of her purple sweater and starts writing our admit slips.

I sneak a glance at Leah. She's entering our tutoring appointment into her phone. How am I going to do this? With her? I don't even want to think about the fun Mitch and Dave are going to have when they find out. And am I going to have to pay for it? "What about—"

Miss Fraser glances up, waiting for me to finish.

"How much does it cost?"

"The school pays for peer tutoring, Declan. You just have to show up."

I close my mouth and nod slowly. They have it all covered, don't they?

Miss Fraser hands us our slips, and I watch my brand-new tutor head down the hall, her perky hair bouncing. I hate perky people even more than I hate perfect little suck-ups. And Leah is both.

But at least I didn't have to give up my recess.

SEVEN

Great. I'm finally home, ready to crash in my room and listen to Black Sabbath, but there's a note from Mom on the table. *Dekkie, Plese make a box of spageti. Sauce is in the frige. Put it in the med. pot and leave it on simmer. I'll make a salad when I get home. Kate and Mandy coming for supper.*

I feel like heading right back out the door. I'm not in the mood for company.

I could go out, pretend I didn't see the note, but Mandy will be disappointed. She's always happy to see me. She's so beautiful, man. And smart. She won't need a Little Miss Perfect tutor when she's in high school.

I fill the big pot with water and put it on the stove to boil. It's freezing on the deck, but at least I can take a few minutes for a cigarette. I've got Mom's note in my hand to make sure I know what she wants. She really can't spell. Add her to the list of high school dropouts in my family. Did any of us

learn anything in school? I don't even know if Dad graduated. Anyway, who the fuck cares?

What if I don't want to finish high school? What do I
need with a locker and a tutor? Isn't it just going to mean
more work for me? I dread the idea of all the extra homework as much as I dread the idea of spending my time with
Little Miss Perfect. It better be worth it.

Imagine me being the first one in the family to
graduate.

I take a drag off my cigarette, and when I exhale, the
smoke comes out with a laugh. Instinctively I look around
to see if anyone heard me. *You live in the middle of nowhere,
Dickhead. No one heard you.*

Even though it's only March, there've been some warm
days, and a lot of the snow around our place has melted.
The banks are all crusty and dirty on top. It's quiet as hell.

That's why my parents wanted to live in Rigaud, away
from the big-city hassles of Montreal, like parking and
traffic and noise. Dad's family has lived out here since the
1800s. His great-great-grandfather was a farmer on Rigaud
Mountain or something, and his parents used to live in
town. So, back when Dad and Grandpa were still talking,
Mom and Dad bought a mobile home and plunked it down
here. The acreage used to belong to some relative from
his family, only they died, and luckily Dad got the land.
How else could we afford a huge yard like this? I was glad we
didn't have to move after my parents split.

Yeah. Before my parents split, they both worked in my grandpa's landscaping business, and they said one day we'd have enough money to build a house. The company was supposed to go to my dad. Instead, my grandparents sold their house and the business and moved to Florida.

When I was little, we had a big garden in the back. It's all grown over now, but Dad's a landscaper, and he grew all kinds of things: vegetables, flowers, raspberries. I take Mandy back there in the summer to pick the berries off the few bushes that haven't died. The yard used to be beautiful, green grass and lots of space for us to play, with the forest behind it. I still mow the lawn, but I can't make it look like my dad did.

Before Kate moved out, Seamus and I shared a room, back when he was a normal human. He had a transistor radio, and he used to say to me, "Let's go fishing." I'd crawl into bed beside him and we'd search for radio stations in the dark. I loved it. We'd find stuff from all over the place: baseball games from Boston, traffic reports from New York City. We had a favorite hard-rock station that came from Ottawa. Music is one of the few things Seamus and I still have in common.

I take the last drag off my smoke and drop it into the coffee can that's been sitting on the picnic table since last summer. It sizzles as it goes out. The can is full of sand and all kinds of other crud that's crawled in there over the winter. Now, on top, there's a bunch of soggy dead cigarettes sitting in sludge. The filters are all puffed up from the water, but I can still tell them apart. Seamus and I smoke the same brand—Player's—my sister's have lipstick on them, and Mom's are Craven Export Menthol. There's even a couple of Old Ports from my brother-in-law. Dad used to let me taste the plastic tips of those when I was a little kid. I actually went digging in the ashtray for them when no one was looking. Yuck.

I jump down from my perch on the picnic table. Time to get going with the spaghetti.

The water's boiling in the big pot, which is all blue and speckled on the outside because Seamus put it in a fire once to cook corn. He and his buddies had a party last summer and trashed a whole bunch of stuff. I throw in the box of spaghetti and catch my reflection in the damaged pot. It makes me look all scrambled. Sort of like how I feel.

I push aside all kinds of crap and pile up five plates on the dining room table. One each for Mom, Kate, Mandy and me, and a fifth one in case Seamus shows up. Mandy has cute little Winnie-the-Pooh dishes with spoons and forks and everything. There's a stack of five cups, and I stick five forks in a mug. I put hot pads down so the spaghetti and sauce pots don't make marks on Mom's nice table. I miss sitting down together for meals at the big wooden table like we used to.

We stopped setting the table for meals after Dad left. Usually it's just Mom and me for supper, so we eat in front of the TV. But why do we have to do that when people come over? We should eat sitting down at the table. Like a family.

The big farm-style dining room table is the one nice thing my mom has. Dad knocked down a wall between the kitchen and the living room so it would fit. Mobile homes aren't exactly made for farm furniture. She's always talking about how we have to be careful of it because it was her grandma's. I know she's proud of it. What's weird is that it's always totally covered with crap: notices from school, old newspapers, unopened mail, Mandy's toys, fish food, a random leather winter glove. It bugs me.

I go feed the fish. The first one home always does it, unless it's Seamus. I doubt he even knows we have them. I watch as the three fat goldfish swim to the top and suck in their food. Mandy named them—SpongeBob, Patrick and Squidward. She doesn't know they're not the same fish all the time. We scoop out and replace a lot of dead ones before she sees them. The whole time I'm feeding the fish, I'm thinking about the table. And then I decide that I'm damn well gonna set it properly.

I start to make two piles of junk on the floor. I find a basket in the hall closet and throw Mandy's toys in it. I add a few toys lying around the living room and leave the basket by the TV.

I dig around in the drawer where we keep the dishtowels and find what I think is a tablecloth. It's been folded up for years and smells musty. When I spread it out, there's a squished moth stuck to it, so I chuck it in the hamper. Back to the kitchen. Hiding under a set of old dishes are five mismatched plastic place mats—Niagara Falls, the Habs, SpongeBob—all from when we were little. They'll do. I set five places at the table. Mandy's stuff on the SpongeBob place mat reminds me of a birthday party.

Which side do the forks go on? I decide it makes sense to put them on the right, but then it seems wrong and the table still seems empty. I switch the forks and rummage through the cupboards to find a jug, which I fill with water and place in the middle of the table like a centerpiece. Around it, I arrange salad dressing, a shaker of parmesan cheese, salt and pepper. At the last minute I add a bag of white bread from the freezer—at least it won't be all stuck together at suppertime—and a tub of margarine.

I like it.

I'm a bit nervous about what Mom's going to say, but the hell with it. It makes the trailer feel like a family lives here.

I drain the spaghetti and put it back in the pot on the stove, and make sure the sauce is on low so it doesn't burn on the bottom. I check the time. Mom won't be home for another twenty minutes or so. I still have time to chill for a bit. I take a detour to the utility room to get my clothes out of the dryer, and I'm sock-skating past the kitchen on the way to my room when Seamus scares the crap out of me. I barely miss smashing into the wall. He's standing at the stove in his underwear and a T-shirt, eating spaghetti sauce out of the pot with the big wooden spoon.

"Shit, you scared me!" I say.

Seamus turns around, his mouth full, blinks and turns back to the pot.

"Why are you eating out of there? That's for supper."

He opens and closes the cupboard door with his left hand while scooping spaghetti sauce with the other. "No plates."

"They're on the table."

He looks past me to the five places I set for supper.

"What the fuck?" He sneers. "Did you do that?"

Instead of answering, I grab a plate and take it to him. He has serious bed head, and he smells like dirty laundry. "Forget it—I'm leaving anyway." He puts the lid back on the pot and drops the spoon onto the stovetop. It leaves a trail of red sauce on the white enamel.

I rinse the spoon and clean off the stove. Why does he have to be here? I didn't even think he was home, and frankly, I was counting on it. I don't want him around when I tell Mom about tutoring.

Seamus slams the bathroom door and turns on the shower. While the water runs, I close the door to my bedroom partway, flop on my bed and pull out *Killing Joke*, even though I've already read it. I want to be able to hear what's happening with Seamus, so Ozzie will have to wait.

* * *

Right when the water in the shower stops running, I hear Mom's car, so I jump up from my bed and speed-walk to the front door. I want to get to her before Seamus does. On my way I pull ten bucks out of my wallet and stick it in my jeans. I'll offer it to Seamus before he hits Mom up for cash.

I watch Mom get out of her car. She's five foot fuck-all and about as skinny as the mangy foxes that run around our place. She has on a big, puffy winter coat that makes her look like a kid wearing her mother's clothes. It's secondhand from the church, just like my jacket, but not as nice.

She comes up the steps with two grocery bags, and I unlock the door. "Oh, hi, Dekkie honey. Take these?"

I kiss Mom on the cheek and bring the two grocery bags to the kitchen while she takes off her boots and yells at me from the mudroom, "Did you get my note? Did you do the spaghetti? I hope you got here in time to do the spaghetti. Kate's coming, and I want to have something ready for Mandy. You know how Katie hates—"

She stops midsentence when she comes into the kitchen and sees the table. "This is very nice." She's forcing a smile with closed lips, her chin almost touching her chest. Her forehead is lined like loose leaf. I know the look. I've known it since I was a little kid. She's wondering why I did something nice, and whether it means I'm trying to butter her up before I give her bad news. "Did something happen at school today?"

"No, Mom. Does there have to be some major reason?"

She shakes her head slowly, and there's a little grin on her face like she's saying, *Aww.* I almost expect her to pat me like a dog.

Seamus barges in. The scent of shampoo and my after-shave follow him. Too late for my plan to intercept him. "Hi, Ma." Mom's startled, but she smiles at my brother, probably because she thinks he's staying for supper. "I need twenty bucks, Ma. Where's your wallet?"

"I don't have twenty bucks. I just went to the store. I thought you were staying for dinner."

"Nope. I'm leaving. Who's coming?"

"Kate and Mandy. I wish you'd stick around."

I notice my brother can't stand still, and his hands are trembling, like that thing that happens to alcoholics. The DDTs or whatever.

"Look, do you have a fuckin' twenty or not?"

"No, and watch your mouth!"

Seamus rolls his eyes and turns toward the front door. Mom follows him. "Where are you going? Are you going to be drinking? Don't you dare get into a car with someone who's drunk, Seamus. And call if you need a lift home."

Better yet, don't come home.

"Yeah right, I'll call Mommy."

"Seamus!"

"Fuck off." He's bending down to pull on a shoe, an unlit cigarette dangling from his mouth.

"Don't you talk to me that way!"

My brother stands up and looms over Mom. She steps back and crosses her arms. I can see the whites of her eyes, and her lips are parted.

My fists clench and unclench as adrenaline starts to pump through me.

Seamus spins around and pounds the paneled wall of the mudroom on his way out. The screen door bounces behind him, then latches quietly as the spring catches. He pauses on the porch and lights his cigarette before sticking his hands in his pockets and taking off. A white cloud of cigarette smoke trails over his shoulder.

Mom stares at the closed door, her arms still crossed. Her lips are now thin, straight lines. One foot taps. Annoyed, angry, upset. Her fists drop to her sides and make muffled clapping sounds against her thighs. She watches as Seamus gets smaller and smaller. Finally, she shuts the inside door so we can't see him anymore.

I guess she forgot I was behind her, because she jumps when she realizes I'm standing in the doorway to the kitchen. She sighs heavily.

I feel useless. I watched the whole thing happen. I've never seen him purposely intimidate her like that before. And I stood there—what do they call it? A *bystander*—while my brother bullied my mom. But all the tension empties from her body when she sees me. She tips her head to the side and shrugs. The thin lip lines turn down slightly. She holds out her hands like, *What am I supposed to do?*

I reach out and rub her skinny arm. "I know, Ma."

In a blink, her old take-care-of-business self is back. She checks the spaghetti and the sauce and gives the table one last nod. Then she says, "Please get Mommy's cigarettes, honey." She doesn't usually refer to herself as Mommy. It's just with her cigarettes. It's always been a thing— Mommy's cigarettes. We all call them that.

I get Mom's smokes from her purse on the front-hall table, take one out of the pack for myself and follow her out the back door to sit on top of the picnic table. She takes a few drags and tries to act calm, but that foot is tapping again where it rests on the bench. Her face is serious, and she's staring off into the forest. The only thing you can hear for a while is the hiss and crackle of burning paper and tobacco each time one of us takes a drag.

"It's not fair, Mom."

She comes back to reality and flicks a long column of ash into the snow. "What's that, honey?"

"He makes everyone nervous. I knew when I found out he was here he was going to upset you. I knew exactly what was going to happen. I even tried to get to him first, to give him this"—I pull the ten out of my pocket—"so he wouldn't bug you."

"I don't want you giving him money."

"Why? Because you have lots?"

"Declan."

"Sorry. But it's not fair. There's something wrong with him." I watch for her reaction. "I think about Seamus all the time, and I bet you do too. But we never talk about it."

"He's just in an angry phase."

"Are you serious? A phase? It's more than that. He's been messed up ever since—"

"Drop it, honey. It's not your problem." She leans away from me and crosses her arms over her knees.

"Of course it's my problem. How is it not my problem? He makes it my problem. He's always in my face, screwing things up for me. He showed up at the rink on Saturday, drunk, asking for money. What if Mr. Bergevin had been there?"

She's quiet, trying to get lost in the forest again.

"Okay," I say. "You don't want to talk about it. I get it. I'm sorry. But what's it gonna take?"

Her head shakes slowly back and forth, eyes closed. Now I've upset her. I wait for her to take a couple of drags, then change the subject. "Mom, I spoke to the guidance counselor today."

"Mmm-hmm."

"She thinks I can finish high school." I glance at her. "She got me a tutor."

Mom looks at me like I've grown another head. "A tutor? Don't you have to pay for that?"

I explain that it's free and I'll be taking the bus to Leah's house on Tuesdays. We're both quiet for a moment. Then I say, "So maybe I can graduate next year."

"Hmph. A high school graduate in our family. That'd be a first, eh?" She slaps me on the leg. "It's too bad about the other two." She blows smoke out slowly through her nose. I watch it make a cloud in the cold air, then gradually fade. "Maybe I shoulda got them tutors."

That's it? She doesn't even seem interested. I almost wish I hadn't told her. All she can think about is Kate and Seamus. I try again. "Mom, maybe I can actually pass—"

She pats my hand. "That's good. You never give me trouble like the other two. Just do your best, Dekkie, and that's good enough for me."

I don't know what I was expecting. Maybe some encouragement? A vote of confidence? But a pat on the hand and *I'm glad you're not a loser like your brother and sister, Dekkie?* That's it?

I turn away from her. I don't want to say anything, especially after how Seamus treated her before. While I'm staring at the ice on the bench, a little feeling of excitement pokes through all the other crap. What if I actually *could* graduate?

Mom laughs her smoker's laugh, flicks her ash and elbows me. "You always were a smart little kid. Do you remember when we used to call you Little Einstein? You got all upset because you thought Einstein was a monster."

Ha. Very funny. "Whatever."

When I was little, I collected insects but wouldn't kill them, which was fun when spider eggs hatched and tiny, hairy babies infested the kitchen. And I made Kate do science experiments with me. That was before she became a bitchy teenage mom. I found a condom in her room once and thought it was a balloon. I attached it to the top of a beer bottle and made it inflate and deflate by changing the temperature of the bottle. I thought I was brilliant. I even got everybody together in the kitchen, like it was a show. I couldn't figure out why they were all splitting a gut. Dad had to take me aside and explain it. Yeah, sure. A real Einstein.

There are only two classes I bother with at school—science and art—because I actually like them. I even get perfect scores in most of my science labs. I'm failing it because I never do the homework or study. But I probably could pass. It's easy.

I stamp out my cigarette and stand on the bench. I wind up and pitch the butt as far as I can. It almost reaches the forest.

"Sorry, honey. It's good what you're doing, and I'm proud of you. I guess I've sort of stopped hoping for things."

My brother and sister screwed up. I'm the one who's been here the whole time. I have a job, I go to school, I help her out—I boil the fucking spaghetti. I was going to give Seamus my money! Seamus and Kate cause all these problems, and Mom gets all worried because things are difficult for *them*. I wasn't expecting a party, but I'm trying to do something good here, and it doesn't even seem like she's taking it seriously.

Well, I guess tutoring is *my* problem. I should have known. Why do I care what Mom thinks? She can't even spell *spaghetti*.

Mom's butting out her cigarette. "I better get that salad made. Kate and Mandy are going to be here any minute, and you know Kate hates having supper late."

"Aw, Kate bitches about everything. She's getting a free supper. Maybe she could show some appreciation for once!"

"I know, I know, honey. But things are hard enough for Kate and Ryan. I just like to do what I can to help."

If I squawked and complained more, would she want to help me too? Suddenly I feel bad for being angry at Mom. Maybe it's easier for her to relate to Kate because Mom was pretty young too when Kate was born. Besides, it's probably Mandy who really pulls Mom's heartstrings.

"Dekkie?"

"Yeah?"

"Please watch your language when the baby's here."

"*Baby!* Mom, she's almost five!"

"You know what I mean."

I hold the screen door open for her. "Okay, Ma. Let's go cook."

EiGHT

I got my permission slip from Mr. Peters, and now I'm sitting beside Little Miss Perfect on the bus. It's super awkward. I hate school buses.

Some idiot is blowing spitballs through a straw at the nerdy kids. Leah's holding her phone and her earphones are dangling out of her jacket, like she wants to plug herself in but doesn't want to be rude. She's trying to smile at me, but it looks fake. She's not used to talking to someone like me, I guess. "Nice bus," I say. Brilliant.

Just then a tiny ball of chewed-up paper whizzes past her head and sticks to the window. The bus driver yells at us in French. Some kid's lunch kit opens, and stuff rolls all over the floor. We both start to laugh. Then we stop. Neither of us knows what to say, so we go back to being uncomfortable.

"It won't be that long a ride. I don't live far from school."

I pretend to stare out the window. She plugs herself in.

I know where she lives—in one of the big houses right in Hudson. Not out in the country like me. And there's a lawn and a garden in the summertime. In her neighborhood, there's no broken bathroom fixtures out front. No pickup trucks or old tires or mobile homes or chain-link snow fences.

I know which house is hers because I rang her doorbell when I was trying to get shoveling jobs in Hudson the winter I was saving for my Xbox. She actually answered the door. I figured there'd be lots of people living in those nice houses who could pay a kid for something like that. I walked up and down Main Road, but everyone, Leah's parents included, already had snow-removal companies plowing their driveways and clearing the sidewalks for them. They'd rather pay some old dude like my dad to drink coffee in a heated cab. It's what he does now, in the winter anyway. Drives a snow plow, robbing little kids like me of a rightful living. Just one more reason to hate him.

Leah's standing up to leave. Her eyes dart from me to the floor to the seat. "You don't have a bag?"

What can I say? I stopped carrying a schoolbag about the same time I stopped doing homework. She rolls her eyes and raises her hands like she has a direct line to God. Looking over the top of her head as I walk off the bus behind her, I'm sure I can see the tip of her Little Miss Perfect nose in the air.

Leah's house is long and white with green shutters. Like most of the lakefront houses, it probably has stables and buildings in the back where the workers lived a long time ago. A long driveway leads all the way to Lac des Deux Montagnes through the trees. What a spot.

My hands are shoved into the pockets of my jacket about as far as they can go. I'm watching Little Miss Perfect search through her schoolbag for her keys when I hear voices behind me. Instinctively I turn.

Shit!

Seamus, Robbie and two other kids are leaving a house up the street and walking to Robbie's car, which is parked out front.

What are they doing here?

I try to shield my face with my hood while I watch them. Robbie chucks a cigarette butt onto the street. As he's gawking around, he looks right at me! I duck my head down and try to melt some holes in the snow with my eyes.

Leah's still fishing for her keys in her overstuffed backpack. She stops to take her mittens off.

Hurry up, dammit!

She's scrounging way down at the bottom, even though there are pockets on the outside. I can't stand it.

Car doors slam. *Bam.* One. *Bam.* Two. *Bam.* Three. I wait. No fourth *bam?*

I sneak another peek across the street. Everyone but Seamus is inside. He's walking around to the back of the car, toward me and Leah! I can hear the blood rushing in my ears; my hands are sweating in my pockets. Leah's still kneeling on the ground with her fucking backpack.

Why couldn't she have put her keys in one of the outer pockets? We need to get into the house now!

Seamus stops at the curb, looks both ways like he's going to cross the street, coughs and horks into the gutter. Then he turns on his heel and heads back to the passenger door. I exhale, and my face tingles as it changes from hot to cold.

My heart's pounding in my chest. What's taking Leah so long? "Why don't you keep them in a pocket?!" I blurt out.

She looks at me for a second from under her hat, which matches her mittens and jacket perfectly, and goes back to digging. She mumbles, "Why don't you have a schoolbag?"

Oh for fuck's sake.

Robbie guns the motor. It roars on the quiet street.

Finally, Leah pulls out a set of keys on a butterfly key chain and sorts through them for the right one.

The Taurus makes a noisy U-turn, and fishtails before passing in front of Leah's house. Over the rumbling exhaust I hear, "*Blah, blah, blah,* fuckin' *blah, blah,* dickhead, *blah, blah, blah!*" as Seamus screams at me from the car. He obviously does see me. His arm arcs out the window. A spray of little red cylinders flies from his hand and rains on the street and Leah's front lawn. On impact, the cylinders explode about fifteen feet away from us. *Pop, pop, pop, pop, pop, pop, pop!!*

God fucking damn my stupid asshole brother! I want to run after the car and rip him out of his seat! I want to punch the shit out of him! I've lunged in front of Leah without thinking, and now I'm frozen in place. She's watching the car speed up the street, its exhaust spitting and popping as it goes. Her eyes are huge, her mouth open wide like she's screaming, but there's no sound coming out. She's halfway up from crouching, and she's holding her hat on top of her head. The butterfly keychain is dangling from her other hand.

We both stare as the brake lights brighten at the corner. The blue car gives a final roar as it turns and disappears.

Dead. Silence.

"Who was that?"

Her voice startles me. "Huh?"

"He was yelling at you, wasn't he? Do you know who it was?"

I don't want to say it was my brother. I decide to focus on the driver of the car and not mention Seamus. "Sort of. He's a kid from school." I shrug my jacket up around my shoulders and ram my hands back into my pockets.

"One of your friends?"

"Not exactly."

"Well, that was insane. I can't believe it. What if someone had been walking by?" She shakes her head, and her voice is hard and angry. "What a jerk. He could kill someone driving around here like that. What were those exploding things?"

"They're poppers. Firecrackers." Mr. Helpful. I couldn't have pretended I didn't know?

She grunts and shakes her head, like she's not surprised. "I've seen that blue car there before." She gets busy unlocking the door.

Does that mean she's seen Seamus too? My heart slides into my stomach. I don't want her to know we're related. Boy, if she only knew. She probably shouldn't be letting me into her house at all. If he's hanging around here every time I show up, something even worse *is* going to happen.

What's it like to be a smart, normal person who lives in a nice house and cares about school? With no crazy family members who can show up any second and ruin everything?

I make a mental note to murder my brother in his sleep.

"Declan? Are you going to come in?" Leah's waving her hand in my face like she's trying to bring me out of a trance. The door is open.

"Sorry. ADD moment."

"Do you have ADD? Is *that* your…uh…is that a problem for you?"

"Not officially. I think my official diagnosis is *stupid asshole*. At least, according to my friends."

"Nice friends."

My stomach flip-flops as I step into the entranceway of Leah's house. The first thing I notice is the smell of something cooking. It's awesome!

Curls spring out when she takes off her hat. "Uh-oh, I smell stew. My mom is with a client—she's a real estate agent—and Bubby's not supposed to be cooking. Stay here." She leaves me standing in the hallway.

I take off my boots and hang my jacket on a hook. I think that's what it's there for.

Leah comes back and motions for me to follow her. "Come meet Bubby."

Old people make me nervous. I'm always afraid I'll say something offensive by mistake. What if this bubby of hers doesn't like me?

There's a lamp in the corner of the living room, behind a reclining chair. It's shining on a little old woman who's fast asleep with her mouth open, a book face down on her chest and a clicker in her hand. The news is on the TV, but the sound is off. Leah gently takes the clicker out of her grandmother's hand and pulls a blanket right up over the book. She holds her finger to her lips, and we leave Bubby sleeping in her chair.

"Sorry. I'll have to introduce you another time," she whispers, like she means it.

I try to contain my disappointment.

We go into the dining room, and Leah turns on the chandelier over a large table. There are these huge brass candle holders on a lacy thing in the middle of the table. They're really shiny and have carvings all over them. They've gotta be two feet tall. She sees me looking at them. "Those are for Shabbat. We light them for dinner on Fridays and high holidays." She moves them over to a buffet one by one, using both hands.

I'm just staring.

"I'm Jewish," she says, as if it should be obvious.

I know what Jewish is. But where do the candles fit in? *Shabbat* sounds like a racket sport.

"Oh, right. I forgot. You didn't bring anything with you. How do you manage with no books or anything?"

"Look, if you don't want to do this, we don't have to. I'm sure there are lots of other people you could tutor instead. Maybe this isn't a good idea. I'm sure Miss Fraser can find someone else."

She stifles a smile. "Sorry. I know this isn't your idea of a good time. I'm sure you'd rather be doing... "

She has no clue what I'd rather be doing. I help her out. "Just about anything."

She nods. "So did Ms. Fraser make you get a tutor?"

She calls her Mizz like they say on the school intercom, not Miss like the non-suck-ups do. "Not exactly. Mr. Peters made me go see her because I got in trouble. Tutoring was her idea, but I have to or it's back to Mr. Peters."

"Oh." She nods and smiles. "So what'd you do?"

"A lot of things, I guess. I think this is, like, a last resort."

"Well, what kind of things?" I'm pretty sure this is how rumors start. Why is she so interested in my life?

"Stupid stuff, like smoking on school property, being late, refusing to take off my jacket. Stuff like that."

"That doesn't seem so bad."

"I know, right? But he says I've had twenty-one detentions, and most of them I skipped."

Her jaw drops. There's a silver filling in one of her molars. "What?!"

I thought things were going a bit too smoothly.

She laughs. "How does anyone get twenty-one detentions? I mean, that's ridiculous."

"Right." I feel like I'm the entertainment. Does she practice insulting people, or does it just come naturally? I'm sure she thinks I'm a loser, the whole thing about not having my stuff. What business is it of hers why I don't have my stuff? She's my tutor, not my mother.

I'm obviously not as amused as she is. She stops laughing and says, "Cool. I've never even had *one*."

"Why would you want a detention? They're boring and stupid. That's why I stopped going to them."

"I don't know. There are some things maybe you should have to go through in high school. Things you don't get to when you're…"

When you're what? Too good for detentions? She really is lame. The only people who think it's cool to have a detention are people who never get one. You get detentions because you suck at something—or like, in my case, everything. Little Miss Perfects don't suck at anything. Well, too bad. I don't want them there anyway, stinking up the DT room.

I don't go off on her though. I settle for some sarcasm. "Sounds rough, never getting in trouble."

She wrinkles up her nose. "Oh, some days nothing I say comes out right. I didn't mean it that way. Sometimes it seems like there might be more to high school than I'm getting, that's all."

Right. I'm sure she's a rebel at heart.

She checks the time on her phone. "We'd better get down to work. I'm just going to get my old history stuff from last year. I'll be right back."

I watch her as she leaves the room. A perky rebel. With long bouncy hair and a cute ass. I wish she'd quit leaving me alone. That old woman is still in the next room.

There's a lot to look at in here. Everything's big and old. The table, the chairs, the buffet. The doorframes are trimmed in thick, dark molding. As I'm casing the joint, my eyes land on those candle holders. They look heavy. Really heavy. I glance over my shoulder to check for bubbies, push my chair out silently and walk the few steps over to the buffet so I can get a better look. I reach out and feel the cool metal, run my hand over the curves and angles of the decorations. I check both doorways and pick up one of the candle holders.

I was right.

This baby weighs a ton! I hold it in my right hand like a barbell and do some bicep curls—one, two, three. It's kind of hard to grip because of all those decorations, and it's long and wobbly.

The candle holder starts to roll out of my hand. I try to grab it with my other hand and miss. I'm afraid it's going to crash onto the buffet, where there's all kinds of breakable stuff. Instead, it lands on my foot and rumbles onto the hardwood floor.

"Shit!" I yell. It's out before I can stop it, but my hand flies to my mouth anyway. My foot hurts like crap. I'm hopping on the other one, with my hand covering my mouth, when I hear something behind me.

I whip my head around to see Leah's bubby standing with one hand on the doorjamb. With her other hand she's pointing accusingly at me, looking like she's caught a home invader in the act.

Too bad Leah's not here to introduce us.

"Sorry, Miss...Bubby...Uh...I'm not going to hurt you or anything," How do I explain the candle holder on the floor? I heave it up and wave it at her, but because it's so heavy, it seems more like I'm swinging it at her. "These are beautiful!" She looks terrified and steps back, bracing herself on the doorjamb. "Oh, sorry! It's okay. Leah's my tutor. I mean, I'm here with your granddaughter." I put the heavy brass candle holder back beside its twin. "We just came in. She—"

"Declan? What are you doing?"

I'm actually happy to hear Leah's voice, even with that hint of snarkiness.

"I was just looking—"

She squinches up her face like she's having trouble figuring out what's going on, then sees her grandmother standing in the doorway. "Oh, hi, Bubby. You're—have you two introduced yourselves?"

The old woman lets go of the doorjamb, and her eyes return to their normal shape. She attempts a smile, but she has no top teeth, so she looks more like a fish in a flowery housedress. She's wearing socks and men's slippers.

I want to die.

Leah puts her stuff on the table and goes straight to her grandmother, hugs her and kisses her cheek. She takes her by the elbow and leads her closer to me, so I hold out my hand, pretty sure an introduction is about to take place.

I step toward them. Pain shoots through my foot. I don't flinch. I don't even blink.

"Bubby, this is Declan. I'm going to be tutoring him in history."

Bubby nods and shakes my hand. "Oh, that's nice, dear. So you're not here to rob the place." She jokes! Or at least I think she's joking.

"Sorry about that, Miss…" I look to Leah for help.

"Mrs. Zimmerman. Bubby used to be a history teacher. She'd make a much better tutor than me. And she tells great stories." Leah elbows her so hard I'm afraid Bubby will fall over.

"It's nice to meet you, Mrs. Zimmerman. I'm really sorry for scaring you." We're still shaking hands. Hers feels tiny and fragile in my nicotine-stained paw.

"Oh, that's all right. I don't know who was more scared, you or me." She smiles her toothless smile. "Declan. That's a good Irish name, isn't it? You don't meet many Declans nowadays. Very nice."

Yeah, that's me—I'm one of a kind. "Thank you. My dad was Irish."

Her bony little fingers slip out of mine. "Oh, I'm sorry."

It takes me a second to realize she thinks he's dead. "I mean, *is*. We just never see him."

Leah's eyebrows are scrunched up in the middle of her forehead.

Leah's grandmother nods. "Well, you two carry on. I'm going to go read." She starts to turn around, steadying herself again on the doorjamb. "Oh, there's russela on the stove, dear."

"I know. It smells great." Leah's words sound loving, but she's shaking her head at the same time. "You know you're not supposed to use the stove, Bubby."

Leah's grandmother ignores the scolding and asks, "Will Declan be staying for dinner? There's plenty."

"Oh, I can't stay. I…my mom expects me to be home for dinner. Thank you." The idea of eating with Leah's family terrifies me.

"As you wish." Bubby shuffles back to the living room in her corduroy slippers.

"She makes the best russela in the world."

"Russela?"

"It's a Jewish name. It's what my family calls beef stew."

"It smells great."

"It is, especially when Bubby makes it. Unfortunately, she knows that. If you *want* to stay for supper, no one here will mind." But I get the impression she means no one but her.

"Thanks, but my mom really does expect me to come home."

"Bubby's a great cook. She taught Mom to cook, and now I'm learning too. That's one thing Jews know how to do—eat! Bubby used to have a friend who kept food hidden in all the drawers of her dresser. She was in a concentration camp during the war, and she learned to hide food so they wouldn't starve. After the war she just couldn't stop. So sad."

"You mean you actually knew someone who was in a concentration camp?"

"Knew someone! I *know* someone. Actually, so do you. Bubby was in a concentration camp during the Second World War."

"No shit?!"

"No shit, Declan." She's trying to look pissed, but she can't keep a small smile from twitching at the corners of her mouth.

Okay, so maybe that wasn't the greatest choice of words. But it's kind of cute the way she's pretending to be a tough guy.

"She was just a teenager. Her family was in Theresienstadt. It was a special camp the Nazis used to fool the world into looking the other way while they killed Jews, homosexuals, political prisoners."

"The Nazis killed gays?"

"Yes. It wasn't just Jews. Bubby's parents were eventually sent to Auschwitz, where they died. She and her brother were left behind, but her little brother died of tuberculosis in Theresienstadt. She's the only one who made it out."

She looks away and shakes her head. I know a bit about Jews and the Holocaust from history class, but I obviously haven't been super keen on history. It's different when you meet someone who was part of it. And I had no idea there were gays in concentration camps. Maybe I should have paid more attention in class.

"Wow," is all I can think of to say.

"My grandmother had a beautiful voice. She sang in a children's choir in the camp. There were a lot of artists and musicians there. When the Danish Red Cross visited, the Nazis made the prisoners clean up the camp and put on a show. They thought it would stop the Allies from looking for the death camps. But you can see pictures online. It was terrible."

"Wow," I say again.

"When I said my bubby was a good storyteller, I meant it. Once I was old enough, she started to tell me everything. It scared me at first, but my parents thought I should know."

I have to be honest: I'm enjoying listening to Leah talk about her grandmother. Learning about history never felt like this in a classroom. "Your grandmother seems awesome."

"I'm really proud of her," Leah continues. "She's been through a lot. She's very strong. Well, she was. Now she lives with us because last year she had a stroke. She can't live alone. And she can't read or write anymore. I hate that, because it meant so much to her."

"But in the living room, wasn't she reading?"

Leah smiles, but she wrinkles her forehead at the same time. It makes her smile sad. "She acts like she's reading, and she's trying to learn again. A speech and language therapist comes to the house to help her. Right after her stroke, she didn't know who *we* were, but she never forgot her stories."

"Wow." I shake my head.

"You say *wow* a lot."

"Yeah." Little Miss Perfect's back.

"It's getting late, Declan. Since you didn't bring books or anything, maybe for the rest of our time today we'll just make a plan—get organized. The final exam is in less than three months. We should see each other at least once a week, right?" She's looking at the calendar in her phone. "Okay, that means we'll get to meet about ten more times before the end of term, and if we throw in a few quizzes…"

Back to tutoring. Back to reality. Time to prove I'm not a loser lowlife.

NINE

Why the hell do there have to be so many different kinds of pens? I just need something to write with. And a notebook. I grab a light-blue notebook off the pharmacy shelf. It looks like the Hilroys we used when I was a little kid, but thinner. I guess they don't make 'em like they used to. Where's the list of things Leah said to get? I pull the crumpled note out of my jeans. *One-inch binder.* Check. *Loose leaf.* Check. *Notebook.* Check. *Pen.*

How are you supposed to choose a pen? What the hell is a gel pen? Red pens. Purple pens. Sharpies. Mom used one of those to write my name and phone number on my clothes when I was in elementary school. Why? I guess she thought if I got lost, the first thing someone would do is look inside my underwear for contact information.

At this rate, Mom'll be done getting groceries next door before I find a pen. She brought me along to carry the bags. Here's a blue ballpoint pen. Perfect, but it's in a package of twenty-four! Here's one for $6.95. Why can't I find a goddamn plain, ordinary, normal ballpoint pen? Finally I see a package of Bics—two blues, a black and a red. I snatch it off its hook and head for the cash, where there's a lineup.

One cashier is talking to another one, who's on break. The line moves very slowly as they blab and laugh about some guy who puked all over his girlfriend at some party.

I'm getting excited because there are only two more people in front of me when I hear someone call my name. "Declan? Declan O'Reilly? Declan, how are you?" The man reaches out to shake my hand, and I realize it's my soccer coach from the summer I was ten—the last summer I had a normal life. He's tall and has a big chest and shoulders, but I'm looking him straight in the eye. Last time I saw him, I probably came up to his belly button. He was a giant to me.

"Hello, Monsieur Lavoie." He's still shaking my hand, and I can feel it yanking my shoulder.

He finally lets me have my hand back and tips his head to one side while he gives me the once-over. He's wearing a green canvas winter jacket and a striped scarf that looks like someone made it for him. His cheeks are red above a wicked five-o'clock shadow, and he still has the bushiest, blackest unibrow I've ever seen. Only now it has white hairs in it.

"Mon Dieu, Declan, you've grown so much! What are you, fifteen? Sixteen?"

I smile. "I'll be sixteen in May." I feel shy, though, like when I was ten.

Coach Lavoie's kids go to French school. But we all played soccer together in the summertime. He was a great coach. We made fun of his accent. He'd say, *'Ow do you expect to get de ball if you don't get your hasses in dere?!* His face would get red, and that unibrow would wriggle like a big caterpillar. We laughed, but we got our *hasses in dere* and won!

"I was thinking about you the other day, Declan. I need someone to help me with one of the boys' teams, the U8s. I'm coaching my youngest—"

He stops because I can't believe his youngest son is eight, and I guess it shows on my face. He was three when I played with his older brother, Stephan.

"Yes, it's true! The thing is, I asked Steph, and he's too busy with intercity. So I thought about you."

"Me?"

"Yeah, sure. You were such a good little soccer player. A natural. I thought you'd play intercity, like Steph."

I'm amazed he remembers. We did talk about me trying out for the intercity team. He and Dad were going to take Steph and me. Then shit happened. "Thanks, sir," I say, "but I haven't played since..." My voice trails off. He knows what I'm talking about. "We kick the ball around at school sometimes."

He nods and says, "How is your dad? Is he still living in that cottage in Coteau-du-Lac?"

"Yeah."

"Please say hi to him for me."

I nod, but I know I won't.

"What do you think about helping out?"

"Uh, I don't know, Monsieur Lavoie. I'm working at the rink. Can I think about it?"

"*Bien sûr!* It would only be a couple of evenings a week. And sometimes on Saturdays."

"At the same field?" The soccer pitch is about a kilometer from my house, right next to the rink.

"Yes, yes."

"I guess I could think about it."

"Like I said, Declan, I'd love to have you," he says.

I look out from under my hair. Someone told me once my hair reminded them of Kurt Cobain, because of how long and scraggly it is. I don't think I've had it cut since. Suddenly I'm self-conscious about my frayed, slush-soaked jeans and my nicotine-stained fingers. I don't want him to see me this way. It's my turn at the cash, and neither of us seems to have anything else to say.

"Tell Steph hi," I say as I get out my wallet. "I better get back to my mom. She's getting groceries." I nod in the direction of the grocery store. "I'll think about what you said."

"One minute, Declan," he says. He finds a piece of paper in his pocket and writes on it, gives it to me, then shakes my hand again and slaps me on the back before waving goodbye.

After I've paid for my stuff, I pull the crumpled note out of my jacket. Under his phone number it says, *Please call me. I'd love your help.*

Who knows? Maybe I will.

As I'm walking next door to meet Mom, I hear yelling. My brother is having a screaming match with a man who's barring the entrance to the liquor store. Seamus is unsteady, and his clothes and hair look like he just crawled out of bed. I should probably step in, get Seamus out of the guy's face, but I know my brother. He won't go quietly. I don't want Mom to know he's even here. Besides, I'm still riding pretty high after talking with Coach Lavoie. I decide to simplify my life and deke into the grocery store.

TEN

"If you want the table set, Dekkie, then set it." Mom's buzzing around in the kitchen, getting supper ready for Sunday dinner with Kate, Ryan and Mandy. I'm hooking up a new Nintendo Wii to the living room TV. Mom splurged, with a little help from me, and got the Wii on Amazon for Mandy. My niece is going to love it. It's Ryan's first time here for dinner since he went on night shift at the medical center, and Mom wants everything to be perfect.

So then why did she tell Seamus to be home by six o'clock? He'll sabotage the whole thing. Doesn't she know that? Add my lunatic brother to the normal craziness of an O'Reilly family gathering, and you've got a recipe for nuclear war, not quality family time.

"Declan! Come do the table. They'll be here any minute!"

"Do you want me to set this thing up or not?" I connect the last of the wires and feel bad about being rude. There's no point making things harder for Mom. As far as I know,

I'm still the good kid. She's at the sink, tearing lettuce into pieces for salad. There's a chicken on the top of the stove ready for me to carve. I tap her on the shoulder.

She jumps and yelps. "Don't sneak up on me like that! You want to give me a heart attack?"

"Oh, Ma. Why're you so jumpy?" I open up my arms to give her a hug. She reaches around me (as far as she can, at least), with a piece of lettuce in one hand and the head in the other, and hugs me back with her elbows. She's so tiny it's like wrapping my arms around a stick person. She smells like cigarette smoke and hair conditioner, same as always. "I love you, Ma. It's going to be a nice dinner."

"Oh, of course it is, as long as *it's* not dry." She nods in the direction of the headless, brown bird. "It'll be nice to see Ryan. You know, he hasn't been here for supper since Christmas?" She's quiet for a few moments. "So, did you get the thing hooked up?" I can tell she's excited about giving Mandy the Wii.

"Yep. Mandy can play her new game as soon as she wants to. By the way, I've been meaning to ask, how come you never bought me a Wii? I had to buy my own game console." I'm teasing, but she takes me seriously.

"Oh, Dekkie. I know. Things were different back then." She looks at me out of the corner of her eye to see if I'm serious. "Besides, I couldn't have done this without your help."

"That's our secret."

I reach above her head to get plates from the cupboard. "It's all right, Ma. I know you love her more than me.

At first it bothered me, but I'm okay with it now." I'm only half joking.

She rolls her eyes.

We used to torture Mom by asking her over and over who she loved best, me, Kate or Seamus. She would always say, *All my children are different and special, but I love them all the same.* Then we'd ask her who she loved best, us or our friends, us or characters from TV shows, strangers on the street, dead relatives. No matter how hard we tried, we could never trip her up.

I stuff a bunch of paper napkins into a glass. Like Martha Stewart, right? Mom tells me the chicken is ready to carve. I sharpen the big knife and am just starting to work on the wings and legs when we hear Kate and Ryan come in. She goes to the door.

There's a lot of chirping as Kate and Mandy and Mom hug and kiss each other. Ryan's deep voice rises above the others. Mom is flitting around like a hummingbird, hanging up their coats, taking Kate's dish from her, listening to Mandy's latest story. I want to be there when she shows Mandy the Wii. I put down the knife and grab a towel. I'm wearing an apron so I don't get grease all over my clothes from the chicken. Ryan sees me first.

"Oh, look, it's Dekkie Crocker!"

"Fuck off, man!" I slap him on the back and give him a hug.

A look from Mom says, *You're not too old to spank.*

My niece runs to me with her arms up. "Dekkie, Dekkie, Grammy has a s'prise! Do you know what it is?"

I pick her up and squeeze her, then settle her on my hip like I've done since she was a baby. "Do I know what it is?" She kicks me in the thigh like a horse, the signal she wants to get down. "It was me who picked it out for you. You are gonna love it!"

"Declan, what is it? What is it?" She pulls me by the apron into the living room.

"Hang on to your shorts, girlie. As soon as Grammy's ready."

"I don't wear shorts! Shorts are for boys!"

"Oh, sorry. Hang on to your Disney Princess panties then."

Kate walks over and smacks me on the side of the head, hard. "*Underwear*, Declan. *Panties* is disempowering. I ain't bringin' up no girly-girl."

I kiss my sister on the cheek, rubbing the spot where she hit me.

"Oh, I forgot you turned all feminist since you took that self-defense course. I think Mandy's underwear should be a feminist-free zone. Besides, doesn't she play with Barbies?" I walk around the living room on tiptoes, sticking out my chest like I have huge boobs. The apron adds a nice touch. My niece attacks me with her little fists, and I pretend to fall over, grabbing her and flinging us both onto the sofa. She wriggles away, too excited to stay still. But she manages to turn and stick her tongue out at me before escaping.

Mom's standing in front of the TV set, finished with twittering around. She crooks her finger at Mandy to come, then points at the doors of the TV stand, motioning for her to open them up.

Mandy looks inside and sees the Wii, the controllers and the Mario game, all ready to go. Her face lights up, and she screams a string of words none of us can make out. It doesn't matter. All Mom needs to hear is how happy she is. The nearest neighbors are half a kilometer away, but I'm sure they can hear her. She's doubled over with her hands on her knees, and she's turning red because she hasn't come up for air.

Of course, she wants to play right away. She rips the cellophane off the Mario game in seconds and slides the disc into the console. "Play with me, Uncle Dekkie," she says as she picks up a controller.

"Later, monkey. I have to finish Grammy's chicken. But after supper, we're on! Now, you get it going and practice— 'cause yer gonna need all the help ya can get!" I do my best evil-cowboy impression, with bowed legs and fingers in my belt loops, and head back to the kitchen and the half-carved bird. Kate and Mandy follow me.

"No way you're going to beat me, Dekkie! I beat Daddy all the time. I'm really hot!" She licks her finger and pretends to make it sizzle by holding it on her four-year-old butt, then runs giggling back into the living room.

I look at Kate, horrified. "Who taught her to do that?"

"She comes home from daycare with these things. Why do you think I'm concerned about girlie crap?" My sister is hovering over the table like a vulture. She swoops down on the veggie platter.

"I told you. School is evil."

"For sure. She's even asking to go on Facebook, because her friends are on it. What kind of parent lets a four-year-old kid go on Facebook? Shit for brains, I tell ya."

"Language, Mrs. Massarelli," I whisper.

Her fingers fly to her mouth, and she looks for Mom, pretending to be worried. When she sees Mom is nowhere around, she leans in and continues whispering. "Where's Seamus?"

I shrug and whisper back, "He went out this afternoon. Mom told him to be home by six." It's almost six thirty on the kitchen clock. He could still show up.

Kate presses her lips together and shakes her head. "Asshole. Mom's going to be disappointed. She's been gearing up for this all week."

"I know, but..." Am I the only one hoping he stays away?

My sister returns to her normal voice. "Hey, speaking of school and evil, Mom tells me you got a tutor?"

"Yeah. Remember Miss Fraser, the guidance counselor? She wants me to try to catch up and pass history. If I do, she thinks maybe I can actually graduate next year like I'm supposed to. Go figure."

"Wow. It's possible you're not the idiot we thought you were."

"Thanks, sis. Knew I could count on your support."

"Well, the rest of us seem to be doing fine without a piece of paper saying we're legit." She's crunching on a carrot stick. "Don't you have to pay?"

"She's a peer tutor. Free."

"Oh." She's nodding like she just solved the mystery. "It's a she! Is she cute?"

"No! She's a pain-in-the-ass suck-up." Cute, yes, and she's not as much of a suck-up as I thought she was, but it would be suicide to tell Kate that.

"Well, if you do pass, it'll be the first convocation for the whole family. You better reserve an entire goddamn row of seats. Mom's going to want everyone to be there." She looks nervous, like she said something wrong.

"Settle down. It's not next year yet. I'll probably fail everything anyway."

"Graduation isn't such a big deal. I didn't graduate, and I'm happy." She waves her carrot in the air.

"I don't know. I like to picture myself walking across the stage to get my diploma. Then I open my gown and..." I turn toward Kate, pretending to flash an audience.

"Oh, you're such a pig!" She smacks me again, on the other side this time. "Forget it. There's no hope for you."

I pretend I'm seeing stars, then shake my head. "Seriously, I'm gonna give it a shot. I may as well. The VP and the guidance counselor are making me do tutoring, so I don't have a choice. It's a"—I make air quotes—"consequence."

"Ah, now I get it."

Ryan comes in and takes a beer from the fridge.

"Grab me one too, Ry," my sister says. "Hey, the brat's doing tutoring after school."

He swings around. "You?" Half a smirk and one raised eyebrow. Not a complete dis.

I shake my head and roll my eyes. "Thanks, guys. Your support is overwhelming."

"No, Declan. That's great. I was just surprised. Thought you hated school," Ryan says.

"This doesn't mean I like it. I just think it would be cool to say I graduated, that's all."

"Oh, don't take him seriously, Ryan. He's just doing it because he got in trouble. I thought there was something fishy when Mom told me."

Like the only way I could care about school is if I'm forced to. Like I couldn't want it on my own, or I'm not smart enough. I feel red creeping into my cheeks.

"No!" He elbows her. "Go for it. It's a good thing. You'll get better jobs, maybe even go to college. I'm proud of you, little bro."

"Thanks." How'd this guy ever end up with my sister? I smile at him, grab his beer out of his hand and take a swig before he knows what's happening. He grabs it back, and then *he* smacks me on the back of the head. At this rate I'm headed for a concussion. I don't care. Ryan makes me feel like a little brother again.

Mom wants to eat while everything's hot. When we finally sit down for supper, no one says anything about Seamus, even though there's a space at the table where he should be. I catch Kate checking her watch. I know Mom's thinking about it too, because she's all quiet and distracted. "The chicken's great, Ma. I love the outside crispy part. It's the best."

"Yeah, Barbara. It's delicious. I've missed dinner with you guys! It'll be great to be on days for a while. I'll be back next Sunday!" Good old Ryan.

"Oh, thank you, boys. Thanks, Dekkie, for all your help getting things ready. And look at us all sitting around the table."

I stare at my plate like I never noticed how interesting roast potatoes are.

"I like it!" Mandy chirps in.

"Me too, honey." Mom puts her hand on the back of Mandy's head and tickles her neck so she pulls in like a turtle and laughs.

"It's nice not to have the TV on for a change." Kate's always complaining about the TV, mainly because Ryan and I like to keep it on sports. And if it's not sports, it's some kids' show. "So Mom, can we borrow your car on Tuesday morning? Ours has to go into the shop. We'll drive you to work and bring it back the next day."

"Sure, that's fine, dear. I'll ask Janice if she can give me a lift home."

Mandy opens her mouth to say something, but a burp escapes instead. She hides her face in Mom's arm and laughs. If anyone else is thinking about Seamus, they're not saying so.

* * *

Mom and Kate are in the kitchen doing dishes. Ryan's reading the newspaper on the sofa. I'm lying on my side on the living room carpet, playing Mario with Mandy, when I hear it. A cough. Outside on the walk. Seamus is here after all.

Without moving my head, I glance at Ryan. He heard it too. I sit up.

Mandy's worried I'm going to stop playing, but I threaten to beat her at the game if she doesn't pay attention. I keep my eyes on the TV, my ears tuned to the door.

Click. Seamus unlocks the outside door and slams it. There's a pause while he takes off his shoes. He walks in and chucks his coat on a chair.

"Where's Mom?" He's squinting while he scans the living room. His cheeks are red and his socks are soaked, and by the smell of them, he hasn't changed them in a while. He must have walked from somewhere.

"In the kitchen. You missed supper with everyone," I answer, turning my attention back to the game. I can feel the muscles in Mandy's little body get all tight. I put my hand on her back. "Mom made you a plate. It's in the fridge." I want to get rid of him.

"Great. I'm starved." He slurs his words.

What a jerk. Why'd he bother showing up at all? If we're lucky, he'll just eat and go to his room.

Seamus walks carefully into the kitchen, trying to seem not drunk. Mandy holds her nose and pretends she's going to die from foot stench. I look at Ryan. We do a sort of mind meld, like we're agreeing to join forces. He nods.

I hear dishes and the microwave, and for a while I think it's going to be okay. Sometimes when Seamus is drunk, he just gets quiet. Doesn't open his big mouth. Now, if only Kate can stay out of his way and keep hers shut. They have this pattern that neither of them can resist. Like bugs flying into a zapper.

Seamus settles in at the table to stuff his face. The back door grinds in its track. Mom and Kate go outside for a smoke. Ryan takes the newspaper to the bathroom. Mandy and I continue to play till we finish the level, and of course she beats me. She's excited, and for a minute I forget that Seamus is there. I get caught up with Mandy. She's such a gorgeous kid. I high-five her.

Then I feel Seamus looking over my shoulder.

"What the hell is that?" He points at the Wii and belches. Mandy laughs. Seamus doesn't.

"It's a Wii. Grammy got it for me. And I beat Declan at Mario! I'm Daisy." She has trouble containing her excitement, pointing at the screen. She just looks at Seamus, waiting for him to reply. He doesn't even react. She glances at me and turns back to Mario, who's bouncing up and down on the TV screen and prompting, "Let's go! Let's go!"

"She never got us no Wii."

"I paid for it." It's only a half lie. I hope Mandy doesn't catch on.

"It's really fun, Uncle Seamus. You wanna try?"

"A baby game? Wii is for babies. PlayStation's way better." He picks up the clicker and switches the TV to sports, as if Mandy's not even there. He's smirking.

Mandy looks down, shoulders slumped, like he's knocked the air right out of her. My body starts to vibrate. I make fists, dig my fingernails into my palms. The pain calms me down.

"Aw, Seamus is just afraid you'll beat him, Mandy. Don't worry. I had fun playing with you, even if you did beat the pants off me!" I cover up my privates like I've got no clothes on, and she laughs.

"You're pathetic," Seamus drawls without taking his eyes off the TV.

I ignore him.

"Did you hear what I said to you, man? I said you're pathetic." He's raising his voice. What's his problem?

"I heard you, Seamus. Thanks for your opinion." I start to get up from the floor and take Mandy's hand to lead her to the kitchen. "Mandy and I are going to the kitchen to have some more of Grammy's chocolate cake."

"Fuckin' loser asshole who does tutoring. Ha! Mom told me that's what you were doing when I saw you the other day. Fuckin' loser. You're so stupid, prob'ly won't even help. Fuckin' gay asshole!"

The memory of firecrackers popping outside Leah's house launches me the rest of the way to my feet. I've dropped Mandy's hand, and I'm standing right in front of him. He smells like alcohol, B.O. and putrid socks.

"Declan's not stupid!" Mandy's little voice pipes up behind me.

"Shut up, runt!" He lunges around me toward her. She jumps back and screams. Seamus laughs and stumbles in front of the sofa.

"Go to the kitchen, Mandy. See what Kate and Grammy are doing." But she doesn't go. She's stiff, like a statue. I don't take my eyes off Seamus.

"Why don't you just go and leave us alone?" I say through clenched teeth. "Watch TV in your room. Let Mandy play her new game in here." I position myself between him and Mandy.

"No. I wanna watch in the living room." Before settling back down on the sofa, he reaches around to grab the clicker and looks right in my face. "Who's gonna stop me? You?"

Something snaps, and I lose track of my body. I watch my right fist catch him, completely off guard, on the left side of his face. He tumbles back onto the sofa, and his hand flies up to his cheekbone. It takes him a moment to realize what's happened. He struggles to his feet and lunges at me. Behind me I can hear Mandy shrieking and Ryan coming out of the bathroom, but I'm not thinking about anything except doing as much damage to my brother as I can. I block him and swing back, hard.

It's like there's a power surge to my arms. I swing again and again, into his chest, his face, his stomach. He's making no sound. He doesn't have time. He can't even catch his breath. My body just does what it has to do. I'm deadly strong. Punishing. Unstoppable. I'm Donatello. I'm Batman. I feel a scream building up inside of me. Or is it laughter? I could soar.

Seamus gets free and lunges at me again, tries to get both hands around my neck. I see the room, Mom, Ryan spin around me, and a comical thought pops into my brain—that they're watching us dance. I get my balance and push him off me with all my weight.

Seamus goes flying backward into the table by the door. The lamp topples and falls, and the bulb bursts. Keys and cigarette lighters and travel mugs and loose change fly everywhere. He comes back at me, flailing, but I'm waiting for him, and he's still slow and unsteady. His face smashes right into my fist, and there's an explosion of blood on my hand and on his face. This time he falls down, holding his nose.

Then I'm on top of him. I push him onto his back. Over and over I punch him in the face, I don't know how many times, until I hear my mom screaming, "Declan! Stop! You'll kill him! Please stop!" I feel Ryan grabbing the back of my shirt, trying to pull me off.

I stop, my breath rasping out of me, my shoulders heaving. Seamus is whimpering and trying to cover his face with his hands. I take my knee off him and grab a big handful of his shirt in my fist.

"Get up," I growl, low and slow, twisting his shirt in my bloody hand as I yank him up. Hair is stuck to the sweat on my face. My heart sounds like thunder. "Get up! Get up, you fucking asshole! Get your coat and get out. Get the fuck out of this house or I'll fuckin' kill you. Now! You piece of shit! Go!" I push him backward toward the front door, releasing his shirt from my grip.

Seamus stumbles again into the table with the tipped-over lamp. He turns around and pauses, leaning on the table to get steady, then moves carefully to the door, his back to the living room. I hear Mandy crying. She's with Kate in the kitchen.

"You're taking too long!" I grab the back of his shirt with my right hand and open the door to the mudroom with the other. He doesn't fight back because his hand is stuck in his pants pocket. We stumble over boots and shoes while I unbolt the front door. With all my strength I shove him out, and my brother is suspended in midair. Time stops.

He crash-lands in a pile of snow.

I spin around, grab his soaked shoes and his jacket and fling them out the door. They land beside him as he struggles in socks and bare hands to get out of the snowdrift and stand up.

I don't wait to see how it ends. I shut the door and bolt it. When I turn to face my family, the room is deadly silent.

"Where will he go?" Mom's voice is tiny, almost a whisper.

ELEVEN

Where the hell is my wallet? I can't find it anywhere, and I'm going to miss my bus. I figured it landed on the floor last night when everything flew off the table, but it's not there. Mom must have cleaned up. The broken lamp is back where it belongs, its shade balancing on what's left of it, and the keys and cigarette lighters and loose change are all in their usual places. No wallet. I grab the coins from the change dish and stuff them into my pocket.

Our driveway's about the length of a football field. A few centimeters of fresh snow have covered Seamus's tracks from last night, like he was never here. Running for the bus is tricky. It's so icy underneath the snow, I break into a full glide a couple of times, surfer style, to stop myself from wiping out. I get there just as it's pulling up to my stop. No time for a smoke. I put the unlit cigarette I've been holding into my pocket.

Like I do every morning, I walk all the way to the back, but I keep my hood up. There's an ugly cut on my left cheek from my grandfather's ring. Seamus wears it on his right hand.

My fingers are puffy and swollen, and my knuckles are bruised. I bet Seamus left with a broken nose, the way the blood spurted out. It doesn't seem real. Like it's my imagination or a dream.

It felt good to hit him. Shouldn't I feel bad about that? Because I don't. Where *did* he go? And what's going on in *his* head? I hate to think about how pissed he is at me now.

I waited till Mom left this morning before I got up, so I wouldn't have to see her. What am I supposed to say to her? He may have had it coming, but she still loves him. She's stressed out enough already. I'm sure I just made everything way worse, and that's not what I'm supposed to do. She counts on me.

I pull my hood around my face, lean my head against the window and close my eyes. I make a fist with my sore hand and squeeze until I can't stand the pain anymore. When I let go, my whole body cools, like I'm floating in water.

As the bus gets closer to school, the kids around me get louder. To tune them out, I focus on the acceleration and deceleration of the bus's engine, and the shifting of its gears in between long stretches of road. Brakes. Door. Low gear, accelerate, shift, accelerate, shift. *Whirrr...*

I'm jolted awake as the driver throws the bus into Park in the school parking lot. The diesel engine settles into a grumbling idle. As usual, kids from fifteen different buses are all trying to get through the front entrance of the school at the same time. Chirpy girl voices grate on my nerves. What's everyone so excited for?

Another one of Mr. Peters's stupid rules: no hoods or hats in the building. I slip off my hood and keep my head down to hide my face. I track what's in front of me out of the corner of one eye. So far, no sign of Mitch or Dave.

I sense I'm about to bump into someone and raise my head enough to see Miss Fraser in her purple sweater, smiling at me. She zeroes in on my face, and her smile droops. She switches to emergency mode. "Come to my office?"

I don't want to talk in the hallway, so I tag along with my head down. The warning bell rings and the hall starts to empty as she unlocks the door. She motions for me to sit.

"Miss, that was the bell."

"Don't worry, I'll give you an admit slip. This is more important. What happened?"

What's with her and admit slips? I tell her about the fight.

"Oh dear. I guess it was just a matter of time."

"What do you mean?"

She hesitates, like she's choosing her words carefully. "Last time we spoke, you were pretty fed up with your brother. *The scary one*, you called him." Again, she takes a second to think before she speaks. "*A total dick*, I think you called him."

My eyes open wide. "Yeah." I can't believe she said *dick*.

She's sitting in her chair, turning a little pink plastic dinosaur over and over in her hand while I stand beside the desk. She stops when she sees me looking at it. She seems different this morning. Nervous, like there's something on her mind. My boots are leaving dirty puddles of melted snow on the tile floor.

The second bell startles me.

"Relax, Declan. Why don't you sit down? It's the morning after your first fistfight with your big brother. There's lots to talk about. It's not an ordinary day."

"Frankly, Miss, nothing in my life is ordinary lately. Trouble with Seamus is the most normal thing about it."

"Seamus started to act out when your parents… separated?"

Separated? That makes it sound so gentle, like pulling apart pieces of frozen bread. It was more like a war. I look down and rub my sore hand. "I guess."

"So?"

"So, I don't know. So, he went into his room nice when my dad left, like big-brother nice, and came out three weeks later mean."

She raises her eyebrows.

I decide to step back from my puddles and sit after all. Why not? I'm not that crazy about going to class anyway. I explain how Seamus stopped going to school, and how Mom had to take food to him on a tray or he'd have starved. "My sister finally kicked his ass, dragged him out. She told Seamus to stop sulking, because he had to be the man of the house now. That it was up to him because Dad was…gone."

The word *gone* hangs there when I finish speaking. I bend my neck from side to side and then back, so that I'm looking up at the ceiling tiles. On two of them there's a big coffee-colored water stain with jaggedy, brown edges. Heaviness is spreading inside me like that stain, like cement is filling up my arms and legs. I take a couple of deep breaths and let the last one out slowly through my lips. For a while, nobody talks.

"Was there something...specific...that upset Seamus?"

This seems like a stupid question. Wouldn't most kids be upset if their father pulled a vanishing act? It makes me wonder if she already knew what was going on with my family back then.

My leg starts to bounce. We just sit, and it's real quiet. Pressure builds up behind my eyes. My face flushes, and I get this big lump in my throat. For once, I wish she'd say something. Did she run out of stupid questions?

Maybe I could change the subject. I'd like to change the subject, but my brain has shut down. I don't want to talk at all—I'm afraid words will come out and cause trouble. I look for anything else interesting to read on the walls, but there's only the gay-sex poster, and I don't feel like looking at it right now. Two pigeons peck at the concrete ledge outside the window. One glides away, the other follows.

Miss Fraser uncrosses her legs and crosses them the other way. I notice her glance at a Kleenex box sitting on her desk with that little pink dinosaur and a bunch of other stuff: piles of papers, a mug that says *Mommy*, one of those squishy stress things filled with sand that you can squeeze, a chain of colored paper clips all jumbled together. Nothing like Mr. Peters's desk.

She finally speaks. "Do you want to talk about how you're feeling right now?"

Do I look like I want to talk about my feelings? I shake my head and fake a smile, but it's not working. It feels like gravity is pulling the corners of my mouth down. I lean forward with my elbows on my knees and stare at the floor. Swallow hard. Man, I need a smoke.

Finally I calm down enough to make eye contact. She's leaning toward me with her elbow on the armrest. "Okay?" She has that concerned eyebrows-up look.

"Phewww." I blow out air for a long time. I just want to get out of here. "Yeah. I'm an idiot, Miss. I'm pretty sure I shouldn't be talking about this. I never do."

"Like we said before. Things aren't ordinary."

She doesn't know the half of it. When I think back to that time, it's like a war. And we were collateral damage, like civilians in that war in Afghanistan, only in my house. Maybe I do need to talk about it. About how your whole world can turn upside down in a single day. One bad day, like in *Killing Joke*. How things are not always what they seem...

"The funny part is, I never knew there was anything wrong. Nobody did. Not even Mom, I don't think. We were just going along, being a family..."

"...and?"

"I don't want to talk about it."

TWELVE

Ripping down the stairs from the guidance office, I run right into Mr. Peters. I'm sure I'm going to get into trouble for running, or being in the hall during class time, or something. I wave my admit slip to show him I was with Miss Fraser. His eyebrows move about halfway up his forehead when he sees my face.

"What happened to you? Did you get attacked by a tree on the highway?"

Funny.

I tell him it's a long story and I've just been through it all with Miss Fraser and I shouldn't miss any more of my class. I'm hoping he'll be impressed by my improved attitude and just let me go. He opens his mouth like he's going to protest, then closes it. Pauses. "Okay, Declan, but no running. Get rid of that jacket, and straight to class."

"Yes sir!" I can't believe it. No social-worker comments about my hard life or anything.

Dave's already sitting in English. When I walk in, his eyes pop out of his head. *Where were you?* he mouths.

I put my admit slip on the teacher's desk. She has a page of a book up on the Smart Board, and she's making red circles around examples of how the author uses sentence structure to create mood. Seriously. How am I supposed to concentrate on that? I grab the book she's talking about from the shelf at the back of the class and sit in my usual spot beside Dave. I flip to the page the teacher's on and pretend I'm fascinated, to keep her off my back but also to put Dave off my trail.

The bell rings, and Dave drags me to his locker. Mitch is waiting there, an unlit cigarette hanging from his mouth.

When he sees me, he grabs the cigarette from between his lips. "What the fuck?!" They're both staring at my messed-up face.

"Okay, let's have it. Where'd you get the cool tatts?" Dave asks.

"Tatts?"

"Your face, stupid. Looks like you got in a fight."

"Yeah."

"Whoa! With?"

"Seamus."

"Holy crap!" Dave looks at Mitch. They can't believe it.

"What happened?"

I go through the basic story, but they want more, so I launch into a play-by-play with all the gory details.

Mitch says, "Cool!"

Dave smacks me on the back and sends my English books flying across the hall. "I'm proud of you, man!"

I don't feel proud exactly.

At recess we head outside. When you walk around with a smashed-up face, people assume you have a story to tell. I get a lot of fist bumps from guys who know my brother. Everyone's interested. Everyone except Theresa, that is. She doesn't even ask. She wouldn't care if I was black and blue and bleeding out as long as I listened to her problems.

As we're walking back into the school for third period, some chick I don't even know comes up to me and touches my face! I jump back and hit a signpost.

"Oooh, black eyes are so hot!" She flips her hair over her shoulder and looks back to watch me as she's walking away with her friends. She makes sure I'm looking at her before she turns to talk to the girl beside her. She keeps watching me out of the corner of her eye. Through their giggling, I hear, "Adorable!" "Oh my god!" "Cute!" I hope no one can tell I'm turning red. What is wrong with them?

Mitch and Dave think it's hilarious and start to paw at my face. "Oh, *adorable*, oh my *god*! Your bruises turn me *on*!"

"Shut the fuck up!" I lunge at Dave, but he's faster than me.

Sometimes Dave reminds me of a monkey or a boxer, always bouncing around. One moment he's on my right. Then he's behind me. Then he's talking to someone else. It's like keeping track of a fruit fly.

By the time the dismissal bell rings, I'm sick of my own story.

After school Mitch and I kill some time together. He and Dave are going to his place after the variety-show rehearsal. Dave's been doing his crazy backflips for years, and he gets in trouble for it all the time. Now that he's in the variety show, the same teachers who give him shit are making him a celebrity. I've decided to drop in at Kate's later. I keep hearing Mandy crying in the kitchen after the fight. I want to see her, tell her it's okay. Besides, I really don't want to deal with Mom.

I'm in the hallway, laughing at old graduation pictures of goofy-looking kids who went here in the sixties. Mitch is sitting at the back of the gym, watching the rehearsal. He sticks his head out the door and gestures wildly for me to come in. Normally, Mitch is sloth-like. There's only one thing that gets him that riled up.

"There's chicks d-a-n-c-i-n-g, dude. C'mon!" I can tell by the way he takes a long time to say *dancing* that he thinks they're hot. Rhianna is playing on the sound system. I drag myself over, my hands in my jacket pockets, shuffling my boots.

A bunch of girls are on the stage doing hip-hop. Two are in front with their hands over their heads, turning while they swing their hips around in circles to the music. Their sweats are rolled down at the waist, and their shirts are tied above their belly buttons. Pretty hot, all right.

Then I realize one of them is Little Miss Perfect.

"Whoa! Dude! It's your tutor!"

I try to act cool, but I'm in shock. It's hard to take my eyes off her. She looks so…different. I pretend I don't care and hope Mitch hasn't seen my eyes become saucers. "Yeah. So?"

"So! So she's like, whoa." He's gesturing the outline of a curvy female body with his hands, grinning like a total sleazeball.

"Don't be an asshole."

He gawks at me like I've lost my mind. "What's wrong with you? Since when are you Mr. Appropriate? She's hot, man. I don't care what you say."

She *is* hot. And the way she's moving her body, those hips! But I can't let him know what I'm thinking. I'll never hear the end of it. They tease me enough about what I do with Little Miss Perfect. Besides, I'm pretty sure I shouldn't be feeling this way about my tutor.

"Whatever." She's not the only hip-hop dancer I've seen. It's no big deal. There's a lot of good-looking girls at school.

Mitch shakes his head, but his eyes are fixed on the dancers. Especially on Leah. It bugs me the way he's staring. She's *my* tutor.

Bam! I'm bodychecked from behind, and the breath is knocked out of me. I belt out a horrible gagging sound and go stumbling into the gym. Behind me, Dave is doubled over laughing. Why are my friends such assholes?

"She's pretty cute, eh?" He's been watching us watching her.

The music's still playing, but the girls onstage and the teacher in charge of the rehearsal are squinting and glaring at us under the bright stage lights. We've completely shut down their practice. The rest of the gym is almost dark. I'm hoping Leah won't be able to tell it's me. The three of us trip over each other trying to sneak out.

"Boys!" The teacher is shielding her eyes. She's not letting us off that easy. "I'd like to see you, please, up here under the light." She motions for us to come forward. My heart starts pounding even faster. Mitch, Dave and I come out from the shadows, heads down. "David? Is that you back there?"

Dave mumbles sheepishly, trying to be cute. "Yes, Miss." She threatens to make us come up onstage and rehearse with the girls unless we beat it. Some of them giggle. Leah shoots daggers at me.

We leave the gym as quickly and quietly as we can, eyes on the floor, apologizing under our breath. But I can't help it. I sneak another look. She catches me. She's got her hands on her hips, and she's shaking her head. My feet keep walking, but my mind is in the gym, stuck on Little Miss Perfect. She's not supposed to be hot.

Mitch and Dave are giggling like little kids who just got in trouble. I don't find it as funny, so I hang back. They're pissing me off. They realize I'm not laughing along, and they start acting all proper instead. I still don't laugh.

"Hey, man. We're sorry. I guess that was kind of immature, in front of your tutor and everything." Dave hangs his head, mocking me. Mitch is smiling.

"Forget it. I'm just tired. It's been a long day." We start walking together again.

"So you really decked him?" Dave asks as he shadow-boxes around Mitch.

"Yup."

"Dekkie the Decker!" He jabs my bicep—right, left, right, left.

"Cut it out. I probably broke his nose."

"Gimme a break. A lotta guys wish they could break your brother's nose." He fakes an upper cut into Mitch's jaw. Mitch swats him, and Dave flies across the hall like an insect.

"And if they tried it, I'd break theirs." Forgetting I'm not actually the Hulk, I smash my sore hand into a locker. Stupid.

Dave recovers from being airmailed and drops his imaginary gloves. "Man, when are you going to stop being all 'he's my big brother'? We get it. But he's an asshole. I'm sure he's sittin' around with his buds worrying about you! It's about time somebody broke his nose." He goes back to annoying Mitch.

His words sting, but I know he's right. He's been with me through everything—the divorce, Seamus…everything.

He shrugs. "I swear, Declan. If either one of us saw him lay a hand on you, we'd kill him."

Mitch grabs me in a headlock and rubs his knuckles on my scalp so hard it hurts. Dave rams his shoulder into my back. They act like it's a joke, but I know they mean it. They'd kill him.

We stay far away from the gym, but we're not supposed to be wandering around the school either, so we have to keep a lookout for Mr. Peters. Mitch writes *Dekkie + Leah* with a big heart around it in every open classroom in the math hallway. I try to keep up, erasing his artwork behind him as he goes. Luckily, Mr. Jamieson's door is locked, because the guys want to trash his room or piss in the garbage can or something. That's all I'd need.

Dave sits down at the piano in the dance studio. He took lessons when he was a little kid, but he wouldn't practice, so his mom stopped paying for them. He taught himself instead, and he's pretty good. I honestly think he's some kind of a genius. It makes me wonder why he still hangs around with us.

We listen to Dave play "Paradise" by Coldplay for a while, but Mitch and I ruin it by singing along with the *ooh-ooh-oohs*.

In one of the classrooms we find a yardstick and pretend to be Mr. Jamieson, smashing it on desks, until we hear someone coming. We crouch behind the teacher's desk. When it's clear, I see a mug on the desk and get the great idea to use it and the yardstick for a game of mini-putt. I turn the teacher's coffee mug on its side and crumple paper from the recycling bin into little balls. I win because Mitch and Dave both suck and can't get a single ball in the cup. Now who's the genius?

Walking together to the bus stop, Dave asks me why I came late to class this morning. I tell him Miss Fraser dragged me into her office. "She wanted to know about Seamus and the fight. I guess she knew Seamus before all the crap with my parents. Anyway, she freaked me out, asking all these questions about my family like she knew something." I lock eyes with Dave. "I couldn't wait to get out of there."

"What about your family?" Mitch asks.

Dave's eyebrows shoot up, and his eyes dart from me to Mitch, then back again.

"My parents' divorce."

"It was complicated," Dave says.

"Most divorces are," Mitch replies.

"*Really* complicated," Dave says.

"It's nothing," I say to Mitch. I don't want to go there. I never talk about the divorce and what happened to my family. Only Dave knows why my dad really left. Just thinking about it gets me upset.

"It doesn't sound like nothing. You're making it seem like this big thing."

"It *was* a pretty big thing." Dave's nodding wildly.

"It wasn't that big a thing." I push Dave out of the way, but he pushes me right back. He's not going to let up.

"It *was so* a big thing."

"Fuck off. It wasn't." I'm lying, and Dave knows it.

"Will one of you weirdos tell me what the fuck is going on?"

"My dad had—" I try to say it, but I get stuck.

"His dad had an affair." Dave nudges me to keep going.

"Yeah, an affair."

Mitch is waiting for more. "So? That's it? Your dad had an affair? That's the big family secret?"

Dave pushes me aside now and stands square in front of Mitch. "Declan's dad had an affair with a dude. His dad turned gay!"

I freeze. I can feel those words in the air.

Dave looks relieved.

Mitch's mouth widens into a huge, silent O. After a few seconds he speaks. "Oh! Crap! That is big. I had no idea!"

"Yeah. I don't talk about it. Now you know why."

"Yeah, he doesn't talk about it."

I glare at Dave. "Shut up."

Mitch faces Dave. "You knew."

"It was fifth grade. I was there for the whole thing."

Mitch has his hands in his pockets. He swings back to me. "You could have told me. I have a gay uncle, you know, so I'd have been cool with it."

My turn for the jaw drop.

"So, like, in five years you've never talked to your dad because he's gay? I just assumed he was in jail for murder or something." It sounds stupid when Mitch says it. "You should talk to your dad. What if he's really cool, like my uncle? You'll never know."

Mitch has a great relationship with his dad. They go shopping and smoke up together and shit like that.

"I'm not ready for that." I'm not sure I'll ever be. I have to admit, the last thing I ever wondered about my dad was whether he was cool. It's not cool to ditch your family, especially not for some gay asshole.

Mitch slaps me on the back, then keeps his arm around my shoulders. "If you ever do want to talk, I'm here, bro, anytime."

I nod. "Yeah, sure." I'm stunned. I've held this inside for so long. I expected there to be more of a bang when it all came out. Instead, it's just a fizzle. I was always afraid of being ditched or hassled if people knew about Dad. Kids get teased and humiliated for way less than that. I've been mocked for living in a trailer. But with Mitch, it seems like the opposite is true.

We make our way outside in time to take a couple of drags. Leah's nearby, waiting for a lift with her friends from the variety show and laughing, which makes her curly hair jiggle around her shoulders. She's not wearing her matching hat and mittens. I'm embarrassed after what happened in the gym, but I finally screw up enough courage to nod and wave from the curb. She gives me the smallest smile, like she's hiding it from her friends, then turns her back on me.

A wolf whistle peels out, long and clear. I spin around and catch Dave grinning proudly, and then I turn back to Leah. There's no question that she knows who whistled and who it was meant for. She acts all disgusted, and her friends give us the evil eye. I'm relieved when a fancy big-ass SUV picks them up and drives away.

Screw her. I felt stupid enough going to tutoring. What a waste of a Tuesday night. It's hard to imagine making things any worse than they already are, but my friends found a way. On the other hand, I'm still stunned by Mitch's reaction to my secret. Apparently, true friendship has no limits.

I wave to the guys as the bus pulls away and leaves me standing on the street alone. There's a storm building inside me. A ball of energy is sitting in my chest, making me want to cry or laugh or scream at the top of my lungs like I'm a crazy person. I want to understand why I feel this way. I want to know why life has to be so confusing, how you can expect a bang and get a fizzle, and how you can want someone and hate them, all at the same time.

THIRTEEN

It feels good to be on my own, breathing in the winter air as I walk to Kate's. Even though it just snowed, you can tell it's getting warmer. Next Thursday is March 21, and it'll officially be spring. Every year at Harwood High the Little Miss Perfects and all the other suck-ups organize a stupid dance called the Spring Fling. Everyone knows it's next Friday, because some peppy girl talks about it on the intercom every morning.

Yeah right. I'm going to go back to school on Friday night to stand around and watch drunk people grinding in the gym. The only thing flinging would be my supper.

It's still sunny as I walk down the hill into town. Kate and Ryan live in Hudson too, in a condo right near the park. They should all be home now. If I play my cards right, I can score an invitation for dinner—as long as they let me in. I have no idea what they think after last night. There's fresh, sticky snow everywhere. Perfect for snowballs.

Before turning down the street to my sister's place, I pack a good one and wing it at the stop sign. *Bong!* Snow sticks to the sign so it says *STUP*. Yes!

Ryan's car is out front, and the lights are on in the living room. I clear the steps by kicking aside as much snow as I can on the way up and ring the bell. I'm nervous.

Kate answers the door. She doesn't even say hi, and the look on her face tells me she's not exactly happy to see me. She notices the cuts and bruises on my face and wrinkles up her nose.

"Hi, Kate. Can I come in? I thought I'd come and take Mandy to the park."

She still hasn't opened the door all the way, and for a second I think she isn't going to let me in. She must be really mad. She looks behind her and says, "It's Declan" to someone inside. There's a pause, as if she's waiting for an answer.

She opens her mouth to speak and then changes her mind and exhales. "Sure, Declan." She finally opens the door all the way.

I untie my boots in the front hallway. When I stand up, she motions me into the living room, where my eyes land on a man who is holding Mandy. Not Ryan. This man's older. Balding. With thinning, long blond hair, same color as mine, pulled back in a ponytail. Bushy reddish-blond mustache. Wide-set blue eyes.

He looks like me. Our eyes lock for a moment.

Dad.

Of course. It's the only thing that hasn't happened to me yet today.

Mandy has her hand up like she's going to wave, but she senses something's wrong and stops. My instinct is to do an about-face and run out the door. But first I turn to Kate, shocked.

Dad's eyes travel from me to Kate, then to the floor. He's not enjoying this surprise any more than I am.

"Declan! Mommy, look at Dekkie's face! Ooh, it's got a boo-boo! Grandpa, Dekkie and Seamus had a fight. Look at Dekkie's boo-boo!"

Grandpa?

Mandy's wiggling around, so Dad's having trouble holding on to her.

"She's been worried about you, Declan. She keeps asking if you're all right," Kate says.

I ignore her. "I'm fine, Mandy. I came to say I'm sorry. For fighting in front of you. We shouldn't have done that. Sorry, kiddo." While I'm speaking to her, I have to look at my father, because he's holding her. He nods at me and seems to be trying to smile.

"It's okay." She reaches her hand out to me. "Love you! Grandpa's here for supper. Are you coming for supper?" She's expecting me to stay. But I can't. Her little hand drops, and she looks back and forth between me and Dad.

"Nah, I gotta go. Grammy's waiting for me. I just wanted to say hi." I blow her a kiss, which she catches in her hand.

She throws one back at me, but her forehead is wrinkled and her head is tipped to one side.

Dad puts her down but keeps his hands on her shoulders. She reaches up to hold his wrists. He lets her pull off his watch so she can play with it.

I can't stand being here, watching him with Mandy. I'm crawling out of my skin.

The minute it takes to get my boots back on is the longest minute of my life. You could play guitar on the tension in Kate's front hall. Kate keeps making these little sighing noises, and it pisses me off. I can't wait to leave, and as I'm rushing I break a shoelace. I stuff the loose ends into my boot. I can't get out fast enough.

I turn and open the door. Cold air hits my swollen face. I take a deep breath and shoot Kate a *how could you* look before I walk out, but I don't even know what for. Having him over? Not telling me? "Ciao."

"Declan. Please! Stay. Come back. It's okay, Declan! Come back. We can talk! We *need* to talk, Declan! Declan…"

But I'm already halfway to the corner. Her desperate voice trails off behind me. Because of the broken lace, my boot feels like it's going to come off, but I don't stop running. Past the stop sign, around the corner, past the park and the houses and the post office. I don't stop until I get to the top of the hill. I'm out of breath. Walking, I backtrack toward the school.

Not bad for a smoker. Fuck the smoking pamphlets in Miss Fraser's office! Fuck guidance counselors, and vice principals, and tutors, and stupid-fucking-asshole gay fathers! Fuck everything!

When I reach the school I realize I've been talking to myself, because kids carrying instrument cases are staring at me as they arrive for a school band concert. Shit. I just want to be alone.

I walk around to the staff parking lot in the back and start pounding on a big red Dumpster. I pound and I pound and I pound, with both fists. I pound because I feel stupid. I pound because I feel betrayed. I pound because nothing makes any sense. I keep pounding until I can't lift my arms anymore. Limp, exhausted, I turn around, brace my back against the bin and slide down until I'm sitting in the snow.

And then there are tears. I can't stop them. And huge sobs from way inside my chest. My whole body shakes, and I bury my head in the arms of my big jacket and cry like I've never cried before.

FOURTEEN

I'm not sure how long I've been sitting back here. It's dark, and the parking lot lights came on a while ago. I saw the door of the loading dock open twice. It was the janitor, piling up garbage bags before bringing them to the Dumpster; both times, he gave me the evil eye. He probably thinks I'm going to graffiti the Dumpster.

I'm cold—in fact, I'm starting to shiver. I pull my cigarette package out of my pocket and take out a smoke.

There's band music coming from the school, and the front parking lot has gone from empty to full. Cars are squished together right up to the part of the driveway I can see from back here. As I stand up, my knees feel like they aren't going to unbend. My jeans are frozen and wet and stuck to my ass. I head inside to warm up before walking home.

Kids from the Ghana project are selling cookies and chips and drinks in the main hall. It smells like coffee. I scan the girls behind the table. Thankfully, no Leah.

The school feels different when there's people in it at night. It reminds me of winter carnivals at elementary school. I never cared about the lame bingo games and face painting or the fish pond where you held a yardstick with a string on it over a giant cardboard box so some mom from the parent-teacher group could attach a crappy dollar-store surprise.

My friends and I would wait for the right moment and sneak into the hallways where we weren't allowed. We loved running around the school when there was nobody there. The principal always found us and kicked us out eventually, but trying not to get caught was part of the fun. We'd write rude things on the blackboards or draw pictures of penises, hoping they'd still be there when everyone arrived for school the next morning.

After I use the washroom, I decide to check out the concert. On the way to the gym I walk past the door of the main office, and I notice too late that Mr. Peters is sitting at his desk. His head's down, but he hears me and looks up.

"Declan?"

Shit.

"This is the last place I would expect to see you, at"—he checks his watch—"7:04 at night." He pauses, staring at my face. "Are you okay?"

"Yes, sir. I went to visit my sister in town. Just came in to warm up before—"

"Are you walking home? Now?"

"Sure, sir."

"Declan, it's cold and late. And dark."

"Not that cold. Or late. I do it all the—"

"Yes, I know. Look, I'm leaving in about twenty minutes. Why don't you go see if the guys need help in the gym, setting up and taking down chairs between band sets." He's been trying to get me involved with the techie geeks all year. "I'll come get you when I'm ready to go."

"Thanks, sir, but I don't know—"

"Declan, let me drive you home. You don't look too good."

Great. Why'd I have to go and walk past his door? I wish I had a do-over.

"I don't suppose you'd tell me now about that nasty gouge on your face? It's obviously not from squeezing pimples. You in a fight?"

"I figured Miss Fraser would've told you."

"No. She doesn't tell me anything. She needs your written permission to tell me if she passed you in the hallway." He waves his arm like he's fed up with all the rules.

I nod. "My brother."

"You wanna talk about it?"

"Nope."

"Fair enough." He clasps his hands on his desk and tips his head to one side. His eyes are kind. "The offer to drive you home is still on the table. I promise I won't ask you any questions. I'd just like to see you get home. You look tired."

As soon as he says it, I realize how tired I am. A lift would be cool. But I don't want the third degree. "Sir, no questions? You won't make me talk about anything?"

"No questions. Scout's honor." He crosses his right arm over his chest and holds two fingers in a peace sign against his left shoulder.

"For real? You were a—"

"Boy Scout? That's not fair. If you get to ask questions, so should I."

"Sir, I bet you were a Boy Scout. You seem like the, like the—"

"The Boy Scout type?"

"Yeah, sort of."

"You mean like a dork?"

He thinks I just called him a dork! I'm not sure whether he's insulted or just messing with me. He's smiling a lopsided smile and has one eyebrow raised. I always wanted to be able to do that.

"No, Declan. I was never a Boy Scout. I sang in my church choir though. Now it's my turn."

I brace myself.

"Were you?"

"What?"

"Were you ever a Boy Scout? You seem like the Boy Scout type."

I exhale and laugh. "Good one, Mr. Peters."

"So, it's a yes for the lift?" He looks at me over the top of his glasses.

"I guess so. Sir?"

"Yes?"

"Thanks."

FiFTEEN

Mr. Peters slows down at the end of my driveway. We've been making small talk, and he keeps his promise—no questions. It turns out he's thinking of buying a house out here, so he drives around looking for *À Vendre* signs. Maybe he's not a pedophile after all. I think about telling him Leah's mom's a real estate agent, but I decide not to.

"Here is fine." I don't want him to drive me to the door and see the trailer and the junk on our front lawn. He thinks I'm enough of a case already.

"I'd like to see you to your door." He's peering into the blackness beyond the beam of his headlights. The front light of the trailer glows through the trees in the distance. "You have a long walk to the bus every morning."

"That's the way it is out here, sir." I shrug my jacket onto my shoulders. "I'm going to have a…" I hold up the cigarette I took out of my package while he was driving.

"Okay, Declan. We'll see you tomorrow. Get some rest, eh?"

"Thanks, sir. Bye."

He makes a U-turn and heads for the highway. I take my time walking to the house. There's a lot on my mind: Little Miss Perfect, Seamus, Mitch, Dad.

Yeah. Dad. My famous vanishing father. I guess his new act is reappearing when you don't expect it.

It was like he went into exile after he came clean with us. At the very beginning of the TMNT story, Yoshi, who becomes the Turtles' sensei, is exiled after he brings shame to his family by breaking an honor code—he disappears to protect his family. I mean, we knew where Dad lived and everything, and we saw him a few times at first. But Seamus and Kate acted like they hated him, and there were huge fights whenever he was around. He caused total chaos, and Mom was a wreck. Now I wonder, was it vanished or banished? Maybe he thought he was doing us a favor.

I've never met anyone who's dad or mom is gay. I never thought about it before, but there must be other kids with gay parents, maybe even at my school. How do they deal with it?

That poster in Miss Fraser's office, the sex one. Lots of times I've wondered, because of Dad, if I might be gay. I know Seamus does too. He doesn't have to say so. I can tell because of how homophobic he is, and because he calls everyone *fuckin' gay asshole* when he's mad. Could having a gay dad make you gay? What if I—how would I know? *Calm down, dickhead. You get a hard-on practically every time a cute girl gets near you.* That's got to mean something.

Never got a boner with a dude, and the idea gives me the creeps.

Does that make me homophobic? Do all kids with gay parents go through this stupid shit in their heads?

So which is it? Vanished or banished? I'm more confused now than ever. It was easier when I just didn't think about it, about Dad. My parents had to divorce. I get that. But lately I've been asking myself, did he have to disappear?

I feel the pores of my face open and little beads of sweat form around my eyes and on my upper lip. What if he hadn't been gone the last five years? I don't want to think about it. I throw the last of my cigarette into the ditch. The cherry fizzles out in the damp snow.

Mom's car is in its spot, and the lights in the living room are on. She meets me at the door with a gasp. It's the first time she's seen my face since last night. She doesn't say anything, just stares.

"Hi," I say, "nice to meet you. My name's Declan." I reach out to shake her hand. "And you are?"

She crosses her arms in front of her and rolls her eyes, but I got her to smile.

Out of habit, before taking off my jacket I reach into the pocket to take out my wallet. Of course, it's not there. "Damn. I can't seem to find my wallet. I've looked everywhere. Have you seen it?" I hang my jacket on the hook on the back of the door.

She shakes her head, and I scan the table again just in case. Nothing's changed since I left for school.

The lampshade is still propped on the broken base; I guess we'll need a new one.

"Maybe it's in my room and I just didn't see it."

I turn to face her under the light in the hallway. She gets a good look at my cheek. "Oh my god, Declan! Come here." She reaches out like she wants to examine my cheek.

I pull away. "It's no big deal, Mom."

She steps back and shakes her head from side to side, biting her bottom lip. Obviously, she's uptight about something. "Katie called."

Of course. She knows I went there. I wonder if she knows who else was there? I was planning to pretend the whole thing never happened, make some excuse for being so late. I wait for her to finish her sentence, but she doesn't.

"Yeah. I stopped by to see Mandy."

"I know, Dekkie. Katie told me everything."

"Can you believe it? Dad was there. Fu...freakin' unbelievable." I shake my head.

"Well, Declan, he is her father, and Mandy's grandfather."

What? What is she saying? "This is bullshit! Sorry, Mom." I'm stunned. It feels like they've changed the rules on me. "Are you *for* this? Is this okay with you? Wait a sec. Did you know? That she...? That he...? Mom! What the hell's going on?!"

Silence.

My face is getting hot, and that feeling like I want to punch something is creeping back in. "I can't believe you wouldn't tell me! I can't believe she didn't tell me!"

"You should have called first, before you showed up at her house."

"Called? I never call! It's not what we do! Why didn't you tell me? Did you think I couldn't handle it? Like I'm ten? I'm not ten! Nobody tells me that—that he goes there for supper. That Mandy calls him Grandpa! Well, let me tell you, it was a pretty fucking big surprise!" I don't even care anymore about my language.

She's cringing. I lower my voice. "Okay, Mom. I'm not going to hurt anyone. I'm mad, all right?" I flop down onto the sofa and let all the air escape through my lips. With my head in my hands, I take a second to calm down. I need to think.

When I raise my head again, she blinks a few times.

"How long have you been hiding this from me? You and Kate?"

"Not really hiding—"

"Oh fuck! Mom! What the…?" I smash my fist into my thigh. Pain shoots through my right hand.

"I should have told you, I guess. I just figured you'd find out sooner or later."

That's Mom—don't get too excited about anything. Always patting our heads to make things go away.

Doesn't she realize this is kind of a big thing to just *find out*? He's not supposed to be there. There are reasons. I close my eyes and remember Kate yelling at Seamus that Dad was a piece of shit, that he wasn't our father anymore. I remember Seamus punching walls and throwing things, and Mom just standing there, tears streaming down her cheeks.

"I thought Kate hated him. We all hated him."

She joins me on the sofa. "No, Declan. We all loved him. It tore us up. He took our life away, like that." She snaps her fingers. "I wish I could've hated him. It would've been easier. He was my best friend."

"Yeah right. *I love you, and you're my best friend. I just forgot to tell you I like to fuck guys!*"

Before I have a chance to regret what I said, pain sears my cheek, and my head jerks to the right. Everything is black. It takes me a second to realize that she slapped me! Her hand flies to her mouth. Her eyes are huge.

I stand up with my hand on my cheek and start to walk out of the room. Tears prickle at my eyes.

She follows me. "Stop! I'm sorry. You crossed a line, Declan. You don't understand. You couldn't understand. You were too young. Come back here. We need to finish this."

Still holding my left cheek, I return like a robot to the couch. I don't know what else to do. She sits down beside me. Reaches out like she's going to put her hand on my leg, then pulls it back.

"Things change, Declan. People change. It gets easier, and you move on. Thank God. Because I couldn't have lived feeling that bad forever. I had to take care of you kids, find a new job, and then Mandy was born. So you just keep moving. And one day you realize it's gotten easier."

Easier? We just pushed it away. But it was still there, working its magic. Look at us! Seamus, *acting out* as Miss Fraser calls it. Me, failing at school. Kate, pregnant at seventeen. Mom, who was a business manager, working in an animal-testing lab, for Chrissake. We're all just living in our own private versions of hell, trying to survive, pretending we're fine. It's not easier, just quieter.

"You missed him too. You don't seem to remember that," she says.

She's wrong. I do remember missing Dad. At the time, I couldn't figure out why he left. They never fought, like other kids' parents did. They actually seemed to like each other. I remember wondering why being gay meant he had to disappear. He was supposed to be my dad. But everyone else thought it had to be that way. Nobody ever talked to me about it. I just followed along like a fucking puppy dog.

"You wouldn't leave me alone," she continues. "You didn't want to be away from me. Do you remember sleeping in my bed?"

Oh my god. All those times Seamus locked himself in his room—*our* room—I had to sleep with Mom. Seamus teased me about being a mama's boy. How did I forget that? I swallow hard because there's a huge lump in my throat, and my nose is starting to run.

Mom says, "You were always trying to cheer me up—you still do that. I guess I told myself because you seemed okay, you were okay. Maybe it was wrong for me to do that, but what else could I do?"

I squeeze my eyes shut to fight back tears and see the day Dad left, and all the screaming. It's like a nightmare. I'm watching everyone—Kate, Seamus, Mom like she's in a trance, Dad. Me? I can barely see me. It's like I'm not there. *Don't worry about him. He's just little. He has nothing to say.*

The ringing phone brings me back. Mom answers, "Hello…Yes. He's here." She glances at me, then turns away, nodding while she listens. "No. He got a ride home…I don't know…Well, he's very upset." She's almost whispering, but I can still hear, "Yes, tell Katie. Okay, goodbye, Patrick."

The hairs stand up on the back of my neck. She said his name. *Patrick.* She was talking to Dad.

There's a pause, and her voice changes completely. For the rest of the call, I can tell she's talking to Mandy. I walk to the bathroom to get a wad of toilet paper for my runny nose.

When I come back, she hangs up the phone.

"He's still there?"

She nods. "He visits. Has done for a while now."

I shake my head. How long is *for a while now?* Mandy was so comfortable with him. And yet he's a stranger to me.

"I thought you hated him. Because he's—"

"Not hate. I felt betrayed. I didn't want to believe it. But by the time he left, I already knew. I always had my suspicions. I just kept them to myself. I thought if we got married it would go away. Then we had kids, and you just kind of forget." She takes a sip of water from a glass on the coffee table, then uncrumples and folds a Kleenex she's had balled up in her hand. I can hear the fridge motor whirring in the kitchen, and the fish tank bubbling. Even the lamp on the table next to us seems loud.

She crumples the Kleenex back up again. "We lost so much. Not just each other. We lost our family." Her voice cracks. "It was just easier to get the divorce over with and push on."

Push on? Really? Because it seems like we just buried it. Like we were hiding a dead body in the backyard. Heroes push on. Face things. I'm not so sure pretending nothing happened, hiding it all, was heroic.

"You weren't disgusted?"

"No. I don't know. I probably said that at the time. It gave me an excuse to reject him. I felt a lot of things. Don't forget, he also had an affair. That made me feel like I'd been living a lie. It made me doubt everything...how he felt about me. I was angry—angry doesn't even cover it—and confused. But disgust?" She shrugs, and her lip trembles. I notice tears in the corners of her eyes. She rolls her eyes to the side, trying to make the tears evaporate. After a few seconds she calms down, reaches over and strokes my face. Her fingertips make tiny cool spots on my bruised cheek.

"I'm sorry for slapping you—"

"It doesn't matter." I grab one of the cushions and hold it against my chest.

"You have a right to feel whatever you feel, Declan. But you shouldn't have said that."

I know I should apologize, but I can't. I'm mad, and I don't know for sure about what. And so tired—too tired even for a smoke. I want to be alone. "Ma, do you mind if I just go to bed? I didn't sleep much, and it's been a long day."

"Of course. Go. I'm going soon too."

"Ma?"

"Yes?"

"What if I'm not sure how I feel about—that?" I picture him holding Mandy, her playing with his watch, her little fingers holding his wrists. *My uncle's gay, he's really cool...*

"It's okay, honey. You have to feel what you feel. But I think we all..."

She trails off. I wait for her.

"Maybe for Mandy, we all have to put that aside."

My shoulders drop. "I don't know, Mom. I just don't know. I don't know what I think anymore."

Before I leave the room, she asks if I've heard from Seamus. She seems small and sad. I shake my head. I can't help her. The truth is, I'm not sure I care.

"He's out wrestling with the devil, I guess. I hope he's safe." She's trying to look brave, but I can tell she's terrified.

"Yeah, I guess. Good night, Ma."

"Good night, Dekkie."

I sit on the edge of my bed, too tired to take off my clothes. Too confused to focus on anything. Vanished. Banished. These words keep rolling around in my head. I keep going back to that TMNT story. I know what shame feels like, what Yoshi felt, and what his family must have felt about him. Without Yoshi's exile, there would have been no Teenage Mutant Ninja Turtles. Was there any other way? For Yoshi, the alternative was hara-kiri. For us? Was there an alternative for us?

He is her father, and Mandy's grandfather. My father. What does that word even mean? I guess exile is better than hara-kiri. I still have a father. And he doesn't live in a sewer on the other side of the world.

SiXTEEN

I'm coming in from having a smoke after lunch on Tuesday, walking—*walking*—around a corner to get to my locker before the second bell rings, and *wham!* Leah smashes right into me.

"Whoa!" I grab her shoulders before she assaults me again with her books. In her hands, those things are like weapons.

She shakes her hair back and makes an annoyed sound in the back of her throat. "Figures you'd be somewhere you're not supposed to be!"

"Hey! Figures *you'd* be tearing around a corner not looking where you're going—again." I still have her by the shoulders. She has to look up to see my face because she's so close and she's a lot shorter than me. There's this electricity between us, and for a second it's awkward. Her eyes dart away, and I let go.

"You're not supposed to be on this side. You walk on the other side in case someone's coming around the corner! Like driving?" She curls her lip like, *duh.*

I've seen the damage she can do walking with a pile of books. If she was behind the wheel of a car, no one would be safe. "Yeah? Well, fortunately this isn't driving. Watch where you're going."

She shakes her head and acts all pissed off. But she's flustered. For once, I'm the cool one.

Then she notices the bruise on my cheek. Her face changes, and she loses the impatient routine. Little Miss Perfects aren't supposed to be bitchy when people are hurt. I liked it better when she was snotty. At least it was honest. She's trying not to stare, but her eyes keep sneaking up to my face. Today, my whole left cheek is black and kind of a smooth marbled purple, and there's a crunchy, rust-colored scab on my cheekbone. It makes me irresistible. "Aren't you gonna ask? Everyone else does."

She presses her lips together, probably annoyed I caught her staring. "What happened?"

"I got in a fight. I was the good guy."

She nods, but her raised eyebrows say she doesn't believe me. "Are you all right?"

I consider telling her what a beast I was, and how I tossed Seamus out like a bag of garbage. Chicks dig that sort of thing, even though they pretend they're all superior. You can tell because their eyes get like heat-seeking missiles. I decide not to. I'm nervous enough about going to her house again, especially after we made fools of ourselves in the gym. I shrug and flex my sore hand. "You should see the other guy."

She rolls her eyes and calls me a jerk. I'm smiling inside at how easy it is to mess with her. Her arms are crossed in front of her over her books, and she's wearing a low-cut top. Being tall has some advantages when it comes to certain things. I can't help looking at her boobs. I'm afraid she'll notice, so I change the subject. "We taking the bus to your place later?"

Her eyes open wide, like she expected me to blow off tutoring. "Yeah, sure."

"You'll be happy to know I actually have my stuff this time." I hitch my schoolbag, just excavated from under a pile of stuff in my closet, onto my shoulder the way I've seen the real students do.

"Great. I'd better get to class." She starts walking away backward.

"Better look where you're going." I don't know what gets into me, but I wink. It's like my eye decides to do it without running it past my brain first. Her forehead wrinkles up, and a corner of her mouth sort of twitches.

Her fingers let go of their grip on her books and flutter "bye," and then she pivots gracefully on one canvas sneaker and walks away. I'm watching her walk—the smooth swing of her hips—and she looks back and catches me. My stomach does some major dance steps. But she turns and continues down the hall, hugging her books as she makes the distance between us grow. Not perky. Just smooth.

I pull myself away. Two minutes till the final bell. I can make it to class on time if I run. I do a quick check up and down the hall—no Mr. Peters, no Miss Fraser—and beat it to my locker to ditch my jacket as fast as I can.

* * *

"Done."

I push my chair away from the table and stretch out my legs. Leah takes the cap off her red pen. I've just finished my first history quiz. She said she wanted to see how much I know, where the "holes" are. I tried to convince her I wasn't ready, but she doesn't take no for an answer. When she thinks something should happen, it does. I'm learning it's kind of how she sees the world.

She puts on her teacher face and reaches for my paper. I slide it toward her slowly. The red pen gets to work.

There's nothing on the stove today, but I hear a clock ticking somewhere. Leah's grandmother has the TV on low in the living room. It's dusk. The chandelier over the table isn't on yet, and it's getting darker in here. The candlesticks on the buffet are catching the last of the light through the dining room window. I shudder at the memory they bring up and go back to following the red pen. Isn't she done yet? My legs are jumpy from sitting for such a long time. I could use a smoke.

Check. Check. Check.

Leah stops to put her hair up in a pink elastic. She twirls it around and twists the elastic into place and voilà, like magic, there's a loose pouf of hair on top of her head.

Now I can see the little bone of her spine sticking out above the collar of her sweater; escaped curls rest on the back of her neck. Little soft ones you could put your finger through, soft like the pussy willows that grow in the ditch near my house.

Snap out of it, dickhead. "So how's it look, teach?"

"Well, Declan." Hearing her say my name has a surprising effect. My insides turn to mush. "Not bad. I'm just about done." She writes something on the paper and motions for me to move my chair closer. I hesitate, shy about pulling up beside her. I bite the inside of my cheek and stare at the red marks on the page.

"Oh, get over yourself."

I grab my chair and scoot over. I have to scrunch up my legs so our knees don't bump. *Just keep your eyes off those curls.*

She gives me this long story about how I did well on some of the questions but makes me feel like an idiot about the long answers. "You have to write more than two or three words."

I strain to see the page. Some of them have four or five.

"Did you understand this stuff?"

What does she mean, did I understand it? Why wouldn't I? "Yeah." I know I sound kind of huffy.

"Okay, okay. I just want to know if you get the big picture."

I have no idea what big picture she's talking about, but it's no problem. She can tell by the clueless expression on my face.

"It's okay. We'll go over it. You'll get questions like this on your final exam. Haven't you had to write any essays?"

How do I tell her I've never done one? That I've handed in squat the whole year? On the other hand, what makes me think she'd be surprised?

"They don't just want you to memorize stuff. You kind of have to show that you can use your brain."

I start picking a hangnail. What the hell time is it anyway? Shouldn't I be going home?

"Is something wrong?" She sounds like she's actually trying to be nice.

"No." I look at my watch. "It's getting late."

"I thought you wanted to pass the exam." No more Miss Nice Guy.

"I do, I do. It's just—"

"It's just what? You don't want to work?"

"What? No! I'm here, aren't I?" It's only my second week of taking things seriously. I'm still getting warmed up.

"Well, you have to work!"

"I know. It's just…"

"Hard?"

"Tiring!"

She's shaking her head.

"You think I'm a…a loser! I know you do."

She's about to say something, but she stops herself and settles on a scowl.

"Well, I'm not. I'm just not like you. Little Miss Perfect—"

Leah straightens like a rod in her chair. I think she might slap me. Two slaps in a week. "Little Miss Perfect? What's that supposed to mean?"

"You know, straight As, the Ghana project, the guidance counselor's little pet—"

"You're insulting me because I'm a good student? And helpful? Oh my god! It's better than being a loser stoner whose friends walk up walls for attention because they're too stupid to do anything else!"

I'm pissed that she called me a stoner. But I'm not going to sit here while she insults my friends. Especially since Dave's a freaking genius. "You know what? My friends've got my back. They're loyal *and* smart. You probably can't see it, because you're too busy with all your popular shit, but Dave's a freakin' genius. The girls you hang around with are all nicey-nice to your face, but they have shit for brains, and they're real bitches."

"Yeah? Well, your friends are immature jerks. They whistle and objectify women."

My jaw drops. "They whistle because they think you're cute! 'Cause they saw you dancing and think you're hot! And *objectify women*? What the hell does that even mean?"

"Well, if you weren't so…"

"C'mon!" I dare her to finish.

She freezes.

"Say it!"

She presses her lips together.

"You were gonna say *stupid*."

She looks down.

"Don't bother. I know you think it anyway. Little Miss Perfect, helping the poor loser! Good for you! I guess you think you deserve a Nobel Prize or something." My hands are tripping over themselves getting my stuff together so I can leave.

"I don't think you're stupid! But you are lazy, or maybe you just don't care. Anyway, it seems like that's what you want everyone to think. Why do you act like you're so tough all the time?"

"'Cause I *am* tough?" I stop shuffling papers. Did I really say that?

"You're all *fuckin this* and *fuckin that*. But you were sweet to my bubby, and you go home to have supper with your mom."

She stops, and my ears ring in the silence. It's like the walls are stunned too, it's so quiet. "Careful. You'll ruin my reputation," I say.

"You're not such a bad boy." She has her arms crossed in front of her again.

"And you're not such a Little Miss Perfect. Yesterday in the gym, the variety-show thing? That was a surprise."

Neither of us says anything for a few moments. She's quiet, but her eyes are fiery. Her chest rises and falls a few times. "Your friends think I'm cute?"

I have to decide whether to rat out Mitch and Dave or let her think they're jerks. "Look, I'm just saying, they liked it. Hip-hop isn't exactly Chinese folk dancing."

I glance down at her arms, crossed over her—you know—boobs, and she notices! Little Miss Perfect tilts her head to the side and curls fall over her shoulder. Her eyes are slits.

I'm a boy. She's a girl. What does she expect?

Quickly I look away, ready to get blasted.

"Oh."

I've been holding my breath. I exhale. "Oh?"

"Yeah. No one's ever said that before, that I'm—cute."

"Seriously?"

"Well, yeah," she says, like it's obvious. Like she's really surprised they think she's hot.

Funny. Guys always think girls know. They put so much work into how they look—makeup, clothes, their hair. How could they not know? It seems like they do a lot to get us to notice. Then when we do, they act all pissed off. I shake my head and change the subject. "So, what about the quiz? I actually should go soon. I have to walk, and it's pretty far." Notes and books and pens are jumbled up, sticking half in, half out of my bag.

"You live in Rigaud and you were going to *walk*?" she asks, like she thinks I'm crazy. She starts again, several decibels lower. "Look, if you wait till six my dad can drive you. You won't get home any later."

She wants me to stay? I feel my heart pumping in the back of my throat. "Thanks, but after sitting all this time, I think I need to move, stretch my legs." I don't want to meet her dad! Isn't her grandmother enough? What dad wants his daughter hanging around a guy with a black eye?

"Well, I have a great idea then!"

Oh boy, here we go.

"I usually take Bubby for a walk around this time. After we go over your quiz, you'll come with us. We'll all stretch our legs."

I hear *you'll come with us* and realize it's another one of those times when there's no point arguing. It's what's going to happen. I'm going to stretch my legs with Leah and her bubby. "Are you sure? Last time, the candlesticks and everything. Maybe it's not such a good idea."

"Don't be ridiculous. She'll love it. Maybe we can even get her to tell us one of her stories. By the time we get back, my dad will be home, and he can give you a lift. See? It's perfect."

Yeah, perfect.

* * *

We work for another hour, and I head to the washroom, thinking there's got to be some other excuse I can come up with to not go on this walk. The washroom distracts me while I'm in it.

It's filled with old stuff. The sink is made of an old washbasin like the kind we saw on a field trip in Old Montreal, and there's an antique chair with crackled varnish in the corner, holding a plant in a pot that looks like it's from the Stone Age. On a wooden shelf above the sink, there's a cracked dish with a lid that says *Atkinson's Parisian Toothpaste.* It looks ancient! I start to open it. I want to see if you can still brush your teeth with it, but then I decide I'd better leave it alone. My history with Leah's family's souvenirs hasn't been so good. I go back to worrying about the walk.

Leah's not at the table when I get back, so I go to see if she's with her grandmother. The living room looks out over the lake, and the sun is setting. The snowy hills on the other side are outlined in bright pink. There's a fireplace along one wall. If this was my house, I'd spend all my time here. Leah's grandmother is in her recliner, talking on the phone. She smiles and points to the chair beside her. "Yes, dear. Thursday will be fine."

I sit on the edge of the chair with my elbows on my knees. I notice she has a tattoo on her arm, the one that's holding the phone. At first I think she's even cooler than I thought; then I realize it's a number, and it's probably from the concentration camp. I feel like I'm not supposed to see it, like I found her in her underwear, so I look away and start scanning the room. But it takes a moment for me to shake it off.

There's more old stuff on shelves and hanging on the wall. Really old, like arrowheads and something that looks like a cave painting, only it's carved into wood. There's a creepy little stone statue with no face or arms and really long legs, and angels and crucifixes. Isn't it against the rules to have crosses if you're Jewish?

Bubby takes a couple of seconds to focus on the keypad's huge buttons. She clicks the phone off. "Good afternoon, Mr. O'Reilly."

"Hi, Mrs. Zimmerman." I'm surprised she remembers my name. Let's be honest. I'm even more surprised I didn't screw up hers. Should I shake her hand? She doesn't hold out hers, so I decide it's okay not to. I push my hair out of my face and nod.

"Oh my, what happened to you? Looks like somebody beat you up." Her little bird eyes are darting around my rainbow bruise. I forgot about that. I give her some story about bashing my face on the coffee table, to play down my resemblance to an actual criminal. I'm sure she doesn't buy it, but she leaves it alone.

"How is tutoring coming along?"

"It's okay. I'm not the greatest student."

"Well, there's always room for improvement. Leah's students seem to do quite well in the end."

"I believe it. She's a slave driver. She gave me a quiz today."

"Oh my. You did all right, I hope?"

"Not too bad. Like you said, there's definitely room for improvement."

Leah comes in carrying a bunch of winter stuff— coats, hats, scarves. She lays them on the sofa beside her grandmother. "Hey, Bubby. Declan's going to join us for our walk today."

"How nice!"

Leah's grandmother slides her feet out of her slippers. She's wearing men's woolen socks. Leah helps her with her boots and her coat. Her flowered housedress sticks out under the coat. She almost disappears under all those layers.

Outside, Leah holds Bubby's elbow. I check for the blue Taurus across the street and exhale when it's not there. I'm beginning to wonder where Seamus is. I'm used to him turning up everywhere and giving me trouble. We haven't crossed paths once since I threw him out of the trailer.

I shove my hands in my pockets and walk on the street beside the curb where Leah's guiding Bubby along. What is it with Leah and that curly hair? I could watch her all day. She catches me and smiles in kind of a shy way. I'm glad it's getting dark, because I can feel myself blushing.

"Look at the nice clear sidewalks. It still amazes me how they have machines to do that nowadays." Bubby means the little tractors the city uses to clear the public sidewalks—unless, of course, you live in the middle of nowhere on a highway. Like she read my mind, Bubby asks me where I live. I tell her about our place in Rigaud, away from the road, and how there's forest all around us. Leah's eyes get big when I say my parents bought a trailer instead of a house.

"How clever," Bubby says. "It sounds like paradise." Maybe it's because I left out the part about the tires and the broken toilet, but she made me feel good about where I live and why I love it. She really listened to me.

"Declan's going to be studying World War II and the Holocaust in history. I promised him you'd tell us a story about what happened to the Jews, like maybe about Kristallnacht and the yellow stars? He'll need to know it for the exam." Leah helps her grandmother around a patch of ice as we cross the street. I see now why she went ballistic when Robbie and Seamus sped past her house.

"Kristallnacht. Declan, do you know about Kristallnacht?" Bubby asks.

I love the way she pronounces the word, with a hard *ckt* sound at the end. I try it myself, but it sounds more like a cat coughing up a hairball. Leah and Bubby stop themselves from laughing out loud, but Leah has to turn her head away.

"Don't worry, Declan. That was a good try," Bubby says.

"Yeah, great!" Leah's still trying not to piss herself.

Bubby continues with her story. "It started with the Nazis painting yellow stars on the windows of Jewish businesses to discourage people from going in. Germany was in a bad way economically, and the Nazis publicly blamed the Jews for it. During Kristallnacht, Jewish businesses were vandalized, windows broken, stores looted. Do you know what *Kristallnacht* means?"

"Isn't it 'crystal night,' because of broken glass in the street or something?"

Leah tips her head in an approving nod. I've redeemed myself from my hairball.

"Right! And vandals used the yellow stars to identify which businesses belonged to Jews. No one stopped them. The government, the police. Everyone stood by and watched. It was the beginning of cleaning the streets of anyone who didn't fit in with the Nazis' plan. And it was where the idea of forcing people to wear identification badges came from. First it was Jews and the yellow star. But then other badges started to turn up, on the streets and especially in the camps. There were all kinds of people the Nazis wanted out of the way. Political people who spoke out against the government, communists, blacks, Poles—"

Poles? I must look confused, because Leah whispers, "People from Poland."

"Our choir director was a lovely gay man who wore the pink triangle on his sleeve."

"The pink triangle?" I've never heard of the pink triangle.

"Oh, there were quite a number of gay men in the camp. They wore a pink triangle instead of the yellow star. There were many different badges, actually—red triangles, black triangles. They all meant something different."

"But the pink triangles. What were they for?"

"Homosexual men. I think in some ways it was worse for them, because not only were they singled out by the Nazis, but they got very little sympathy from the rest of the prisoners either. Somehow, homosexuals didn't fit with anyone's plan."

"You knew them?" My voice sounds jittery.

Leah motions for me to take Bubby's elbow while she bends down to tie a bootlace. So I'm actually holding Bubby's arm while she's talking to me. I can barely feel it, deep in the layers of her winter coat. It's bony and weighs nothing.

"I sang in a children's choir in Theresienstadt—that was the name of the camp. The Nazis put us on display, paraded us around to make the rest of the world believe we were all happy and healthy." She stops walking and looks right into my face. "Can you imagine?"

I shake my head. I can't imagine living through any of that. I can't believe I'm holding her arm. It makes me feel connected to her story—to her—and I like it.

"He was wonderful, our choir director. It may sound odd, but we felt lucky. He'd been an opera singer before the war.

Of course, there were other prisoners who couldn't stand what he was, you know. But I loved him. He was so good to my brother and me after our parents were taken away." She puts her free hand on her throat, raises her chin in the air and turns to me again, proud. "He told me I had a beautiful voice."

"Oh, it's true, Bubby, you do," Leah says, and Bubby starts to sing, right there in the middle of the street. She hums a clear, sad tune—not anything I've ever heard. Her voice is a bit shaky, but it's beautiful.

I try to imagine being in that concentration camp. Forced to pretend in front of people who could help. Not screaming about what was really going on because if you did, you'd be killed. And at the same time, feeling lucky or happy that someone liked your voice. How do you feel lucky when you've lost everything?

"What happened to him?"

"Oh, he was killed—beaten to death and violated. They left him in the yard, with his hands tied and his pants down, for everyone to see. A lesson. They liked to do that. What was he supposed to have done about being gay? How could he have hurt anyone? I prayed that there was a heaven, because I needed to imagine him there. I couldn't think of him, such a good man, like that."

A good man. I'm supposed to be steadying Bubby, but I'm pretty shaken, and I don't want her or Leah to know. I clear my throat and take in a big breath of fresh air. Leah's house is up ahead. We're almost there.

Bubby's smiling. I can tell she adores Leah. "Thank you so much. That was really lovely. Soon it'll be spring, and you won't need to prop this old woman up. Thank you for your help, Declan."

"You're welcome, Mrs. Zimmerman. That was an incredible story. I never met anyone before who…"

"Of course, dear. And that's probably a good thing. But as I say to Leah, soon we'll all be gone. It will be up to you youngsters to remember."

Leah puts her arms around her grandmother and kisses her. "I love you, Bubby." She unlocks the door, and we make our way back inside. The house feels warm and familiar.

SEVENTEEN

Turns out Leah's dad was the one driving the big white SUV I saw at the school. It even has heated seats. He's an archaeologist, which explains all the old stuff in their house. Leah rolls her eyes when I ask him, "Like Indiana Jones?" But he says yes and tells me about *artifacts* like the Parisian toothpaste that they dug up right in Old Montreal.

He asks me about my parents. I say they're divorced and that I never see my dad, hoping he won't ask me any more questions. Leah has this strange look on her face. I pretend I don't notice.

I get them to drop me at the rink so I can pick up my check before I go home. It's payday. I'll get Rita, who works the afternoon shift at the canteen, to cash it for me. It'll be nice to have some cash of my own again. I still can't find my wallet, and at lunch I had to borrow from Dave just to get a cookie.

The automatic doors open to the usual smells: ice, French fries, Zamboni exhaust. The Rigaud rink is one of the old rinks with wooden benches that freeze your ass. Not part of a big rec center. No gyms. No bars. No heaters. No hockey parents drinking beers and yelling at the refs. Just one flat-screen TV attached to the wall in the waiting area, and some wobbly tables and chairs. And you can see your breath when you're on the ice. The canteen's cozy, but it's a basic burgers-and-fries operation.

I unlock the reception-booth door and find my check in my cubby. Phil is on the rink with the Zamboni. Parents are chilling around the TV, watching sports highlights from the latest Habs game, checking stuff on their phones. I jostle through them on my way to the canteen.

Rita's standing on a chair, up to her elbows in the slushie machine; it's jammed and making an ugly grinding noise. When she sees me coming, she smiles like I'm her long-lost best friend. She needs me. I can fix it.

"I can't believe you're here. Would you mind?" She sounds like she's ready to throw the machine from the bleachers.

When no one's looking, I vault over the counter, just missing a jug full of gummie worms. She screams and laughs. It takes me a couple of seconds to work my magic. The grinding stops and the giant bag of colored syrup gurgles and flops into place. Purple and orange crushed ice swirls around to the machine's familiar *grrr-urrr-urr*.

I leave the canteen with my cash and run into Phil coming off the ice in his hat and coat. "You going out?" I ask, wondering if he wants to join me outside for a smoke.

"Nah, gotta unplug a toilet in the girls' bathroom. Wanna help?" He takes off his coat and hangs it on the hook in the caretaker's office.

"Gee, I'd love to, but I hear my mommy calling."

"Chicken."

"You got it!"

He gives me the finger.

I wave goodbye to Rita, who blows me a thank-you kiss, and head for home. I'm glad for the chance to really stretch my legs. I enjoyed walking with Leah's grandmother, but propping up an eighty-three-year-old woman isn't exactly a workout. I light a cigarette.

I catch myself scanning for Seamus and the car. Where is my stupid brother? I'm not going to lie. I've enjoyed a few trouble-free days, but he should have turned up by now.

For the longest time after Dad left, I thought the worst thing anyone could be was gay. It was the reason my family fell apart. How was I supposed to feel? I always knew not everyone feels this way, and I don't really have a problem with other people being gay. But it's different when it's your dad. It's confusing. What Leah's grandmother said really made me think. She loved that gay choir guy because he was a good person. She didn't care about him being gay. The Nazis did though. *My dad* could have been hunted down, imprisoned, tortured, killed. Because he didn't fit in with some plan?

What if he really is cool, like Mitch says? You can't always trust Mitch's judgment on this kind of thing. His family is different. When Mitch started hanging around with me and Dave, his mom asked both our moms to one of her yoga retreats. My mom's a chain-smoking, coffee-guzzling hummingbird with limbs like dry twigs. She'd rather have her toenails removed with pliers than spend a weekend like a pretzel with a bunch of inner-peace flakes. But she said yes to be polite. She came back amped up and miserable, smoking twice as much as she had before. It wasn't for her. Square-peg-in-a-round-hole kind of thing.

I wonder if I'm a square peg, trying to pass history and graduate? It's sure as hell not an easy fit. I almost blew it today.

And what about Dad? I understand why he and Mom had to end it. But what about the rest of us? Maybe it isn't right to say someone doesn't fit in their own family. This isn't Nazi Germany, but we did kind of push him out, like he wasn't part of *our* plan.

Man, there's too much stuff floating around in my head. New thoughts are trying to find places in my brain, and they're fighting with all the old ones. Everything has to shift. Like it's a puzzle and somebody gives you a bunch of new pieces and says, *Make room for these.*

How could anyone survive living in a concentration camp? And losing your whole family? Watching friends die? When we learned about it in school, I only ever thought about how many people were killed. I never thought about the people who weren't.

I chuck the butt of my cigarette into the snow and turn up the driveway, looking forward to being home. Right away I can tell something's not right. Instead of the usual glow of the trailer's front light in the distance, blue and red lights are bouncing off the trees in the dark. Police! I choke back panic and run as fast as I can the rest of the way, doing my best to avoid patches of black ice.

I reach the yard and almost bash into a cruiser parked in front of the house, the colored lights rotating silently. There's no one inside it. In one giant step, I'm at the door. I grab the handle, take a big breath. *Oh please, oh please, let everyone be okay…*

Mom's perched on the end of the sofa. Two police officers with *Sûreté du Québec* patches on their uniforms are sitting in the living room, one beside Mom and the other in the armchair. They're wearing hats, and their winter jackets are open—I can see flak vests underneath. They both have newspaper under their boots. Mom made the SQ put paper under their boots? That's nuts.

"Mom!"

"Declan. I've been trying to reach you. Where have you been? I called Dave's but—"

"What's wrong?" I'm heaving, trying to catch my breath.

The officers introduce themselves, but their names float by in a blur. All I get is that the one doing the talking has a French name. The other one looks younger. They ask me my name and I tell them. Then the guy with the French name starts firing questions at me. Where was I last night? What's Kate's address? Why was I there? Where did I go after? Did anyone see me? How long was I there? I'm so worked up I really have to concentrate to remember anything about last night, but I give them everything they ask for, except the part about seeing Dad and being upset. He writes it all on a little notepad.

I try to get in a few questions of my own. Did something happen to Mandy? Kate? Seamus? I still don't know what this is about, and they don't tell me anything. They want my answers to their questions first. Mom is stone-faced. If something happened to one of us, she'd be way more upset, wouldn't she?

The French officer's voice interrupts my thoughts. "Please answer the question, Mr. O'Reilly."

I can't remember it.

He repeats it for me. "How long were you sitting by the Dumpster before you went into the school?"

My mind is blank, and then I remember Mr. Peters checking his watch and teasing me about being at school at 7:04. "I saw the vice-principal at 7:04."

"At 7:04?" Maybe I'm being paranoid, but it sounds like he's mocking me. I bet he thinks I made it up. "You're telling us you were sitting—leaning—on this Dumpster from 6:15 to 7:04?" The officers smile at each other like they think it's a joke. They don't believe me. What's worse, Mom's lips are pressed together like she doesn't either. It feels as if the police and Mom are on the same side, and it's not mine.

"Yeah, he actually checked his watch. He—" I stop myself from saying he was surprised to see me. I need someone on my side. "It was 7:04."

"You sat in the cold for forty-five minutes?"

"Sir, I didn't feel the cold. My mind was somewhere else."

"Your mind, Mr. O'Reilly? What does that mean?" He leans forward on the sofa and puts his elbows on his knees. He's trying to get closer to me. Right in my face. It freaks me out that he keeps calling me Mr. O'Reilly. He probably thinks I was stoned or selling drugs.

"I was just thinking." I don't want to go into the whole story about Dad.

"And the vice-principal's name?"

"Mr. Peters. I don't know his first name."

"If we ask him, he will tell us he saw you?" He's trying to catch me in a lie, I think.

I explain that he drove me home. Mom nods her head. Her face relaxes. Did she really doubt me?

"Does Mr. Peters know where you were between"—he checks the little notepad—"6:15 and 7:04?"

Wow. This is a fucking interrogation. They're questioning me like I've done something really bad. "I guess not. What's going on? Can you please tell me what this is about?"

"Mr. O'Reilly, do you recognize these?"

The other officer holds up a student card and a debit card. When I look closely, I see they're both mine. Mom gasps. They're supposed to be in my wallet.

"My cards! You found my wallet!" I'm so relieved I actually smile.

He's not feeling my vibe. "You lost your wallet?"

"Yes. I've been looking for it since yesterday morning. I couldn't find it anywhere." I turn to Mom. "Remember? I told you last night."

Her lips are still pressed together. Her face is hard. What the fuck?

The officer writes in his pad. Why does he have my cards? "This lost wallet. Did you report it?"

"What? No." Do people actually do that?

"Would you like to know where we found these? Maybe you already have an idea where."

I shake my head. None of this makes any sense to me. "No. Where?"

He starts examining my face, ignoring my question. "You have some bruises there, some scratches too. Can you tell us how you got those?"

"I got in a fight with my brother, Sunday night." Mom's nodding again.

The officer looks back and forth between us. "That's how you got bruised and scratched?"

"Yes, sir."

"*Sunday* night?"

"Yes."

"Officers." We all turn toward Mom, who hasn't spoken until now. "I was there on Sunday when my boys were fighting. I saw the whole thing. My other son hit him pretty hard a couple of times in the face." She looks down. "And I noticed Declan was bleeding. When he came home last night, that big scratch was scabbed over." She points to where I got gouged by Seamus's ring. "Not fresh."

Not fresh? What is she talking about? Who cares how fresh my scab is? I realize she knows what they're asking me all this for, and I don't.

"What time was that?"

"About eight, I guess."

I try to make eye contact with her, but she turns her face away. Why? I need her right now. I turn back to the officer who showed me the cards. "Sir, why do you have them?"

He sighs, and the two of them look at each other. The guy with the French name nods, tells the younger guy to go ahead. "They were given to us by the owner of the golf course on Harwood. He found them on his property."

He's studying me, waiting for my reaction.

"Golf course?"

"Yes, Mr. O'Reilly," the French guy answers. "The Harwood Golf Course, where there's been thousands of dollars in damage to the property. Vandalized. Someone made a nice mess spinning tires on the eighteenth-hole green and then took a joy ride in a golf cart—rammed it into the garage wall and left it on its side."

I'm starting to get it now. "And my cards were found there, so you think *I* did it?"

"It seems like you were there, no? It's a ten-minute walk from the school."

"I didn't do it. I've never been there."

All three of them stare at me. Mom shakes her head.

"Mom, honest! I didn't do it!"

Can she really think I did? I try to put all the pieces together. Sunday night. My wallet. Sitting by the Dumpster. How could my cards have gotten to the green? The only problem is, I'm kind of in panic mode. My brain isn't working properly.

I look at Mom. She's drained and tired. I remember her screaming at me the night of the fight. Does she really think I did this? I shocked her when I lost it with Seamus. Does she think I lost it after seeing Dad at Kate's?

It seems like you were there. The officer's words ring in my ears. How did my cards get there? And why couldn't *I* find my wallet the morning after the fight?

Slowly a picture begins to take shape in my brain. I remember Seamus leaning on the hall table on his way out the door. Steadying himself on the same table where I leave my wallet and keys every night. The next morning, no wallet. He's always hitting me up for money. Was he still mad because I said no when they showed up at the rink? Mad enough after the fight to steal my wallet? *Made a mess spinning tires.* The blue Taurus?

Seamus would vandalize a golf course. Just like the shed he and his friends torched two years ago. Just like the wipers on that teacher's car.

I feel sick to my stomach thinking about what my brother might have done to the golf course and to me. "Mom, maybe Sea—"

"No, Declan!"

"But Mom, Monday morning before school, I couldn't find my wallet. It hasn't turned up since. I'm sure it was on the table Sunday night." I open my eyes really wide, trying to get her to see what I'm not saying. She knows I keep my wallet there. It's a habit. I grab it and my keys before I leave the house, every time I go out. Everybody in the house knows that. *Everybody.*

I search Mom's face. I'm sure she knows what I'm thinking. She shakes her head and presses her lips together again. Her eyes bore holes into me, warning me not to go there. It's not the encouragement I was hoping for.

Great. Seamus must be involved in this. But it's obvious Mom doesn't want me to say it. What's going to happen to me if I don't? The police think I did it. It seems she expects me to take the rap for my brother, like she's protecting him.

Who's going to look out for me then?

"Officer." I take a deep breath and turn away from Mom. Both officers face me.

"I think I might know what happened." I wipe my palms on my jeans. Everyone's eyes are on me. "There's a chance my brother took my wallet when he left here Sunday night. He's always asking me for money. After we fought, he stopped and leaned on that table. I think he might have left with my wallet."

"Declan! He wouldn't! How could you—"

I turn to Mom and say, "He would. You know it too."

The French officer holds up his pen to get me to focus on him. "You think he took it? You mean he stole it?"

It's tough to tune Mom out. She's shaking her head, trying to get me to stop. Stole it? I didn't think of it like that. "I guess so. He had his back to us, and there was a lot going on. But he stopped there before he left."

I force myself to look at Mom. She's studying the shredded Kleenex in her hand.

"Your brother is Seamus O'Reilly?" The officers share a meaningful glance. They already know his name, but they turn to Mom for confirmation. She nods, then covers her mouth with her hand. The other hand is balled up around the shredded Kleenex.

"Officer, I'm not saying he did this thing at the golf course. But he could have taken my wallet. It wasn't me at the golf course. I didn't have my cards."

"We'll follow up on this new information. But I'm afraid we will still have to take you to the station—"

"The station? *What?!*" My voice cracks. "Why? I didn't do anything!"

"We don't actually know that yet. We're still investigating. This is interesting new information." He taps his pad. "We're not charging you at this time. But we want to take your fingerprints. In order to do that, we have to take you in, so we're arresting you. Do you understand?"

"Arrested? Charged? No!" This is going way too fast.

"For now, we want to take your fingerprints and your statement. We're not charging you with anything—yet. We're just going to hold on to you for a little while." The officers smile at each other. Pricks.

"There's a difference between being charged and being arrested?" I ask.

"Yes. You have to be arrested first to be charged, but sometimes you aren't charged when you're arrested. It depends on our evidence. But we need to arrest you or we can't take you in for your fingerprints."

"So you're arresting me just so you can take my fingerprints?"

"Yes." He hands Mom an official-looking paper. I can see it says *Warrant* on it. "He'll be at the station in Vaudreuil. You can follow us in your car if you want to stay with him. Or you can call." He takes a small folder out of his pocket and hands her a business card. "Ask for me or Sergeant Reid. We can't take you in the cruiser. Sorry."

Mom's still shaking her head. Ryan and Kate have her car. She can't even come with me. "Mom! I have to go alone? Call Ryan! Call Kate! Please!" She just stands there, shaking her head.

I swallow hard. Breathe. "Sir, after you're done finger-printing me? What happens then?" The contents of my stomach are liquefying. My voice sounds like it did when I was twelve.

"After that you will probably just come home and have breakfast with your mom."

Funny. But I exhale.

"What will you do with my fingerprints? How...when will I find out if you're going to charge me?"

"Don't worry about that now. You need to come with us."

Is he crazy? *Don't worry?* Then I think of something. "Sir, can't my fingerprints also prove I wasn't there?"

"Yes, they can eliminate you from the investigation."

"Oh, they will, sir, they will."

"We're going to see about that." Both officers stand up and motion for me to do the same. One of them pulls an orange zip tie out of his pocket and uses it to tie my wrists together behind me. It seems funny to me that it looks like they get their handcuffs at Canadian Tire. Then the guy who was questioning me says the scariest words I've heard since my parents told us they were getting a divorce.

"Declan O'Reilly, you are under arrest for...*c'est quoi, méfait?*" He actually has to ask his friend for the English word!

"Mischief. Public mischief."

"Mischief. You have the right to remain silent, and you have the right to legal counsel. That means you don't have to talk to us anymore until you speak to a lawyer. A youth-justice worker from Legal Aid will meet us at the station. Do you understand?"

I nod my head.

"Mr. O'Reilly, you have to answer the question."

"Yes, sir." My knees are about to give out. I'm in a cold sweat. I'm so dizzy I almost topple over. The guy holding my arms sits me down so I can put my head between my knees before I walk. He does it like it's all in a day's work.

I catch Mom's face as the officers are turning me around to take me out the door. She looks terrified.

EiGHTEEN

For the second time tonight I'm riding in a stranger's car.

The front seats where the two officers are sitting are leather and really plush. In the back, the seats are like molded plastic buckets, and it smells like someone puked. There's zero legroom, so I'm all cramped. Every time we turn a corner I have to brace one of my shoulders against the window or the back of the seat so I don't tip over. The orange zip tie digs into my wrists.

Well, at least I know what happened to my wallet.

There are three panes of Plexiglas between the front and back. The middle one is open. I don't know whether to be insulted or relieved. Between their two seats there's a laptop, and I can hear a woman's voice on the two-way radio. The officer with the French name is driving. Reid laughs at something he hears on the radio. He picks up the two-way and speaks into it in French, and the two of them smile at some cop in-joke. He keeps glancing back at me in the mirror. I turn my head to look out the window.

The snow beside the road doesn't look the same from the back of a police car; it's really far away and not part of my world anymore. Same road I walk on every day. I turn and watch it disappearing out the back window.

Funny it never occurred to me before that Seamus lifted my wallet. I only had about fifteen dollars in there. For fifteen bucks, I'm sitting in the back of a fucking police car. Unless he guessed my PIN number before he lost my bank card on the golf course. It's 6-2-6-3: MAND. I wonder if he would have figured it out.

I keep seeing Mom's face as I was leaving, trying to figure out what bothers me about it. It's like she's more afraid of something happening to Seamus than to me. Like if it's me, it's not real. But that zip tie biting into my skin? It's real.

What if this gets out at school? Not if—when. I want to vomit. Maybe that's why it smells like it does back here. What about Leah? She would never hang out with someone who got hauled to the station in the back of a police car, even if the cops did get it wrong.

The cruiser slows down and we pull into the parking lot of the Vaudreuil police station. Vaudreuil gets a bit more night action than Rigaud. A couple of cars pass on the road, and a block away there's lights on at the Tim Hortons. Everyone else is just going about their lives.

We walk in together, right through the front door of the station. The guys all say *salut* and chitchat with each other, but even though their conversation's in French, I can tell it has nothing to do with me.

I look around. It's more like a doctor's waiting room than a place for criminals. There's a guy wearing a quilted work jacket and a plaid cap with flaps over his ears, fast asleep on a chair. His head is resting on a table where there's a coffee-maker and Styrofoam cups and other coffee stuff.

Except for the guys in uniforms, the only sign of any security is another Plexiglas window, with holes you can talk through, at the reception desk. The whole place looks really modern. Sergeant Reid takes me to a small room. A sign on the door says *Interrogation 1*. Inside, there's a table and three chairs and a garbage can full of fast-food wrappers and empty Tim's cups. It smells like coffee and old fries. On the table there's a pen and a pad of paper. It's just a room.

He cuts the zip tie off my wrists and then apologizes before he checks all my pockets and pats me down. He puts my keys, my cigarette package, fifteen cents left over from the money Dave lent me for my lunch cookie, and my pencil stub in a little basket. "Sit here, Mr. O'Reilly. We'll be with you shortly."

I sit in one of the chairs.

"Oh, and I'll need your jacket."

I stand up and hand it over, glad that I have my plaid shirt and a T-shirt underneath, and sit down again.

"Have you ever given a statement to the police before?"

What does he think? I make weekly visits?

He explains. "Sometimes people make statements because somebody stole their lawn mower, or someone's threatening them online…things like that."

Oh, not just the bad guys. I shake my head.

Reid smiles at me, but I'm too nervous to say anything. I just nod. He leaves the room with my stuff and the door closes with a *clunk*. My stomach flips. I'm locked in. The only way to get in or out is by entering a code on a keypad beside the door. What if I have to pee?

The fluorescent light hums above me. The walls are painted concrete, and there's a map of the Montérégie region taped up beside the door, just like the one in the main office at school. Figures that schools and police stations would get their maps at the same place.

It's quiet.

Sergeant Reid comes back, and I'm glad to see him. He hands me a cordless phone. It's black and grimy.

"You can call your mom if you like, let her know you're okay. You're safe with us. You can even sleep here."

Was that supposed to be a joke? I take a moment to consider the possible accommodations. I don't remember seeing any cells. I guess they wouldn't be right out in the open like on that old police sitcom Ryan watches.

"Also, the youth justice counselor's going to come talk to you before we do anything. Just so you understand what will happen. You'll write your statement with him."

He pauses. "You know, about the fingerprints. Even though you say they'll show you weren't at the golf course, you have to understand that they could incriminate you. You have to sign a consent form saying you understand that."

"Incriminate me?"

"Well, let's say maybe you didn't do this, but you did something else—stole a computer or a car or something—and we have fingerprints in the database that match. We can charge you with that too."

"Too?"

"Don't worry." He slaps me on the back. "I'm pretty sure we won't be charging you for anything tonight. We just need to ask you some more questions, get your statement. We're going to show you some pictures from the golf course. And we need some information so we can verify where you were last night. All right?"

"I guess so." Does that mean they have to go to my school? It's always a big deal to see cops at school. You know someone's in deep shit. Never thought it would be me.

He says he'll be back later with the youth justice guy, then smiles again and leaves me with the phone. It smells like aftershave and chewing gum. When I try to dial my number, my mind goes blank, and it takes me three tries to get all the digits right.

Mom picks it up on the first ring. "Hello." Her voice comes out fast and worried.

"Hey, Mom."

"Dekkie! Are you okay?"

"Yeah, I'm fine. I'm just sitting in a room. It's really quiet—"

"Did they, did anyone—"

I repeat that I'm fine except that I wish she was here. She answers me with a sigh. It's her way of saying the topic of her coming to the police station is closed.

I try harder to get her to change her mind, but when she says she needs to stay there in case Seamus shows up, I realize there's no use. She's made a choice. I hear her voice, but it sounds a thousand miles away.

She asks me a bunch of questions, almost like she's got a list, and I tell her what's happened so far. She tells me I have to talk to a lawyer, because I'm a minor. I'm surprised to hear her say this, but I relay the information Reid gave me about the youth justice counselor. Then she asks me if I've been charged.

"Why would I be charged? I didn't do anything."

"Well, just in case things don't go the way—"

"No, Mom. I wasn't there, and they're going to find that out when they take my fingerprints."

"And be careful what you say. Don't get them mad."

What? Where is this shit coming from? "Why would I get them mad, Mom? I'm not your crazy son, remember?"

She doesn't answer for a few seconds. "Did he really take your wallet?"

"It looks like it, doesn't it?"

"I can't believe he would do that."

"So you think I vandalized the golf course?"

"Well, where were you?"

"I told you. Why don't you ask Seamus where he was? Oh, wait—don't you think it's funny that he hasn't turned up anywhere for two days? He should have at least been snooping around for money by now, except (a) he's guilty, and (b) he *has* money—*my* money." My voice echoes in the concrete room. I'm almost yelling.

Silence on the other end.

I feel bad for flipping out. But I'm tired of standing back and feeling powerless. And look where it's gotten me. "He's been pulling shit like this for years. He just never gets caught." I think of him driving around drunk with Robbie the Moron. "At least he hasn't killed anyone yet."

"Oh, Declan, don't say—"

"Whatever. He doesn't care about anyone, Mom. He took my wallet. And whatever he did at the golf course, the police think I did it."

"It's just—"

I'm mad now. "*What*? It's just *what*? What about me? You're worried about him? *Him*? Why are we even talking about him? You know what I think? I think you stayed at home so if he shows up you can warn him that I gave his name to the cops. I'm the one sitting at the fucking police station! Doesn't it bother you that I'm the *little* brother? Taking the fall for him?"

"Declan, stop! I've had to worry about Seamus since the day he was born. Not you! I'm sorry. I can't stop being afraid—"

"Of what?"

She pauses before she says, "He's so unpredictable. He takes risks."

"He's hurting people, and you're protecting him!"

"I know. Maybe because I think it's *our* fault."

I'm starting to get the picture. I can tell by the way she says *our* that it's not what she really means. "Say what you mean, Mom. You think it's Dad's fault."

"Well, he needed a father."

"Yeah, Ma. We all did." I close my eyes, and I swear I can hear the blood rushing in my ears. I'm spinning far away from here. Away from Mom, the phone, this locked room, my stupid brother.

The sound of clicking on the keypad outside the door pulls me back. This time the other officer who arrested me lets himself in. He sets a mug of creamy coffee down on the table and motions for me to go back to my call. He'll wait.

"The officer is here. I better go. Can you come get me later?"

"Declan, I don't have the car. I won't until Kate and Ryan drop it off on the way to the daycare."

"Can't you call them? Maybe they can bring it now, and you can drive them back."

"Don't worry. We'll get you home."

We'll get you home? Don't worry? They damn well better come and get me. What is wrong with my stupid family? Is it that difficult to figure out what to do? I shake my head because I can't think about this right now. The officer is looking at me from across the table, letting me know there's no rush. But I have nothing more to say. I sigh.

"Remember what I said. Don't get—"

I interrupt her. "Mom, I gotta go." She says bye, and the phone is dead in my hand.

I hand it to the officer, and he slides the pad of paper and pen toward me. The paper has the SQ logo on it behind the lines you write on. It looks very official.

NINETEEN

They remind me that I can't write my statement until the youth justice guy is with me.

While I'm waiting, they let me walk around the police station and talk with some of the guys. I never knew cops did so much paperwork. Logs for the cars, logs for responding to calls, logging in and out, requisitions for everything. They even write down when I go to the bathroom, and someone has to stand outside the door. What do they think I'm going to do? Drown myself in the toilet? They're more concerned about me than my own mother is.

When the guy we've been waiting for finally arrives, he looks pretty sleepy. His name is Andrew. He apologizes for making me wait for four hours. I'm his second case of the night. I tell him the same thing I told everyone else. He asks me if I've been treated fairly by Officers Lefebvre and Reid (at least I finally know the French guy's name). I say I can't complain. I wish I could say the same about my mom.

He explains a lot of things to me, like what will happen if I refuse to sign the consent form so the cops can take my fingerprints. He says if there's enough evidence, the police will probably charge me and go ahead and take them anyway. I figure since they found my ID at the golf course, they already have enough evidence. So I sign.

Then I write my statement in front of Andrew. It's not such a big deal. It's kind of like English class. I just write down the things I told Reid and Lefebvre in the living room. I sign it too, and he says, "We're done!" He shakes my hand and gives me a *Quebec Youth Justice* brochure and his business card, then leaves for his third case of the night. No one ever gave me a business card before. I put it in my pocket.

When Lefebvre comes to get my statement, he brings me a sandwich and a drink from Tim Hortons. He even offers me a donut from a box the cops are sharing. They're way nicer than I thought they'd be.

I kill time reading the *Youth Justice* brochure, but I can't concentrate on it. Finally, Reid comes back to show me the pictures. First he sets two pictures in front of me: the overturned golf cart inside some kind of shed, and the flat, snow-covered golf green, both from a distance. I shrug. Neither of the pictures mean anything to me.

Next, he shows me close-ups of black ruts cut deep into the green, like the ruts a car makes when it gets stuck and you spin the tires trying to get out. Only you can tell these were done on purpose, because there's lots of them at different angles. I think of the whitewall tires that sprayed me when Seamus and Robbie sped away from the rink.

I murmur, "I'm guessing a blue Ford Taurus," and he asks me what I mean. He writes down everything I tell him about Robbie's car. I say Robbie goes to my school but I don't know his last name, and this makes me feel slightly less like a snitch.

Finally, he shows me the last two pictures, the worst ones. The first is of the overturned golf cart from a different angle, with something on the ground beside it. In the second shot the camera has zoomed in to show the object more clearly. It's round and black.

"What's that?" I ask.

He looks closely at the picture. "It's the gas cap from the cart. We think the cart was tipped over to empty the gas. Maybe someone was thinking of lighting it on fire but changed their mind. That's gasoline there." He points to a stain seeping out from under the cart onto the cement floor of the shed. My sandwich wants to come back up. Seamus may as well have left his signature. I keep this to myself.

They take my fingerprints with a machine like the thing you put your bank card in at the grocery store. The guy presses each one of my fingers on a screen pad. It scans them and beeps. That's it. I was afraid I'd have to go to school with ink on my fingers. How would I explain *that*? Apparently, the scanner is connected to a national database, and my fingerprints can even be shared with the FBI! I feel weird knowing my fingerprints are out there with real criminals'.

Reid and Lefebvre check in with me before they leave at the end of their shift, ask me if I need anything. Surprisingly decent guys. Lefebvre also hands me his card in case I hear from Seamus. He says they just want to ask him some questions, but I think that's cop code for *arrest and charge.*

I sleep for a while with my head on the table in the interview room. They ask me if I want to lie on the sofa in the waiting area, but I say no. I think you have to be plastered to sleep in the middle of everything, like the guy with the plaid hat. I'd rather sleep in private.

A bit later an officer comes in to tell me I'm being released and that they've called my mom. He gives me back my jacket, and my keys and smokes and, of course, my pencil stub. I feel light all of a sudden. It's 6:10 AM. I've been here for nine and a half hours! I sit in the waiting room, hoping someone will show up soon to get me, but it feels like I've been waiting for hours. If Mom's coming, she won't get here till after Kate brings the car back, unless she decided to call them after all. The guy with the plaid hat is gone. Sunlight is starting to come through the front entrance. I feel so groggy. I can't wait to get home to my bed. Screw school. Screw everybody else.

I'm looking out the door at the street outside, sort of dozing, and I see someone in a black cap coming up the walk. As he gets closer, I make out a ponytail over his shoulder.

He's tall and thin. A bushy mustache grows almost under his chin on either side. One bare hand clutches a bunch of papers. With the other he flicks a cigarette onto the freshly shoveled cement, grinds the butt with his boot and kicks it into the snow. I watch as he shuffles through papers with the officer at the window. "Birth certificate, custody papers. It's all there."

Fuck. It's Dad.

* * *

Soins de jardin et déneigement Quatre Saisons. Underneath, in smaller letters: *Four Seasons Landscaping and Snow Removal.*

That's what it says on the side of Dad's truck.

He unlocks the passenger door and walks around to the driver's side. There are two steel shovels, a broom, an ice pick and bags of sand and salt in the back. It's a Chevy Silverado 3500HD, extended cab, four-wheel drive. With a snow plow on the front and a yellow light on top. It's black. It's a gleaming monster. It's awesome.

Fuck.

Papers and a big yellow-and-black remote are on the passenger seat. Through the window I watch him pick everything up in his gigantic hands and put it in the back. He rolls down the passenger window. "Hop in."

"Can I have a smoke first?"

His eyebrows squinch together over his nose, and he looks like he's going to say something about me smoking, but he clamps his lips shut and nods. "Sure. Sure, buddy. Take your time. Mind if I join ya?"

Buddy?

He doesn't wait for me to answer. He gets out and heads around the back of the truck toward me. I turn around and lean on the door. He moves in close, so close I can smell his aftershave, deodorant, whatever, and offers me the flame from his lighter, but I light my own cigarette, watching my hand shake. He steps away, puts his lighter back in his pocket, and the ball of fear in my stomach melts a bit.

A few snowflakes fall around us, lightly, quietly. "This is my favorite time of day." He sweeps his arm in the direction of the same snow-covered mountains I could see across the lake from Leah's living room.

Yeah, well, I like this time of day too. I'm just not in the mood to talk about the scenery.

We smoke in silence for a few minutes. The sun's creeping up the sky. Mom should be making coffee about now. I flick my butt into a snowbank. "I'd like to go home."

"All right."

I take a deep breath and get in. The truck's been running, and it's warm inside. He shifts into reverse, and we leave the police station behind. I lean my head against the window and watch the snow along the road and the paved shoulder whizz by like a white-and-black-striped ribbon. It's hypnotic. I'm dead tired.

"So did they treat you okay? Any problems?"

I'm not doing small talk.

"Declan."

I turn my head slightly, let the sound of his deep, gravelly voice saying my name roll around in my head. Familiar, but it rattles my insides.

"What happened at the golf course?"

I scrunch up my face. "How am I supposed to know? I wasn't there!"

"You don't have to be defensive. I'm sor—"

"Fuck you! You're right I don't have to be defensive! Why would I bother being defensive with you? I don't give a crap what you think. You don't know dick!"

"Okay. Calm down. I'm just trying to help."

"Oh! Oh, I forgot! Oh my god! Thank you SO MUCH for picking me up. What was I thinking? It's only been, what? Five fucking years! Wow! I really appreciate it. Oh, by the way, why the hell are you here? Who the hell are you anyway? You're pretty good at keeping that a secret, aren't you?"

I'm a little bit surprised at myself. He did manage to do more than Mom. But right now all I see is my asshole father who abandoned us so he could hook up with some dude.

He doesn't say anything. He looks straight ahead, pulls the truck over and throws it into Park, right on the side of the highway. We lurch forward, then settle and stare out the front window for a few seconds. His hands on the steering wheel are calloused, and the cracks and crevices are black. Workman's hands. I curl mine into fists. What now?

"I asked your mom to let me come, take you home. I wanted to do something to help."

"What? Why the fuck? You didn't think you're the last person I want to see now?" I'm straining forward, yelling, and I can feel my eyes stretched open, wild.

He undoes both our seat belts, takes a loud, deep breath and exhales through his nose. "You mad? Okay, yell then. Hit me. You wanna hit me? Go ahead. I can take it. You're right. I probably deserve it. Go for it. We're going to have to get past this, 'cause I'm not going away this time."

I'm stunned. Frozen. *Not going away this time?* What does he mean, *not going away?* "You chose what you wanted, and it wasn't us!"

He's shaking his head, his eyes serious, searching my face. "No! That's not what happened. I never wanted that. I thought you guys needed me gone…to deal with…it. But I—"

"Oh, so it's our fault?"

His mouth is still open.

"Right, you protected us! Ha! You fuckin' ditched, man." There's a lump in my throat. It makes my voice crack, and hot tears are starting to blur the gauges and controls on the dashboard. I try to blink them away.

"Declan, no one wanted—"

"Fuck you. Stop saying my name, okay? Just stop!"

"No. And stop swearing at me."

"You're gonna tell me what to do? The hell you are!" I feel like there's a volcano inside me.

"I'm your father—"

I can't take it anymore. I yell, "Nooo!" and lunge at him over the console, laying into him with both fists, my fingernails, my elbows, my own head, anything I can use to hurt him. Snarling, growling, screaming. His head bangs against the driver-side window, and his hat goes flying. But he's huge, like a wall. *Thuck, thuck.* My fists make little sounds against his chest. It's not enough—I want more! Harder! I want to hurt him, smash him, like I've wanted to forever. For leaving, for being gay, for not being my dad, for being my dad, for every time I've hated him and missed him and wanted him when he wasn't there! *I want to hurt, I want to hit, I want...*

He grabs my wrists a couple of times, but I squirm away. I bang my knee on the gearshift; some knob from the dash rolls onto the floor. The leather upholstery is slippery, and I keep sliding back onto my seat. I can't get my boot against anything to push, to hold me in place, but I keep trying. Over and over, I get close enough to smell him, to feel the heat of his body. His jacket twists through my fingers. *My dad...my dad...*the sound of his voice...*Declan.* He's not making any sound, just breathing hard, fast, through his nose. Wait, that's me, panting, wheezing, crying...no more sound coming... my voice is gone. But I go back again and again, until I wear myself out...slip back into my seat...dead heavy.

I can't anymore.

I'm done.

I'm heaving, sobbing, and I don't want to fucking bawl, but I can't help it.

I push myself away from him and face the window. Whimper through snot and tears and spit, my head on the cool glass. It's almost completely light out. I find the window button and open it a crack. Air. I hear cars coming down the road, closer together now. People heading for work on the island. *Whoosh…whoosh…*

I wipe my face on the sleeve of my jacket, and there's blood. I taste blood on my bottom lip, which is hot and swollen. I must have bashed it on something. What? Who gives a fuck. Just breathe…

"Jesus, Declan." He's shaking his head. "I'm sorry. Damn." He bangs the steering wheel. "I'm sorry, man."

I've stopped gasping.

"Look at me," he says.

I roll my head back and forth with my temple still resting on the icy window. *No.*

"Okay. But I'm gonna talk."

Asshole.

"I know you're angry. I understand that. Seems like you bottled it all up inside. And I deserve it." He pauses. "Okay. I've thought about this so many times, about talking to you. Now I don't know what say. Just the fact that you're in my truck…can't hardly believe it."

I wait for him to continue. Breathe. In. Out. In. Out. Making little puffs of steam on the glass.

"Your sister keeps telling me, *Go ahead—call.* But I wasn't sure. I should've called. It woulda been better than surprising you at Kate's. I was afraid I'd lost my chance. So when your mom called last night…I hope we don't have to wait another five years, Declan."

He stops and waits for me to say something. It's so weird to hear him say my name. It makes me feel like I did when I was little, either waiting for something good, like Christmas, or catching shit. I don't know if I want to laugh or run. Little rivers of melted ice run down the window past my eyeball. They collect on the rubber seal at the bottom, overflow and dribble in the direction of the wind. Like tears.

He gets tired of waiting for me to talk. "Anyway, I really dropped the ball with our custody arrangements, my weekends and—"

"Custody?" That's the second time he's mentioned it. First at the cop shop and now here. Of course. Other kids with divorced parents spend time going back and forth between them. I thought we didn't have to because he's gay or something, but now I realize that's stupid. I guess we were supposed to.

"Yeah. Do you remember coming to my apartment? I guess it was only two or three weekends. Kate and Seamus were so angry, and I just didn't know how to deal with things. After a couple of visits they refused to come anymore. I wanted you with me, but I couldn't make you come by yourself. After all the fighting, you just wanted to stay with your mom. So I gave up."

I barely remember this. But now I realize that when Seamus hit me with the chair, it wasn't at the trailer. It was in an apartment that Dad had when he first moved out. It hardly had any furniture in it. Behind my closed eyes I see it all...Bad, bad memories.

For a few minutes it's quiet. The truck idles. I drift to the steady sound of the heater fan.

"Are you awake?"

I jerk my head up from its resting place. Yes, I'm awake.

"I wasn't sure. It would help a lot if you'd look at me."

I don't want to, but I'm afraid if I don't he'll just keep talking, and I really want to go home, so I turn my body and lean the back of my head and my shoulders against the window. I pull my jacket around me, my hands in the pockets. Blood on his forehead catches my eye—and tooth marks. I squint to see better. That's why my lip is bleeding. I bashed it on his head. I can't stop a smile from taking over one corner of my mouth. Good. He had it coming.

He touches his forehead with his right hand, then looks at his fingers and sees blood. He takes a tissue out of a dispenser in the cup holder and swipes it away. Slowly he shakes his head, then reaches to get his hat from behind the seat, puts it on and glances at himself in the rearview mirror.

He stares out the front window, his thumbs tapping on the padded steering wheel. "Well, I do have something else to say. And I may as well just say it. I'm sorry." He sneaks a look at me. "I'm sorry, and I'd like to be part of your life again. I'd like to get to know"—he waves a big paw at me—"this young man you're becoming."

Slowly I shake my head.

"I'm talkin' on your terms—"

"Well, my terms are *no*. I'm not interested in getting to know you or who you are."

He nods his head a few times, narrows his eyes, studies me.

The truth is, I'm not sure how I feel about who he is. But not wanting him is what I'm used to. Right now, nothing in my life is what I'm used to.

"Fair enough."

He brushes his left eye with his knuckle. Then he puts the truck into Drive, signals, and we pull back onto the highway. I'm thinking about what the Joker said, that all it takes is one bad day.

TWENTY

The intercom blares my name at the end of recess, scaring the shit out of me, summoning me to the office. The secretary tells me to wait for Mr. Peters.

Yesterday, after Dad dropped me off, I didn't come to school at all. I slept like a dead thing for a while and then talked with Mom. She took the day off work to make sure I was okay.

At first I didn't want to talk to her, but she camped out on the other side of my door. Eventually I had to pee, so she caught me in the hall.

I was still pissed that she hadn't even tried to come to the cop shop and that she sent Dad. And the whole bit about staying home in case Seamus showed up...I didn't get that. She tried to explain to me about not involving Kate and Ryan, and that what the cops told us had ramped up her worry that Seamus would try to run away from Rigaud altogether. I still don't totally get what good staying home was going to do. Maybe she thought he'd come there first. But what I did get is that she's scared and confused, and he's still one of her kids, and that made me feel bad for her. She's finally starting to accept that something has gone seriously wrong with him.

She tried to make up for it. My favorite beef stew was waiting for me on the stove. She even convinced me to play Scrabble. I don't know why she likes Scrabble so much, considering what a terrible speller she is. We have a blast teasing her. I stopped being mad at her for sending Dad to the police station. It took a lot for her to call him in the first place. She did what she could, I guess.

Today, I've been trying to stay under the radar, and I actually managed to avoid Mitch and Dave until recess. They know something's up. They've probably heard rumors. But I managed to put them off.

Peters breezes in from the hall. "Ah, we missed you yesterday, Declan." Is this some kind of a joke? I mumble something about not feeling well. He leads me into his office, closes the door and throws his pen on the desk. "The police were here to talk with me yesterday. A Sergeant Lefebvre. To ask some questions about Monday evening."

I feel my face going red. I'm afraid to meet his eyes. I have to look down.

"You were here on Monday night, and I was able to verify that."

I exhale. "But what about the forty-five minutes I was sitting by the Dumpster in the staff parking lot? By myself?"

"The police asked me about that. Just hold on for one minute." He picks up his phone, punches an extension. "Lynn, could you page Hal for me, please?"

While we wait, Mr. Peters asks me some questions about my visit with the police. I tell him about the digital fingerprint machine. He says, "Cool."

A few minutes later, a tall skinny guy in dirty coveralls comes to the door. As soon as I see him, I realize he's the janitor who was putting garbage out behind the school on Monday evening. He looks at me, then at Mr. Peters. "Yeah, this is the kid I saw sitting out back Monday. I couldn't see his face that well, but I recognize his hair and his jacket."

"Hal, this is Declan O'Reilly, the student I asked you about yesterday. Declan, Mr. Hinitt."

We nod to each other. He's smiling.

"Do you remember about what time it was when you saw Declan out there?"

"Well, I know I put the bags out while I was finishing up in the cafeteria. I went out a couple of times. So he was there from at least 6:15 to about 6:45, head in his hands. I kept an eye on him. When I went out to put the bags in the Dumpster, just before I finished my shift at 7:00, he was gone. I mentioned it to you on my way out—thought it might be important."

"Well, you were right."

I'm so relieved, fucking tears actually well up in my eyes. Mr. Peters sees.

"Thank you, Hal. What you just said has meant a lot to this young man, I assure you."

I nod, not sure I can speak, but I want to say thank you. I stand up and shake the janitor's hand.

"You're welcome, son." Then he asks Mr. Peters, "Is he in some kind of trouble? I'm pretty sure he didn't do anything back there. I checked."

I *knew* he was giving me the evil eye, worrying about me tagging the Dumpster or something! But I don't care. Now I'm just glad he was paying attention.

"Not anymore, Hal. Thanks to you, not anymore. Thanks for coming down. The police are going to want to speak with you."

"Oh, sure. I'm always happy to visit with my friends from the SQ." He winks at me.

"We'll let you get back to what you were doing, then. And thanks again."

"Okay, Garth. Happy to help."

Garth? Mr. Peters's name is Garth! For some reason it suits a guy who organizes his desk like a checkerboard. I'm so relieved I feel like I could get up and hug the guy. "Thank you, sir, for taking care of all this," I say. "You have no idea." I shove my hands in the pockets of my jacket and think how lucky I am that the caretaker saw me. "Sir, there's something else."

"What is it, Declan?"

"Hal…Mr. Hinitt recognized my jacket."

"Yes."

"Well, that makes this the first time my jacket has gotten me out of trouble and not in it."

"Very true. Now, go take it off and get to class."

TWENTY-ONE

Mitch is shoveling lasagna into his mouth, "Mrs. O'Reilly, as usual, this is the best!" He's eating like he's got the munchies, but he's not even stoned. Yet. He and Dave keep joking that he has a joint in his pocket for us to share on the way to the dance.

Yup. The dance. We're going to the Spring Fling. Dave says it's about time we did some conventional high school stuff. "It'll be fun!" The real reason we're going? Dave's been trying get with a ninth-grade girl named Sophie for the last couple of weeks. He needs us for moral support.

I looked all over school for him today and found him on a ladder, hanging giant butterflies from the ceiling outside the gym. I couldn't believe it. What a dork.

It's not how I want to spend this Friday night. I need a night of nothing except me and my Xbox.

Leah's on the organizing committee, of course. This afternoon at school, she asked if I was coming.

She didn't ask about the golf course or the police. Maybe she doesn't know.

Mom starts clearing away our dishes and offers us ice cream. Dave jumps up and says, "No thanks, Mrs. O. Gotta watch my girlish figure!" He pretends to feel himself up. Mitch rolls his eyes and we both groan, but Dave redeems himself by helping Mom.

"Thanks, Mom," I say. "It was fantastic. And thanks for feeding the cretins."

"You're all very welcome. It's nice to have you boys around."

We finish clearing the table, and Mitch is still sitting there.

"What's up?" I ask.

"Um, I would like some ice cream, please."

"So get it yourself. You know where we keep it."

I leave to take a shower. Dave heads for the living room and flips on the TV. I can hear it and their voices from the bathroom, and for a few moments everything feels normal. I relax and let the warm water run over my face.

When I finish, everyone's sitting in the living room, and the guys start teasing me about my *manly smell*, because I put on cologne. "Ooh, Declan! Getting ready for a certain someone?" I glare at them. They better not say anything about Leah.

"Hey, *smellcome* to manhood, dude!"

"Poor Mrs. O! Old Spice has turned her boy into a *man*."

The guys are on a roll, quoting Old Spice commercials from YouTube. They take turns pushing me around, making

Mom laugh. Dave's been hanging around so long, he's like one of her kids.

I zero in on Dave. "You should talk. Hanging butterflies in the hall? We know why you're dragging us to this thing." Turning to me and Dave so Mom can't see, Mitch makes googly eyes and sticks his tongue in and out of his mouth like gross French kissing.

"What?" Dave pretends he doesn't know what we're talking about.

I pull on my jacket and start to tie my boots. I did put on cologne, but it's not like it's the first time. I say bye, and the guys make a big fuss over Mom, kissing her and complimenting her on her lasagna. They may be cretins, but they're my cretins.

"Have fun, boys. Be good."

It's snowing great big, soft flakes almost like tiny snowballs. There's no wind, and the clouds are low, so it's almost light out. A perfect night. I turn around and wave. Mom's watching us from the front window. It kills me that I'm leaving her alone, and I know how she's feeling about Seamus. She looks sad and like her mind is somewhere else all the time. I turn and catch up to my friends. We light a couple of cigarettes and head down the driveway in the moonlight.

About halfway to the road, Mitch looks back to make sure Mom is gone and then pulls out a nice fat joint. We huddle around while he lights up and takes the first toke. Then he hands it to me. By the time we reach the road we're feeling a nice buzz.

We tramp along quietly, sometimes on the shoulder, sometimes in the ditch. No one's talking. I feel like I'm being filled up by the bright, snowy night. I haven't felt joy like this for a long time. It's not just the weed. It's my friends.

Dave starts to giggle.

"What's so fuckin' funny?"

"It's so quiet!" He's actually whispering. "Shhh, listen to the snow."

Mitch and I look at each other and lose it. "Dude, you're high!" We laugh for a minute. It feels so good.

Mitch jumps on Dave, and they both roll into the ditch. The snow is new and soft. Perfect for snow angels. I jump in and join them. We make a whole bunch of snow angels, all over the ditch. It becomes a quest to find a fresh, undisturbed spot. Man, I love snow angels. It makes me remember being a kid. They're so soft and...and...snowy! I taste some snow from my jacket. It's delicious! Tiny crystals sparkle in the moonlight on my sleeve.

"Hey, guys, look how sparkly the snow is!" They both sit up from making angels to look.

"Fuck, yeahhh, man." Dave washes my face with snow and then runs. I make a snowball and get him in the back of the head. Mitch nails me with one. Then Dave says something about how immature we are, and we both pummel him with snowballs while he turtles in his jacket. He pulls a Kleenex out of his pocket and waves it above his head. We brush ourselves off, pull Dave up off the ground and crawl back up to the road. After we've been walking for a while, he asks what time it is.

"I don't know."

"It seems like we stopped for a really long time. This is taking forever."

"I don't think it was a really long time. I think it's just one of those times when you think it was a really long time because you're high, but it wasn't really a really long time because if you weren't high it would only have been a couple of minutes." I'm feeling like a fuckin' genius. "I mean, because we're high, it was longer. I mean, it was the same amount of time, but it seems longer. Right?"

They stare at me like I have two heads.

"What?"

Mitch and Dave explode with laughter. They're pissing themselves.

After they calm down, Dave is still concerned about the time. He doesn't want to get there too late and miss his chance with Sophie. Mitch to the rescue. "Don't worry, buddy. It's only been about ten minutes since we left Declan's. Your sweetie'll still be there."

"Shut up!"

"Dude, the only reason we're coming to this stupid thing is so we can hold your hand while you do the nasty with Sophie," I say.

"Yeah, you're gonna let us watch, aren't you?" Mitch makes a face with big eyes and his slobbery tongue hanging out.

"You're a sick puppy, Mitch." Dave can't wait to change the subject. "So the cops were pretty chill with you the other night, eh?"

"Yeah. It was okay, except for being up all night. Oh right, and then there was the part about being arrested. That kinda sucked. But otherwise it was a riot."

"That was fucked up, man." Mitch shakes his big curly head.

"Actually, the fingerprint machine was cool." I hold up my hands and wiggle my fingers. "These guys are in the national database now, property of the RCMP and the FBI. I'm famous!"

"Dickhead, you're not famous. You're infamous. That's what you say when you're a criminal." Dave's a nerd at heart.

"I'm not a criminal."

"I know, man, I know. That shit should never have happened." Mitch puts his arm around my shoulders. "You're my favorite deputy!"

"Oh my god, Woody!" Dave pretends to pull a string in my back for more *Toy Story* one-liners, but I'm not in the mood. Instead, I answer Mitch. "There's a lot of shit happening lately. Anyway, I don't want to be a buzzkill. Can we talk about something else?"

Mitch starts making percussion noises with his mouth and playing air drums. The guy doesn't sing, but he belts out, *"Let's change the subject to someone else—"*

Dave yells, "Foo Fighters!" and we join in. *"You know, lately I've been subject to change. Normally I reel in the strange. Hangover, I'm older…"*

We start walking again with our arms around each other, trying to remember the words to "A Matter of Time," but I'm only half there. I'm stunned by how for a guy who seems clueless most of the time, Mitch can totally get it when it counts.

We stop singing and drop our arms when we hear a car behind us. I turn around and get blinded by headlights. *Dumbass. You're not supposed to look at them.* The car slows down and pulls onto the shoulder. Our three heads follow it in unison until it stops beside us.

I know this car. Shit.

The passenger window rolls down. Mr. Peters leans over from driver's seat. "Hello, boys. On your way to the dance?"

"Yes, sir." We answer together, like we're in the army, which makes Dave start laughing again. I dig my elbow into his shoulder.

"Great. Me too. Can I offer you a lift?"

My mind goes into overdrive.

Mitch's eyes pop out of his head. He's scared shitless. Dave and I look at each other. If we accept the lift, we're fucked. He'll know we're blazed. If we don't accept it, he'll suspect we smoked up before the dance and catch us when we're coming in. I'm sure Mitch has pot on him. If I know Mitch, he has loads of it. I decide on my own what to say. "Thanks, Mr. Peters, but we're meeting friends at Tim Hortons."

"I could drop you there."

We're only about half a kilometer away from the Tim's. Could we pull it off? I take one look at Dave's squinty eyes. It's taking all of his concentration to suppress the giggles.

Beads of sweat have popped out on Mitch's forehead. For the first time, I notice he's got more facial hair than me or Dave. *Wait. I have to answer Mr. Peters's question.* As I turn my head back to him, it feels like the scenery is shifting in slow motion, "No. It's okay, sir. Dave has to practice his lines." *What the fuck?* Too late. The words are already out of my mouth.

"Lines?"

"Uh, for the variety show. We're helping him while we're walking. We've been sitting at school all day anyway. Lots of fresh air out here."

I hear Dave mutter, "And sparkly snow." He's starting to vibrate, ready to explode.

"All right then. See you at the dance." Mr. Peters waves and drives away.

"Oh my god. Do you think he knows?" I exhale and break into a cold sweat. I'm high as fuck in front of the VP who just finished proving I wasn't a bad guy.

Dave's doubled over, splitting a gut. "Oh, dude, he knows."

"No, I'm sure he doesn't know. We were fine—Dekkie handled it like a pro." Mitch relaxes.

"Oh yeah! Like a pro! Lines? I don't have lines. I do back-flips, remember?"

"I guess I was thinking of the play." *Wait a minute, what play? I am so stoned.*

"Oh my fucking god, dumbass." Dave smacks me on the back of the head with a soggy Montreal Canadiens mitten. He actually wears mittens his grandmother knit him. You've gotta respect that in a guy.

"I still don't think he knew. Anyway, he likes you, Declan." And since Mitch is the expert on being high and getting away with it, we leave it at that and enjoy what's left of our buzz and our walk.

TWENTY-TWO

We make a quick detour for hot chocolate and a box of fifty Timbits at Tim Hortons and still get to the dance in lots of time for Dave to work his magic with Sophie. The Ghana girls are selling chips and drinks and chocolate-covered almonds under Dave's butterflies. I scan for Leah at their table, but she's not there.

I've never seen so many half-closed, bloodshot eyes and stumbling kids in one place before. How'd these people get in here? I thought teachers checked, but what do I know? A lot of the girls are wearing revealing clothes and heels that have to be about four inches high.

The three of us make our way to the coat check. It's a rule: no coats in the gym. Leah's working behind the table, handing out numbers and hanging stuff up.

Mitch jerks his head in her direction. "Hey, Dec—"

"I know, shithead. Shut up."

"...*low, low, low, low, low, low, low, low*..."

"Apple Bottom Jeans" floats out of the gym. Dave can't help moving to it. I'm wondering if it's possible to hate this song any more than I did in elementary school, when I notice Little Miss Perfect doing her own very *not* Little Miss Perfect interpretation of the lyrics with her shoulders and her hips, just like in the music video.

"...*baggy sweat pants...*" I feel my face get hot.

Finally, it's our turn in line. I nod and hand my jacket to her. I'm sure I'm bright red, and I hope she doesn't notice. She smiles and says hi.

As we're walking away, Mitch keeps tipping his head to the side and batting his eyelashes at me. "Hi! Hi! Hi!" He makes it sound all breathy and sexy.

I punch him in the arm. Hard. "Stop it."

"Sorry. Geez." He brushes himself off, pretends to straighten his shirt. He's actually pretty handsome when you clean him up. He realizes I'm smiling at him. "What?"

"Nothin'. I just love ya, man. Thanks for sharing before. I needed a good laugh."

"No problemo, bro." He fist-bumps me.

Dave disappears with some of the variety-show kids, on the prowl for Sophie. Mitch and I wander into the gym.

Wow. I haven't been to a school dance since I was in elementary. It's a pretty big deal. A few couples are on the floor, and groups of girls are dancing together. A lot of kids are just standing on the dance floor talking, swaying back and forth. The lights are synced with the music. It takes a minute for our ears to adjust to the volume. Talking is out of the question. We plant ourselves against the wall by the door with our hands in our pockets. Wallflowers. At least we match the spring theme.

The DJ puts on "Thrift Shop" by Macklemore and Ryan Lewis, and a whole bunch of people rush in to dance and sing along. Leadership students are working the crowd, trying to get everyone onto the floor. I'm thinking this might be a good time for me and Mitch to split when I see Leah moving across the dance floor with one of her leadership friends.

Her friend turns one way through the crowd. Leah keeps coming toward us. I'm just about to deke when she sees me and Mitch standing by the wall. Her eyes get big, and she starts to smile at us—a sneaky, troublemaking smile— and I just know she's going to try to get me to dance. I glance at the door, and she shakes her head. Our eyes lock. She's coming over.

Just as she crooks her finger at me, Mitch notices what's going on, smiles his biggest *You're fucked!* smile and shoves me toward her onto the dance floor. I shoot him a much-deserved finger behind my back.

I don't dance. I just don't. I like listening to music. But this is my worst nightmare. She pulls me by the hand until we're right in the middle of everyone, then turns around to face me. I know what I'm supposed to do, but I freeze. Leah starts dancing; this is fun for her.

She motions with her arms and mouths, *Dance!* Even on the dance floor she's bossy! She's such a good dancer, and her body is amazing. I'm going to look ridiculous next to her if I try to dance, but I can't just stand here either.

I start to move to the music a little bit, and she flashes me a big smile and a thumbs-up. She must think I'm a loser. She takes my hands. More—she wants me to move more! "Go crazy!" she says and dances like she's really into the music.

I throw my head back and start to laugh. "Noooo!"

We're both laughing when the music changes again. After a few seconds I recognize it. A slow song.

"*...and the saints we see are all made of gold...*"

Leah steps toward me and stands on her tiptoes to say something. She has to hold on to my arms to keep her balance. "Do you want to stay?" I feel her breath against my ear.

I look around us. Some couples are dancing with their arms around each other. A lot of kids are just standing in one place, waving their arms over their heads in time to the music. What do I do? Wave my arms or—

I don't have to decide. Leah reaches up and puts her hands on my shoulders. I just stand there. Totally freaked out. I don't really know what to do. So I do nothing! Just stand there like a dolt. She takes my hand and places it behind her back. I put both arms around her and roll my eyes. But she's smiling up at me.

I don't know how to describe what this feels like. Electricity zings through my body wherever she touches me. I almost can't stand it, being so close to her. It's not like sitting at the same table going over notes or a textbook.

Her body is soft, and she smells so good. She lays her head against my chest. I'm honestly afraid I'm going to pass out, but at the same time I'm happy. Kind of like butterflies—Spring Fling butterflies.

Where's Dave? I wonder. I scan the crowd for him, which is easy because I'm looking over almost everybody's heads. I actually spot him, and he's looking at me, a big grin on his face. He and Sophie are dancing, if you can call it that; they're barely moving. He gives me a thumbs-up behind her back. He's resting his cheek on the top of her head. It gives me the idea to do the same thing.

I lean my head down, but I can't actually reach Leah because there's such a big height difference. Without thinking I pull her a little closer to make it work. It seems like such a natural thing to do, but now I'm afraid of how she's going to react. Will she pull away? She snuggles into my chest. Oh my god! I can't believe this. My body's going crazy! Things are happening. I hope she doesn't notice, because I also don't want her to think I'm a total jerk.

Relax, dickhead. Enjoy this.

"*...it's where my demons hide, it's where my demons hide...*"

We sway back and forth to the song, like we're one body. I realize she's following me, which means that without meaning to, I'm leading. She's letting my body tell hers what to do. This amazes me.

So many times, sitting in her dining room, I've been tempted to touch her hair. Those little curls at the base of her neck. I wonder what she'd do if I did that now.

I slide my hand up her back until it reaches her neck and I'm holding her long, curly hair. She tilts her head back and gazes right into my eyes, smiling, a peaceful look on her face.

She actually looks happy! Dancing with *me*!

Then, very gently with her fingertips, she strokes my cheek where it's black and blue. She shakes her head, and I touch her hand with mine, pressing her fingers to my face. Her touch goes right inside me.

The song finishes, and we stand together holding each other for a couple more seconds. It seems like neither one of us wants to stop. She finally steps back, and I realize her leadership friend is standing beside us. Leah has to go.

She squeezes my hand and mouths, *Thank you*. I hook my fingers around hers as our hands slip apart. She takes a few steps back and smiles, then turns around and walks away, hips moving to the music.

I think I'm going to die. In fact, if I died now, I'd die happy. I can't believe what just happened!

Mitch and I can see that Dave's going to be busy with Sophie for a while. We leave the gym to hang around outside with the smokers. The bass beat of "Don't Stop the Party" throbs from the gym, providing us with background music on the street in front of the school. It's the same group of smokers as always, but the atmosphere outside is different. The girls are dressed up, teetering on their heels, acting older than they do during the day. The guys are nervous and self-conscious. I take out my pack of smokes. Mitch has his lighter ready. Everyone has their arms wrapped around themselves to stay warm. We had to leave our jackets at the coat check.

"I told you, after we got caught in the gym that day. She's cute." He exhales from his first long drag. I knew he wouldn't be able to keep quiet. "Obviously, you think so too."

"Obviously."

"That was pretty hot and steamy." He pretends he's grinding on an imaginary girl for effect.

"Oh, fuck off, man. We danced, okay? Can't I dance with someone without it being a big deal?" But the truth is, I'd do the same thing if it was him or Dave.

"Ah, no, bro. Not her. Not like that. You were into her, and she was into you. I'm not the only one who noticed."

I shoot a *Really?* look at him, but I'm afraid to speak.

"Yeah, her friends were watching and texting." He imitates girls with their heads bent over their phones, speed texting with their thumbs. "I'd be surprised if you're not on Facebook already. She digs you."

"Probably nothing's going to happen anyway." Nothing like this has ever happened to me before. I still can't believe it did.

"You should totally ask her out."

"Yeah right."

"Seriously. She likes you. She'd say yes."

At this point, it's going to take all my guts to show up for tutoring next week. Chicks don't know that rejection is what guys fear most in the world.

Theresa and two of her friends stumble out of the school, yelling back at someone inside. They head over, piss drunk. My danger radar peaks at full volume.

"Hi, Dekkie."

I hate it when she calls me that, like we hang out.

"Hey, Terry," I say.

Mitch raises his eyebrows. He's not drunk, so he hears the mocking tone in my voice.

She's having trouble staying upright on her stupid shoes. "Fuckin' bitch Peters kicked us out...too drunk. Bird-neee puked in the bathroom. Well, actually, she kind of puked all over the bathroom."

Charming. One look at Brittany's bugged-out eyeballs and anyone can see she's not just drunk. There's mascara running down her cheeks, and she's ghostly under the street-light. She could easily be mistaken for a zombie.

Good ol' Mr. Peters, keeping us all safe.

"Brittany looks like she should be home in bed."

"We're walking over there. You guys wanna come party?"

Mitch sticks his tongue out and hangs himself from an imaginary noose. Then he makes a gun with his thumb and forefinger and mimes shooting himself in the head.

"Thanks, but we're heading back to Dave's after this." Under my breath I add, "We have to help him practice lines."

Mitch loses it, and Theresa realizes he's there too. She slinks up to him like she's flirting. What the fuck?

"Hey, Mitch, you have anything to share?" Of course. She wants to know if he has weed. He pulls his pockets inside out to show he's dry. I know he's lying, but obviously he wants her to get lost. She sighs and turns away. Mitch brushes fake cooties off his sleeve.

While she's smoking her cigarette, she keeps asking for a hug, saying she's cold. If Mitch rolls his eyes any farther back in his head, they're going to get stuck there. Because she pesters me, I put my arms around her for a few minutes to warm her up, but she takes it as a sign that I want to make out. She actually tries to plant one on my lips and grabs the inside of my thigh. I have to peel her off and push her away. She gives me the finger behind her back as she and her drunk friends wobble off to put Brittany to bed.

"That's a hot mess," Mitch says.

I shake my head. "Let's go back in. I'm cold."

When the dance is over, Dave intercepts us, squinting under the fluorescent lights at his phone screen. "My dad just texted. He's waiting outside." His clothes are all messed up like he's slept in them, and there's a big red hickey on his neck. Lucky for him, Mitch doesn't see it.

Leah is busy at the coat check, acting like nothing happened. Cool as a cucumber. My legs are like marshmallows. She hands me my jacket, and I break into a cold sweat.

I say, "Bye," and she fakes a smile and nods.

Just get me out of here.

TWENTY-THREE

My cigarette's lit. I like the view of the soccer field from up here on the bleachers. It reminds me of playing with Stephan and the rest of the team. Most of the field is still covered in snow, but bits of brown grass are poking through around the edges. A few more days like today and it'll all be gone. Wet dirt with a hint of melting dog shit. It smells like spring.

Finally, a chance to be alone. And think. It's only been two days since the dance, six days since I saw Dad at Kate's house, five days since my visit with the police, three weeks since I started tutoring, but I honestly can't remember what it felt like to be me before.

Like, fuck! I just went to a meeting to see if I want to be a soccer coach! Me! I still can't believe Coach Lavoie called me and asked me to come. He remembered bumping into me at the pharmacy. I can't believe he didn't try to forget. I'm not exactly a model athlete, unless there's a sport for skinny smokers. But his message said, "Sunday, one o'clock. I 'ope to see you there." I can't believe how the same he is.

I'm glad I decided to come. I don't know if I'll sign up to coach but, like I told him, I'll think about it. It wasn't as scary as I thought it would be. No one cared that I've never coached before. They were just happy I showed up.

I have to undo my jacket, it's so warm sitting here in the sun. I'm glad the soccer meeting ended early. I'm nervous about my big lunch date.

I can't stop thinking about the dance. I can't stop thinking about Leah.

So Dave and Sophie are officially "going out." No wonder Mitch and I couldn't find them at the dance. It didn't occur to us to look in the math-hallway stairwell. On second thought, it's probably a good thing we didn't. I wonder how their *date* went last night, if that's what you call it when your dad drives you both to the movie theater.

What do you call it when you're sitting on the bleachers in the sun, waiting for your dad, who's been a total stranger for five years, to take you for lunch?

Probably a big mistake.

Yesterday Sergeant Lefebvre stopped by our place, told us everything checked out with my fingerprints and where I was the night the golf course got trashed. Of course, I wasn't surprised my fingerprints didn't match anything, but it bugged me that Mom hadn't been 100 percent sure, that she even wondered if I did it. I may fly pretty well on my own, but I still need her on my side.

Now the hunt is really on for Seamus. He's a fugitive, which makes me think of crime shows and cowboys racing away on horses in the Wild West. Lefebvre asked me if I still had his card and reminded me to call him if I hear from Seamus.

It's burning a hole in my pocket.

I didn't want to take the blame for the golf course, but I don't know if I'm ready to turn my own brother in. I can't help wondering about Robbie and the Taurus and where the hell they are.

My watch says 2:05 now. I told Dad the soccer meeting would be over by 2:00. I hope he's not expecting me to talk, because I probably won't.

Why did I let Mom talk me into phoning him? This is totally her fault. They've been speaking a lot lately because of this thing with me and Seamus, and she said he really wanted to talk to me about what was happening with the cops. So I did what she wanted and some other dude picked up the phone, and I called him Dad. Fucking embarrassing. But when Dad finally came to the phone, he was happy. He said he knew it wasn't easy for me to call, and he appreciated it. I told him about Lefebvre's visit, like I was supposed to.

"Thank goodness they cleared you," he said. "You must feel a lot better." He sounded like he meant it. Then he told me how bad he felt about Seamus. He sounded like he meant that too.

He called our first meeting *a disaster*. No shit. He wanted another chance, so I agreed to go for lunch. This time I'll try not to smash my teeth into his head.

Where the fuck is he? He's eight minutes late, and my cigarette is officially done. I give the butt a kick and watch it roll from step to step and land on the ground below.

I'm freaked out about being with him in public. What if someone sees us? I don't want people at school to start asking questions.

I'm nervous.

No. I'm fucking nervous.

I hate waiting.

I'll think about Leah dancing and the way her head felt against my chest, her hand on my face, the way she smiled at me. I'd rather be going on a lunch date with her...or maybe not. This kind of thing can make you crazy.

Dancing with a loser bad boy is probably on some high school bucket list of hers, like getting a detention. She barely spoke to me when we left. In fact, she acted pissed off. I don't get girls.

Finally, the *Quatre Saisons* truck pulls up along the curb and I trade one set of nerves for another. I wave and climb down from my perch, shrug my jacket onto my shoulders and do up the zipper. One last breath of cool, dog-shit-scented air before getting back in that truck.

Dad has the window down, and the radio is blaring. He lowers the volume as I open the passenger door. "So, do you have any favorite places to eat?"

Favorite places? I was hoping to avoid my favorite places. I guess it would be wrong to suggest New York. "Not really."

"I know a great little diner in Pincourt. It'll take a bit of time to get there, but they have breakfast all day. Good and greasy. Are you into it?"

"Yeah, sure." Sounds perfect. I don't think I know anyone in Pincourt.

We don't talk much. He asks about school. I say it's fine. He asks about Mom. I say she's fine. He gives up, and I entertain myself by checking out the truck's interior. It really is awesome. Eight cylinders. Four-wheel drive. All decked out. It's not the kind of thing I picture a gay guy driving. What do gay guys drive?

"Do you mind the radio?"

"No."

"Favorite station?"

"Doesn't matter." I don't tell him it's already on my favorite station. The name of the song is scrolling on the display: *BRIDGE BURNING—Foo Fighters*. Is there anything this truck can't do? I shake my head when I catch the lyrics: "*Down crooked stairs and sideways glances comes the king of second chances...They're all comin' down...it's all comin' round...*" Life is funny sometimes. If he notices the lyrics, I can't tell. His eyes are on the road.

The sun is intense. The glare off the wet blacktop is almost blinding. The snow is melting so fast, water's running in black streaks across the road. Dad's wearing sunglasses, and I notice that his hat says *Like a Rock*. Through his open window I hear the swishing sound of tires on the pavement as cars pass us. Dad drums out the bass line of the song on the steering wheel with his thumbs. The truck seat is so comfortable. I lean my head against the window, close my eyes and listen to Dave Grohl's voice.

* * *

"We're here." Dad's tapping me on the shoulder. I open my eyes as we pull into a gas station parking lot. The attached restaurant is called Chez Bob. *Hot Coffee* is flashing in the window in neon red, and an *Open* plaque hangs from a chain on the door. This is his favorite place for breakfast? A truck stop?

"Breakfast or lunch?" the waitress asks.

Dad looks at me. "Breakfast?"

"Sure." I'm not sure I can eat, so it doesn't really matter.

She grabs two menus and takes us to a table that looks out onto the forest behind the restaurant. There's a woodpecker busy in a nearby tree.

Dad takes off his Chevy cap and hangs it on the back of his chair. I open my menu and hide behind it. I already know what I want. My favorite breakfast is pancakes with bacon and sausages. Lots of maple syrup. Lots of ketchup. Suddenly I'm starving, and I can smell food frying in the kitchen.

The waitress comes back with coffee. Dad turns up his cup, and I order a glass of juice.

"Do you still love pancakes?"

"Yeah." I check the menu. Yes! They have real maple syrup.

The place is pretty full, mostly guys who look like they belong to the semis idling outside. A clump of teenagers huddled around a table staring at their phones makes my heart race. Trying to be subtle, checking to see if I know any of them, I knock my cutlery off the table with my menu. Smooth. In a perfect performance of synchronized head turning, four faces bob toward me, then back to their phones. Luckily, I don't recognize anyone. I swipe my stuff from the ground and bury my head again in Bob's all-day-breakfast specials.

The waitress returns. I give her my order, and Dad asks for eggs, bacon and hash browns. He looks at me over his reading glasses. "You really should try the potatoes. They're famous." So I tell the waitress to add hash browns to my order. What the hell? It's not like I'm watching my figure. She walks away with our menus. Dad puts his glasses in his shirt pocket. "How was the soccer meeting?"

"Fine." I start playing with the salt and pepper shakers, rolling their flat sides against each other.

"That was really great news from the police."

"Yup." It's not news when you knew it already.

He still has tooth marks—two scabs—on his forehead. Great. I'll have to be reminded all through breakfast what a maniac I was before.

"Declan, I owe you an apology."

"Huh?"

"I know I said before that I thought you guys needed me gone. All that stuff in the truck." He waves both arms around his head like he's imitating a crazy person. "You made me think. I told myself you guys were better off without me." His arms land with a thud on the table. "But you were right. I made a decision, and you helped me to see that some part of it was selfish. The truth is, I was afraid to face you. Kate and Seamus were so angry. I just couldn't handle it. It was up to me—your mom and me, I guess—to do damage control, to find a new way to be a family. We—I—dropped the ball." His eyes are down, and he shakes his head. He keeps curling and flattening the corners of his paper place mat.

I just stare at him. Getting an apology is nice and everything, and I can tell he's actually feeling bad, but what am I supposed to do with it? I try to let his words sink in, but the truth is, I don't know what to say. I don't really feel anything. He makes eye contact with me again and continues. "I hope one day you'll be able to forgive me, not for being gay—"

A reflex kicks in and I scan the other tables, especially the one with the teenagers. But nobody's paying any attention to us.

"—but for being selfish and pretending I left because of something else."

I nod and try to keep up with what he's saying about how hard he's had to work to accept himself because of his own homophobia. *He* was homophobic. I want to hear what he's saying, but I can't help glancing once in a while to see if anyone's listening to our conversation. He tells me he hated himself because he thought everyone else hated what he was, and he couldn't change it. That makes me think about us—me and Mom and Seamus and Kate. It makes me think it wasn't fair, what we did, if he had no choice about who he was. He had to learn not to be ashamed.

I'm relieved when our food arrives. I stop checking for eavesdroppers and dig into some of the fluffiest pancakes and most perfect crisp bacon I've ever had. I drown everything in syrup and ketchup. The fried-potato smell reaches my nostrils, and I stab one and pop it into my mouth. He's right—the hash browns are out of this world. Golden and hot, with little chunks of browned onion. Crispy on the outside, soft on the inside. Salty. Spicy. They barely even need ketchup.

He smiles as he watches me, then pokes a potato chunk on his own plate, dips it in ketchup and tells me that when the shit hit the fan at home, they tried to keep the details from his father. My grandfather was about to make Dad a partner in the landscaping business, *O'Reilly et fils*. The company would have been his when Grandpa retired except he found out Dad was gay, and he was so angry he fired him instead. Dad chuckles and waves a forkful of potato in the air. "And then he told me to stay away from the house too. That I wasn't welcome at either place unless I could *straighten up and fly right*." He shoves the hash brown in his mouth. His fork makes a loud clang when it hits the plate. "He sold the business out from under me, and I just let him."

Ditched by your own dad, eh? Yeah, that's tough. But I don't say that. I'm starting to get a picture of what was going on at the time, what we never even knew about. I knew Grandpa had sold the company, and that Mom had to leave because the new owner didn't need her anymore. I guess I could have put two and two together and filled in the rest myself.

"Why did you tell Grandpa—"

"I didn't."

"Then how did he—"

Dad hesitates, his head tipped to the side like he's deciding how to answer. "He and Seamus had a heart-to-heart."

Prickly heat creeps up my neck and into my face as I begin to understand that my brother outed my father. And that maybe this whole fucked-up mess is as much his fault as Dad's. It's getting so I can't keep track of the crap my family has dumped on each other.

He shrugs, like he can read my mind. "I'm not mad at Seamus. He had no idea. He was just an angry, confused, thirteen-year-old kid. From his point of view, I had betrayed him. I don't need anyone to feel sorry for me. I spent years lying about who I was, mostly to myself. After everything else that happened, I had no right to expect you kids to—"

"Wait, are you saying you knew you were gay when you married Mom?"

He nods. "Of course I knew."

"But—"

"Declan, I'm not proud of it. People weren't *out* then like they are now. Marrying your mom was a way to have a life I wanted, with someone I loved, without having to face who I really was. I never thought it would end like it did. I assumed I could pull it off. It was your mom who figured it out." He mimes tipping a drink to his mouth. "She sent me to AA."

I scrunch up my face. I don't remember anything about a drinking problem.

"That's where I met Brian."

I can't help it, but I get this image of my dad having sex with a guy named Brian. What does he look like? What color is his hair? Is he tall? Does *he* wear a Chevy cap? Pajamas? I have to push the image out of my mind. "Did you even love her?"

"I know it's hard to understand, but I did. I still do. I guess there are different kinds of love. From the moment your mom and I met, we hit it off. And all our friends were getting hitched, so we did too. It was what everyone expected. We spent almost every day together until...I think deep down I believed she would accept me no matter what. She's a very special person, your mom."

I can't believe he just said that. He betrayed her, lied to her, took advantage of her. That's how you treat someone you think is special? She even lost her job. But then I remember it was Seamus's fault too. It must have been a horrible time for them both. I lower my eyebrows, get rid of the *what the fuck?* look on my face and try hard to understand what was going on back then. What's going on now?

"Brian and AA helped me see I couldn't keep being dishonest—to everyone, to myself. I couldn't keep living that way. It wasn't fair."

"So that's when you and"—I hesitate, try to make the name in my mouth—"Brian had the affair?" My heart beats fast in my throat. I'm expecting him to get angry, but he barely flinches.

"Oh yeah. That." He looks down, shaking his head. "I screwed up—badly. I should've faced things with your mom first. But I needed some hope." He shrugs with his knife in the air and glances up at me. "Brian was just *there*." For a few long moments he sits, hanging his head over his half-eaten breakfast. I don't know what else to do, so I stare at the top of his head through his thinning blond hair. "I had blind spots, you know? Couldn't see what I was doing. When I look back, I can't believe what an asshole I was." He puts his knife and fork on his plate, folds his napkin over everything and pushes it away. He finds a hangnail and picks at it for a while, his hands in front of him where his plate used to be. I can't help but wonder if he's going to finish his hash browns. "I couldn't handle everyone's reactions, and losing your mom and you kids. It was agony, and I'd caused it myself. I deserved it. So I hid."

It's no gift to be able to see the other side. I always thought of my dad leaving as something *he* did to *us*. Now I can't help but see what *we* did too. Everything is way more complicated than I thought. In a single day, my life had turned into confusion and chaos. But when we pushed him away, he was lost and struggling too.

"I shouldn't have. And I was wrong to say I thought it was better for you. It was a mistake. A big one. When I hear what it's done to Seamus, how off the rails he is…He needed a father—a man—in his life."

"But you're not—" As soon as it's out of my mouth, I realize what an asshole I am.

"A man?"

I wish there was something left on my plate to stick my fork into, but there's not. I drag my finger through a line of ketchup and syrup and try to catch the look on his face without him noticing. This time I'm sure he's going to be angry, insulted, but no. I wipe my finger on my napkin, and he just continues talking. "Being a father, having my family— those were the best years of my life. I like to think I was pretty good at being a dad. I enjoyed it. Your mom and I were happy together. Lots of good memories. I could never regret anything because I'm glad there's a Kate and a Seamus and a Declan in the world. Maybe it's too late to reach Seamus, but Mandy—"

I look up, because he's stopped talking. Little pools of tears brim in his eyes and reflect the lights of the diner overhead, like sparkles. He shakes his head. "You're great kids. It's been hard for your mom with nothing from me but a check once a month."

A check once a month? *Well, of course, dickhead. It was a divorce. That's how it works.* But Mom never said anything about getting child support. I'm shaking my head, and he's still holding back tears. There was real regret in his voice. I have to look away because it's too intense watching him while he tries to get his shit together. It's not about money or responsibility. I see that. It's about time. Maybe he's right. Maybe it already is too late for my brother.

"Well, what about Seamus?" I say.

Dad swirls the rest of his coffee around in his cup. "Seamus is struggling with his own demons."

"He acts like he hates everyone. He doesn't care how much he hurts us."

"I guess he's hurting. Some guys are ashamed of feelings like that. They think it means they're"—he pauses—"*weak*."

I get it. The way he says it, I know he means gay. Seamus is afraid he's gay? "So that's why he's acting like a jerk?"

"Soft on the inside, tough on the outside. Like a crab."

I consider the idea of Seamus as a crab. So he's just hurt and fighting like hell because it scares him? Scares him that maybe he's weak. Or scares him that he's like his father. "So you think he's afraid he's gay?"

Dad shrugs. "There's no reason to think he *is* gay. You can't catch it or inherit it, you know."

"No. I'm not saying that. I'm just saying we were all pretty affected when you"— there's a term for what I want to say—"came out."

"I know, Deck." He sighs. "I'd just like to reboot."

Deck. He called me Deck. Not Dekkie, like Mom. And he listened to what I said, is even thinking about it. All of a sudden it strikes me that I'm having a conversation with him. This must have been what it was like for him and Seamus when they went camping together. I've been lost in it, not thinking about anything else. Just sitting here, having a convo with my dad. It doesn't make any difference that he's gay. He acts like any other dad. Nice, like Mitch's dad, who takes him shopping, or like Dave's dad, who goes to concerts with him, or Leah's dad, who drives her friends around. Only he's mine. Maybe I would like to reboot too.

He still thinks of himself as our dad; that's pretty clear. Wants to help Seamus. I try to picture any situation where my brother would give Dad that chance, and I can't. Who knows though? I never expected to be sitting down for lunch with my dad, and here I am. Maybe he's right about Seamus. *Seamus the crab.* I start to get a worried feeling in the pit of my stomach. Where the hell is he?

"Declan." Dad's voice brings me back to our table in the diner. "I've had five years to think about things. To make sense of my life, past and present. Lots of therapy. Lots of soul-searching. Lots of mistakes. I'm better now. Sober. But it took a long time. And I'm missing my family—my kids." His voice catches.

My stomach is a ball of nerves. I pick up my fork and scratch zigzags into the smudges of ketchup on my plate. I'm not sure what I want anymore. In the truck, I yelled at him, told him I wasn't interested. He still reminds me of so many bad feelings. At the same time, I'm sitting here talking with *my dad.* Like, for the first time in years, I have one.

I put my fork down. "Okay."

"Okay, what?" He looks surprised.

"I don't know. Okay, I hear what you're saying, I guess."

He leans his head forward like he's trying to get a better look at me. Our eyes meet. "We wouldn't be here today if it weren't for Kate. She's trying to make it better. At first I thought it was just for Mandy. But after you left the other night, she told me to give you time. Kate wants this, and I want this, so bad. I thought I'd messed things up for good..."

I still don't get why she never said anything to me. "How did you start seeing her?"

"Total accident. I bumped into her and Mandy at Canadian Tire." He pauses. "I couldn't believe Mandy. Such a gorgeous kid. It breaks my heart." He breathes in really fast, almost gasping.

Suddenly it hits me, what he's missed. It's all summed up in this: when Mandy was born, we were all there except him. He obviously loves her. I remember those times he and Seamus spent together, camping and snowmobiling, and when he coached me in soccer. He made us a garden, and then he was just...gone.

My chair screeches backward. I mumble an excuse and make a beeline for the bathroom. I lock myself in the stall and try to be silent, scrubbing tears off my face with toilet paper. A couple of guys come in to use the urinal. Thank God no one needs the toilet. It's quiet for a while, and then the door opens. I hear my dad's voice.

"Declan?"

"Yeah."

"Are you all right?"

"Yeah."

"Would you like to go home? I just spoke to your mom. She wants me to tell you she loves you."

Home. Mom. Still there. Same as ever.

"Dad?" I haven't said that word to him in such a long time.

"Yes?"

"I'll be out in a minute."

"Okay, son. Bill's all paid. I'll meet you at the truck." He drapes my jacket over the top of the stall door.

I take a few more minutes to calm down and then come out of the stall. The water from the faucet is cold. I splash my face and take a drink.

Dad's having a smoke beside the truck. His shoulders are slumped. He's kicking at the slush. I walk up to him on the driver's side, my hands in my pockets, and stand there. I can't speak. I can't even take out a smoke. He throws his cigarette on the ground and puts it out with his boot.

For once, I feel like I'm not the tallest person around. Slowly, like he's approaching a wild animal, he opens his arms, great big wings, and puts them around me. I don't hug him back. But I don't push him away.

TWENTY-FOUR

"Declan?"

"Yeah?" Leah motions for me to stand up—it's the stop for her house—but my legs have fused with the waffled metal back of the bus seat in front of me. It takes a few seconds to unscrunch my body and come back to reality. I've been lost in my head, wondering why she's acting so distant with me today.

When we get to her house, she fishes her keys out of a pocket on the outside of her bag. She looks to see if I noticed and smiles, but it's a fake smile. I check across the street for the blue Taurus. Worry sits like a rock in my stomach. It's been over a week since anyone has seen Seamus. As I'm taking out my history stuff, Leah says, "I'm going to make tea for me and Bubby. Want some?"

Tea? I've never even tasted tea. Mom hates it. Only coffee at our house. "No thanks."

"Juice?"

"Uh, sure." I pretend to study my notes. We're supposed to be preparing for a unit test on Thursday, and I actually went over my stuff on the weekend. I don't want to be surprised by another one of her pop quizzes. I wish she'd come sit down already. If there's going to be an *I don't like you that way* speech, I want to get it over with.

Leah reappears with a mug of tea and a glass of orange juice. She puts them on the table, pulls out her chair and sits. But instead of getting down to business in her usual teacher style, she wraps her hands around the steaming mug.

"Can we talk for a minute?" she asks her mug.

I brace myself. Here it comes. "Sure."

"Were you really at the police station overnight last Tuesday?"

"Wow. That's not what I thought you were going to say."

She looks confused. "Well, it's the same night we dropped you off. I heard—"

"Yes."

"Yes?"

"Yes, I spent the night at the police station."

"Oh."

"Don't you want to know why?"

"You don't have to tell me."

But I know I do. I sigh, lean my head back and stare at the ceiling for a while. "It's kind of a long story. Remember the guy with the firecrackers?"

"Yeah."

"I wasn't completely honest with you when I said I didn't know who it was. I did. It was the same guy I had the fight with. My brother, Seamus. The blue car belongs to one of his moronic friends."

I glance over to see her reaction. Her brown eyes bug out at me.

"Yeah, we've had—there've been some problems since my parents got divorced. My brother's totally fucked up." She motions for me to go on, so I tell her the rest of the story, about my wallet and the golf course, and what the police station was really like. It's kind of a wild story, and it gets better every time I tell it. She gasps and makes all these shocked faces and says, "That's crazy!" and "Oh my god!" and "Poor you!" It's cool. I leave out the part about my dad coming to get me. I can't tell whether she feels sorry for me or if she even believes me, but it seems like there's still something bugging her. Maybe she doesn't want to hang around with a guy who has sleepovers with the police. I start bracing myself again for *the speech*. "So you hate me now, right?"

"What? No."

"Something's bothering you."

She nods, fakes a cough, takes a sip of tea. She keeps starting and stopping and playing with her mug, like she's trying to get up the nerve to say something, and I'm freaking out. Finally she says, "Friday night, at the dance—" Our eyes lock; hers flit away. "Well, after..." She hesitates. "My friends said they saw you outside."

Saw me outside. So? Smoking? She knows I smoke.

"They said that girl in tenth grade, Theresa…that you guys were, like, all over each other." She looks down at her fingers curled tightly around her mug.

Oh my god. *That's* what it is! Figures her stupid friends would be spying. Oh shit. I'm starting to clue in about what they saw. *She's jealous!* For some reason this makes me really excited. Like maybe it's a good thing. I try to fight a smile that's threatening to take over my face.

"I know it's probably none of my business." She stops staring at her fingers and notices I'm stifling a smile. "It's not funny. I don't dance like that with just anybody." She seems genuinely upset.

I get my mouth back under control and lean forward with my arms on the table, closer to her. I'm nervous. I know things could go either way here. If she believes me, I might actually have a chance with her, and, crazy as it sounds, I want that. If she doesn't, I won't need help anymore with history. I'll *be* history.

"Me neither." I take a deep breath. "I can explain. Theresa and I *used* to go out, like in seventh and eighth grade. But she still hangs around me, especially when she wants attention. She was shit-faced. They got kicked out of the dance. Anyway, she was bugging me that she was cold. So I gave her a hug because we've been friends for a long time. Then she started to get all, you know, so I got mad and pushed her away. She ended up flipping me off and leaving with her friends."

"Really?"

"I swear." Again, I can't resist smiling. I shake my head to try to hide it from her.

She's not enjoying this. "I need to know the truth."

"Sorry." I get myself together. "It's true. I'm not into Theresa *at all*. She's messed up."

I try to read the expression in her brown eyes as I wait for her to say something.

"I liked dancing with you," she finally says.

"Um, me too. You're a great dancer." Under the table I kick myself for giving her such a lame answer.

"Thanks, but that's not what I mean."

"Me neither." I shake my head and move my pinkie so it's touching hers. She's watching our hands.

"You made such a fuss about being pulled onto the floor, but you can dance. You're just shy."

My friends have called me a lot of things, but never shy.

"I can tell you feel the music, because…" She blushes, and it makes little red sunrises on her cheeks. I love that she's nervous talking about us dancing. Maybe I'm not the only one who's been tied up in knots all weekend. "I've been dancing for a long time. You have to feel the beat with your body." She taps her right hand on her chest. Then she puts her other hand over my heart.

I'm afraid to breathe, like her hand is a butterfly and it might fly away.

"You can."

"I can what?" I've lost track of what she's saying because of her hand on my chest.

"You can feel the beat." She takes her hand away, and I breathe again.

"Yeah, but that doesn't mean I can dance. Look at me. Mom says I'm like a human crane with a wrecking ball." She gives me this skeptical look. "It's true. I'm taller than everyone, I'm mostly elbows, knees and feet, and my hair is always in my eyes. I have a special talent for knocking things down from really high places."

Leah leans her head back and laughs, full out, and her neck makes this long curve that my eyes follow all the way down from her chin…I have to look away.

She stops laughing and squints. "You always talk about your mom. Never your dad."

"My parents are divorced. I live with my mom."

"Miranda's parents are divorced, but she does stuff with both of them all the time."

"Well, I don't."

"Never?"

"It's complicated," I say, because I don't want to lie. But I don't want to go into the whole explanation either.

She gets the message and starts shuffling through her history stuff.

"I guess we better make sure you're ready for your test on Thursday." She's back in teacher mode. I have to stop imagining all the other things we could be doing together.

* * *

"Way to go, Declan. I hope you don't mind me saying this, but I'm proud of you."

I brush away her compliment. She gave me another one of her practice tests, and this time I didn't totally suck, but our knees are touching under the table, and that's way more important right now.

Leah groans at my fake modesty and clears our glasses away. It's time for tutoring to be over, but I don't want to leave.

As I'm zipping up my schoolbag, she returns from the kitchen. "Oh, we're not finished." She smiles like she's up to something. Her eyes are dancing. "Just one sec." She disappears and comes back a minute later with her iPhone and speakers, scrolls through her music and taps the screen. Deep bass notes fill the dining room. *Bup, bup bup. Bup, bup bup...*

"It's time for your dance lesson."

"No!" I search for a reason to either stay glued to my chair or run. "We'll disturb your grandmother!"

"She's used to it. I practice all the time." She starts moving chairs to make room.

"Practice?"

"Yeah. For my dance group."

She's holding out her hand. I'd do anything for an excuse to take it, but dancing? Before I have time to decide, she pulls me right out of my chair. "Relax," she says.

I feel a lot of things when she's close to me. Relaxed isn't one of them. So I bend my knees like she tells me to and try to copy her, but my feet get all tangled up. She slows down, I follow her, she picks up the speed, and magically my feet cooperate. I'm getting it! She's beaming. We're actually dancing together in time with the music. *Dickhead's doing hip-hop!*

I smile at her, proud of myself, and immediately trip over both sets of our feet. The human crane lunges and almost crushes Leah. She squirms away, and I get my balance back just in time to stop the chairs from becoming dominoes. I want to crawl in a hole.

She keeps moving to the music. "Don't worry, pick it back up. Kick, step, back; kick, step, back."

She guides me with her hand, and I try to get back into the groove, but I can't seem to find it. I'm saved by Leah's grandmother, who's watching us from the doorway with a big smile on her face.

"Hi, Bubby! Join us?"

Bubby laughs and shuffles around in a circle, groovin' a little in her corduroy slippers. Supercool Bubby.

The song finishes and Leah clicks the music off. Bubby applauds and I bow. Then she continues on her way to the kitchen and Leah and I are alone again. Gently I bump her shoulder with my arm. "I probably should get home. Mom is waiting dinner for me. Besides, the last time I came home late, the cops were in my living room."

"Can you stay for a bit? My dad can give you a lift. One of these days you *will* have to have supper with us so you can meet my mom too."

"Have to? Why? I—I don't think I'm ready."

"You don't need to be ready. My mom will love you. I'd like to meet your mom too. I love that you go home to eat supper with her. It's so sweet. You're like a team."

A team? She actually means it. I never thought of it like that, but we kind of are. I mean, I help her with groceries and stuff, and do all the things she can't do around the house. Leah makes me feel like I could be a good person. I smile at her, but she's lost in thought, so I watch her for a minute, and I start imagining all the things we could be doing together again. She's standing close to me. The back of my hand searches for hers. "I have an idea."

"What?"

"Walk with me partway?"

"I could." Her fingertips flutter against mine. "I can't leave Bubby for too long though."

"Twenty minutes. Half hour, tops. I'll turn you around after fifteen minutes." It's a perfect moment. I check to make sure Bubby's not standing in the doorway and start to move in closer, pulling Leah toward me. She sidles into place.

She turns her face up toward mine and says, "So I guess this is not a good time to tell me about your dad—"

My body, which was shifting into high gear, skids to a stop. I have to clear my throat so my voice doesn't crack. "Wow. That came out of nowhere. I thought I was the one with ADD."

"I know. I'm sorry. It's just—we were talking about parents and everything. I was just wondering. I guess he lives far away or something."

Really? That's what she's thinking about now? I'm truly not capable of understanding girls. I shake my head. "No. He lives in Coteau-du-Lac, actually."

"So it's on purpose that you don't see him?" She's starting to sound like Miss Fraser with all her questions.

"I guess."

"Sorry. You obviously don't want to talk about it. I'm being rude!" She smacks herself in the forehead.

I grab her hand. "No! Don't do that. It's okay. It's just... we don't have to talk about it now, do we?" I try to pick up where we left off, and pull her close...

"I'm sorry." Her shoulders slump.

I scream quietly inside. But it seems mean to leave her hanging, and now she feels bad. Again, not the mood I was going for. I kind of do want to tell her about Dad, and I'm sure she'd be okay with it. "It's kind of a long story..."

"You don't have to—"

"My dad's gay. He had an affair with a guy. So my parents split."

"Oh, Declan!"

I shake my head and cover my face with my hands.

"You found out he was gay and that he was having an affair at the same time?"

All I can do is nod.

"Wow!" She pauses for a second and shakes her head. "So that's why you were so interested when Bubby talked about her choir director."

She did notice. "It was kind of an eye-opener for me," I say.

"How old were you when all this happened?"

"Ten. Right at the beginning of fifth grade. It was a back-to-school present."

"I can't imagine. Poor little guy." She jars me out of my thoughts.

"Who?"

"You, stupid. And your mom. It must have been awful for her."

"Yeah, a lot of things changed. It's been this big family secret for years. But—"

"Oh my god. So *that's* why you don't see your dad? Not because he left, but because he's gay?"

I cringe. "No! Well, yeah. But maybe not really. It's complicated."

"What do you mean?"

And then I tell her that when I was little, I didn't know how to feel. All I knew was my family had blown apart and it was because of him. I didn't really even know what *gay* meant. I tell her how fucked-up my family has been for the last five years. I say the words *vanished* and *banished*, and she actually gets what I mean. As I'm talking, I realize I'm angry about being treated like I was too young to have anything to say about it. I tell her we were collateral damage—me and Seamus and Kate—and it makes me feel sad about Seamus. I even tell her about seeing Dad at Kate's and how it was like seeing myself because he looks like me. And about him showing up at the police station, and his truck, and all-day breakfast in Pincourt. What is it about her that makes me forget I'm talking? She should be a guidance counselor.

"That's so cool," she says. "That he's back in your life again."

"Yeah. I guess." Why does everybody keep saying it's cool?

"And you're not too keen on that."

"Wasn't. Now?" I shrug. "After seeing him, it's different."

The truth is, I'm not nervous anymore about who my dad is. When he brought me home from lunch the other day, I could tell he felt really bad that I was upset. It didn't bug me that he was gay. It bugged me that that he seemed like this normal guy, and I missed him. I had missed him for years.

"You liked Bubby's story about the choir guy and the pink triangle, right?"

Is she going to make me talk to Bubby now? "Sure."

"She used to have a little book called something about the pink triangle. Maybe you'd like to borrow it."

She's not asking if I'd like to borrow it; she's saying I should. What if Dad had lived in Nazi Germany? My face goes all prickly, like when the teacher is handing back tests and you don't know what your grade is going to be. I shake it off. "Okay."

She's surprised. "Really?"

"Yeah. I think it's something I should know about. You know, homophobia."

"Great."

She takes me by the hand and leads me to the kitchen, where Bubby is pouring herself more tea. Leah asks her about the book.

"Oh, yes. You want it for something?"

"Declan might be able to use it for a project."

Bubby looks at me, and I nod because I'm supposed to.

"I'll get it. I know exactly where it is." Bubby's shuffle is more animated as she leaves the room.

Leah takes my hand again. I'm feeling a bit nervous about this book. I muster the courage to meet her eyes. My face is tingly and warm. For a moment it's just me and Leah holding hands. I feel like I should say something, thank her maybe, but I can't get my words out. Instead, I swing our arms back and forth.

We hear Bubby's slippers again. Leah squeezes my hand. I grab her pinkie, then let go. She smiles at me over her shoulder as she turns to her grandmother.

"Here you go, dear." In Bubby's outstretched hand there's a small black paperback with a pink triangle on the cover. In the triangle there's a man's face. Leah nudges me to take the book.

Before she lets go, Bubby's eyes peer out from under gray eyebrows until they find mine. Her wrinkled face is kind. "Now this is not an easy read, Declan. But it's important. Your generation should understand how destructive fear and misunderstanding can be. I lived through or saw much of what you'll read in here, and I want you to know you can come talk to me anytime."

She doesn't know that I have a personal connection to the book. But for a moment I'm speechless. I understand something now I didn't get before. It's all about fear. It's like

Bubby sees the mixed-up feelings inside of me, and sees my family caught up in that same anger and hate and fear. I've never been less proud of my family—and myself—than I am right now.

I glance at Leah. She has a little smile on her face. A week ago I'd have called it *smug*, but I think *knowing* is a better word.

I reach for the book. "Thank you, Mrs. Zimmerman. I will."

The Men with the Pink Triangle is cool in my hand. It smells old. The pages are golden and soft, and curled where a corner of the cover is missing. The musty smell stays in my head after I slide the book into my bag.

* * *

Maybe walking home together wasn't such a good idea after all. My hands are sweating. We're finally alone. I'm afraid if I open my mouth something stupid will come out.

"So tell me about your job." I want to kiss her for starting the conversation. She's so pretty with her curls sticking out of her hat. I want to kiss her anyway.

"I work at the canteen." I check up the street for the blue Taurus.

"Oh. You make French fries and stuff."

"Yup."

"Cool. My friends and I go skating there. Maybe we'll come sometime when you're working. The best thing is French fries after skating."

"The best thing is French fries after anything."

She smiles at me. Our arms bump together as we walk, and I can smell her perfume in the fresh air. I inhale and hold it in, but because I'm nervous, it makes me dizzy. I exhale. "Do you have a job?"

"Well, tutoring, but my parents don't want me to get a job yet. I need a lot of time for schoolwork and dancing."

It occurs to me that she's graduating and will probably be going to CEGEP, a pre-university program, in the fall. Immediately I feel sad and wish we lived somewhere in the rest of Canada, where high school goes to twelfth grade. But I ask anyway. "What're you going to do next year?"

"I applied to the science program at John Abbott. When I'm done CEGEP, I'll go to university. But I'm not sure what I'll major in yet. I like sciences, but I also really love history. Maybe forensic anthropology."

"You mean like on *CSI*?" That's the only place I've ever heard the word *forensic* before.

"Well, kind of like what my dad does. He studies dead people's stuff to learn about how they lived." Then in a scary voice she says, "I want to dig up dead people's bones to see how they died!"

"Wow. You're so, so interesting." *Way to go, Romeo.*

She looks sideways at me and smiles. "Thanks, I think."

We walk for a minute without talking. I try to sift through the usual crap that floats through my mind for something intelligent to say. I find nothing.

"Bubby likes you."

"Huh?"

"Bubby likes you. I told her about the dance."

"You told her?" I try to catch her eye.

She won't look at me. She's staring at the ground. "Yes."

"And she likes me?"

She doesn't get that I'm surprised by that. "Yes, really!"

I hold her arm so she stops, then step in front of her and lean down. "What about you?"

Her face is less than a foot from mine. I can feel the warmth of her breath in the air between us. She smiles nervously, and her eyes flit away. "Why do you think I told her?"

"Oh." Heat creeps from the top of my cheeks to my ears. I get what they mean about knees turning to jelly.

"And, well, also I was upset. I thought you were an asshole because of—"

"Because of Theresa."

She nods.

She actually felt bad? Because of me? "Trust me, the only woman I've been thinking about since the dance…"

"Yeah?"

"…is Little Miss Perfect and how she can move her body!" I pretend to be sexy by imitating her and her friends at the variety-show rehearsal.

She starts hitting me with her mittens.

"Hey!" I hold both of her arms down at her sides, and she gives me a dirty look. She doesn't like being trapped. She squirms for a few seconds but gives up because I'm way stronger than her. I leave my hands on her arms.

"I'm not kidding. You are sexy."

She rolls her eyes.

"Yes, really. But the best part was when…" I pull her close and hold her just like when we were dancing. Close, so our bodies are touching all the way down.

She reaches up and puts her arms around my neck, like it's the most natural thing in the world. I bend to meet her upturned face and kiss her, right on her beautiful lips. They're so soft, and warm, and *real*. I'm kissing Little Miss Perfect, *and she's kissing me back!*

She pulls away. "Wait."

Aw, shit. What now?

"Is this still going to be real tomorrow?" Her forehead is creased, like she's concerned.

"Do you want it to be?"

"Yes. I do."

"Me too."

She smiles at me, and we kiss again, longer this time. A waterfall rushes through me. All of a sudden her eyes spring open. "Bubby! I have to go back."

"I know. It's okay. It's only been about fifteen minutes. Just one more."

I kiss her one last time, hard, like I'm making an imprint of it. Then she turns around, adjusts her hat and heads back in the direction we came from. She flicks her wrist and one red mitten waves at me from behind.

I watch her. Even in her winter coat, I can see the smooth swing of her hips. I shake my head—she actually got me to dance hip-hop with her! I watch till her perfect little body disappears into the gray dusk.

I take out a cigarette and light it, then throw it on the ground.

I'm too excited, nervous. My heart is racing and my legs are jumpy.

I start running home. This time, when I pass the stop sign near Kate's, I jump up and smack it with my open hand. It resonates behind me like a chime.

TWENTY-FIVE

I enjoy the walk home, thinking about Leah. On the last stretch of the 138, I see the blue car just beyond my driveway. After watching for it for days, there it is, idling on the shoulder about forty-five meters in front of me. Exhaust puffs out the tail pipe. It jerks me back down to earth.

The road is empty and quiet. It's dusk. Everything is wrapped in gray. Dark shadows are beginning to color in the spaces between the trees beside the road. Branches creak in the wind. As I get closer, I hear the rumble of the car's engine.

There are two heads in the front seat. One checks the rearview mirror every couple of seconds. If I wanted to turn around and get away, I couldn't. He's already seen me, and he opens the passenger door. A cigarette hits the frosted pavement first. He gets out of the car and grinds the cigarette into the road even though there's no reason to. It's a habit. The right thing to do.

Seamus steps out of the car, zips up his jacket and rams his hands in his pockets. Then he starts walking to meet me.

I can hardly look at him.

He looks like shit.

I'm nervous way down in the pit of my stomach, the way it feels when you pass an accident on the highway. Revolted, scared, but you have to look.

As we get closer to each other, two intense blue eyes search for mine. I turn my head away.

I stop at the driveway and wait for him to reach me. Except for his eyes, I would hardly have recognized him. He's thin and seems so much smaller. His face is gray except for the watery blue spots of his eyes. His hair is greasy. He pushes it to the side in order to see.

I notice he's trembling. Is he sick? Or is it drugs? Or alcohol? Where has he been?

We stand facing each other for a few seconds before he speaks. His voice comes out in a rasp. "Hey."

"You ambushed me?"

"Yeah. Sorry. I didn't think you'd come if I called."

"No kidding. What makes you think I'm gonna stay now?" If I left, would he follow me?

"I have to keep moving. I can't stay, especially here. The cops—"

"I know. Me and the cops, we're pretty tight. Had a sleepover there last week."

He's quiet and looks like he's trying to decide what to say. "Yeah, sorry about that."

He knows! "Sure you are. I'm sure you're just full of fuckin' gratitude. That's what brothers are for, right? Well, I'm happy I could help by getting arrested for you. Fuck!"

He narrows his eyes at me, but not in a mean way. More like he's trying to figure something out. "Look, little bro. I'm desperate. Otherwise I wouldn't be here."

"Did you just call me *little bro*? You have a lot of nerve, Seamus, showing up here." I back off, shaking my head. "What do you want?"

He sighs. A jittery hand covers his eyes, then slides over his nose and mouth, past his chin, and rests on his neck like he has himself in a choke hold. He's struggling to stand up, swaying, unsteady, but I don't think he's drunk. It's something else. It's cold in the wind, but there's sweat on his forehead.

Seamus turns and coughs, and I can hear rumbling deep in his chest. He turns and spits gray phlegm onto the frost-covered pavement.

"You're sick."

He nods. "Pneumonia."

"Have you been fucking sleeping in that car?"

"I need antibiotics. I went to the clinic—" He breaks into a coughing fit. It sounds like he's coughing up rocks. He spits again. Phlegm and blood spew into the road and land with a wet splat.

What am I supposed to do? Watch him cough his guts out, turn around and just head up the driveway? Say hi to Mom when I walk in the door? *Hey, Ma, just saw Seamus. He looks great! Says hi.* She'd die if she saw him like this.

I'm shaking inside.

Shouldn't I call the cops? Sergeant Lefebvre's business card is still in my pocket. I feel it there, cool against the palm of my hand.

Is that what brothers are for?

My brother is standing on the side of the highway, looking like death, with his hands in his pockets, waiting for me to make a decision. I'm sure if I say no he'll just turn around and walk away.

"How much?"

He exhales loudly and tells me sixty bucks, and I give him three twenties from the pocket of my jeans. He's lucky I have the cash on me. Normally it would be in the bank. "If I had my wallet..." I start to say, but what difference would it make? Seamus will have to battle it all out with the cops when they catch up to him anyway.

"Thanks, man." He takes the money from my hand, but he doesn't look at me. He can't. He looks down at his feet and turns one ankle over in the snow, something Mandy would do. I can't watch.

"Where you gonna go?"

He raises his head again, slowly, as if it's really heavy. He levels a half smile at me, bores into me with those blue eyes. "I don't know." It sounds like a warning, but there's something else. He's protecting himself, but he's also trying to protect me. It's better if I don't know. It's better if I can be honest if someone asks.

He leaves me standing on the side of the road and heads back toward the blue car, away from home. He tries to run, and I can feel his anxiety about getting to the car fast, but every few steps he stumbles. It reminds me of Dad calling him a crab. It's pathetic, and I have to turn away. He stops and leans on the trunk to catch his breath. Before he opens the passenger door he raises his arm, so I can see the three twenties flutter in his fist.

I want to call out to him, *Stop!* He should be coming back to the house, where it's warm. To Mom. She'd take care of him. I swallow hard, once, twice, three times.

The Taurus makes a U-turn before it glides by me on its way to the highway. The mags spin slowly at first, so I can see each spoke, then faster as the car accelerates, until each wheel is a blur that seems to rotate in the wrong direction. It's almost dark. I keep my eye on the taillights until the car reaches the exit, then turn up the driveway to the house.

I know I'm going to pretend this never happened.

TWENTY-SIX

It's Thursday. History test. And for a change I don't feel like this is a complete waste of time. I actually know I'm getting some of the answers right. I can hardly believe it. Mrs. Sparks is walking around the room in case we have questions. She's stopped at my desk and nodded a couple of times. She doesn't treat me like a do-nothing anymore now that I have a tutor.

I imagine doing well on the test. How great would that be? Sure, it'd be nice not to be at the bottom of the pile for once. But I'm not going to lie: I'd love to impress Leah. Last night on the phone she said she'd meet me after class to see how it went. Can't think about her right now though.

I'm on the last question: *What was one economic effect of the French government in Paris always controlling the economic decisions of the North American colonies?*

I know this!

Just as I'm about to start writing my answer, the receptionist's voice crashes through the intercom. "MRS. SPARKS." We all jump, including Mrs. Sparks.

"Yes?"

"CAN YOU PLEASE SEND DECLAN O'REILLY TO THE MAIN OFFICE?"

She glances at me and my test paper. "He's finishing the last question on a test. Can he come at the end of class?"

I glance at the clock. Less than fifteen minutes to go.

"AS SOON AS POSSIBLE, PLEASE. THANK YOU."

The whole class bursts into catcalls.

"Quiet, please! Thirteen more minutes and I'm taking your papers in!"

I'm stunned. I want to get this last question. But now I'm wondering why they called me. Am I in trouble for something? Things have been so much better lately with me and the VP. I look at Mrs. Sparks. She nods and points at my paper. Finish up!

Head down, I write everything I can remember about France's economic control of the colonies in Old Quebec. I should read my answers over, but I can't make myself sit still any longer. I decide to take a chance and hand my test in like it is. That I finished it at all is a miracle.

I grab my stuff off the desk and hand my test to Mrs. Sparks. As she takes it from me she whispers, "Good work, Declan." Well, that's a first.

"Thanks, Miss."

I open and close the door as quietly as I can, but once I'm in the hall I speed-walk. I want to get whatever this is about over with before the bell rings. In five minutes I'm supposed to meet Leah.

When I reach the main office the receptionist is expecting me. "Oh, hi, Declan. Ms. Fraser and Mr. Peters are waiting for you in her office. Just go ahead."

That's weird.

I spin around to head back down the hall and take the steps up to the guidance office two at a time. The door is open. Mr. Peters is sitting in the *prick* chair. Miss Fraser's leaning on the edge of her desk.

"Come in, Declan." She motions to the other chair and closes the door. "Have a seat." It's not an invitation. Without taking my eyes off her, I sit, half-assed, my binder on my lap.

"Declan?"

I whip my head around to face Mr. Peters. "Yes."

"Declan, there's been an accident." My stomach drops. "Your brother is in the hospital. Your parents want you to meet them there."

"My *parents*? What? Right now? Is he okay?"

"Well, you're dad said it's pretty serious. I don't think Seamus"—he hesitates—"is conscious."

They give me a second to digest what he's saying. My parents? Both of them? The hospital? I feel like a million tiny fish are swimming around in my body. I can hear my blood in my ears. I just look at Miss Fraser.

My mind is blank. My face is going all prickly. Everything in the room seems fuzzy and far away. I rub my hand on my jeans.

"You okay, Declan?" she says.

"I dunno. Should I be scared?"

"We're not sure. Your dad was pretty upset. He wants you to come now."

I still can't believe she's saying *your dad*. This doesn't seem real.

Mr. Peters stands up and takes a step toward the door. "I'll go with you to your locker to get your things. Then I'm going to drive you to the hospital. I'm sure you won't be back today." He motions for me to lead the way.

I stand up to go with him. "Bye, Miss."

"Bye, Declan. Take care. Please call if you can." Tears well up in her eyes. It freaks me out.

As we're walking to my locker, I remember Seamus and Robbie in the Taurus, driving around drunk. It seemed different then. All I could think of was how angry he made me. I never believed anything bad would really happen. Now it feels like I'm carrying a load of bricks while I walk. I just pray he's okay.

We pass an open classroom door. The art room. A few kids see me walking by with the VP. They call out, "Oooh, someone's in trouble." Walking down the hall with Mr. Peters usually means you're about to get your locker searched. Enough to strike fear in the heart of the toughest stoner. I wish I was in trouble. Anything but this.

"Sir, do you think he's going to be okay?

"I don't know, son. But your brother is at the hospital now, the best place he could be. They'll do whatever they can to help him."

Help him. Help. That's what he needed all along. I shake my head to concentrate on getting my locker open. I'm so nervous I can't remember my combination. I can't see the numbers clearly through my trembling hands. Squeeze my eyes shut. Try again: 56-spin-34-spin-44. Finally, the lock drops open. I put my history binder on the top shelf of my locker and grab my jacket and schoolbag.

Mr. Peters looks at me. "Got everything?"

I nod while I shove my arms into the sleeves of my jacket. He closes my locker door and clicks the lock shut. I swing my schoolbag onto my shoulder, and we leave through the door to the staff parking lot. I glance at my Dumpster.

The automatic door opener chirps, and we get into Mr. Peters's car. On the way to the hospital we pass three ninth-graders, obviously skipping second period. Mr. Peters shakes his head and takes out his cell phone. Then he changes his mind and puts it back in his pocket.

The hospital is in a town called Valleyfield. It's pretty far away. Normally it takes about thirty minutes to get there. Mr. Peters makes it in just under twenty-five.

I reach for the door handle. "Thank you, sir."

"No problem. Do you want me to come in with you? Will you be okay?"

"Yeah. I'll just ask at information for his room number."

"Oh! Hold on. I have it. Your dad gave it to me." With his seat belt still on, he pulls up his jacket and fishes a note out of his pants pocket. "I-201."

"Thanks, sir."

"Okay, Declan, let us know if you need anything."

"Okay, sir. I will."

I close the car door and turn toward the hospital entrance. I-201. I'm pretty sure the *I* is for Intensive Care.

* * *

"All right. Just come with me." I don't want to talk to the nurse as we're walking, so I follow a step behind.

She stands outside I-201 and motions for me to go ahead.

The curtain is pulled around the bed. When I pull it aside, Kate and Dad are on one side of the hospital bed, and Mom is on the other. Ryan's sitting in a chair a meter or so away.

I can't even see Seamus, there's so much medical equipment. Mom makes room for me, and now I can see Seamus better. I start to shake. Mom reaches for my hand and guides me beside her to the bedside.

This can't be my brother.

There are two different tubes coming out of his mouth and one out of his nose. His arms are covered by the bedsheet up to his elbows, but above the sheet his right arm is bruised and speckled with blood. His left leg is in traction. There's a bandage around his head. Both legs are in casts. The toes of his right foot, sticking out of the cast, are blue. There's tape around both arms holding intravenous tubes in place.

More tubes snake out from under the covers, attached to different places: the bed frame, the intravenous pole, machines. His forehead is wrapped in gauze, a bandage covers the left side of his head and his ear, and there's tape over his nose.

Both eyes are black and closed. His chest moves up and down. A respirator sucks and blows and clicks. I follow his heartbeat. Green line on a monitor. *Beep. Beep.*

Suddenly I feel the contents of my stomach rushing up to my throat. The room is fading to white. I think some words come out of my mouth, but I don't know what they are. I turn and rush for the door.

The hallway is cool. I breathe—in and out, in and out. I'm so dizzy. Ryan's right behind me; he puts his hand on my back and pushes my head down, tells me to bend over till the woozy feeling stops. He guides me to a chair across the hall. I lean forward and hang my head between my knees.

"Just breathe, buddy. It's awful, I know."

Head still down, my voice squeaks, "How long...?" I can't get any more out.

"The ambulance brought him in early this morning. He went straight into surgery before your mom or dad got here."

All morning, while I was brushing my teeth, on the bus, writing my test...

"The police took a while figuring out who he was. He had no ID on him. They found your health card in the car and contacted Mom. At first they thought it was you."

I sit up with my eyes closed and shake my head. He had *my* ID.

"What happened?" I ask.

"Well, about 4:00 AM the police tried to pull them over for speeding—"

"Them? Who?"

"Roberto something or other. I don't remember his name."

Robbie.

"He's down the hall. Not as bad. He had his seat belt on."

No seat belt? *You're kidding.*

"They arrested him for DUI. And he was driving with a learner's permit."

"What about Seamus?" I'm starting to breathe more normally again. "How is he?"

"Well, they say it's too early to tell exactly. He lost a lot of blood. There's head trauma. He's in an induced coma. Do you know what that means?"

"Yeah. It's because there's swelling?" I tap my head.

"Right. He has multiple fractures. Let's see if I can remember: right wrist, right leg below the knee, left leg pretty mashed up, cracked pelvis, broken ribs, punctured lung." I can tell he's repeating what a doctor said.

"Is he breathing?"

"Not on his own right now. Actually, there's also fluid in his lungs, like he had pneumonia before the accident. He's getting antibiotics through an IV."

When Ryan tells me about the pneumonia, I nod. Seamus is in bad shape.

"He's gonna live, right?"

"I hope so. It's too soon to tell."

No seat belt. Brain trauma. Even if he does live, what then?

"What kind of accident?"

"They tried to outrun the cops. Lost control of the car and rolled it. The car had no airbags. They ended up in the ditch."

"Ford Taurus. With mags."

"Huh?" Ryan looks puzzled.

"They showed up at the rink a couple of weeks ago. They were drinking." My head drops onto my chest. I wish I'd called someone then. Ryan shakes his head.

"Where did it happen?" I ask.

"On the 342 heading for the Ontario border. Right before the campground."

The 342 is an old highway that runs parallel to the Trans-Canada. We used to take it from Rigaud to go camping in Ontario just across the border. Were they staying at the campground? Sleeping in the car, pulled into some campsite way off the road? It would have been a good place to hide from the cops.

I breathe in and hold it for a couple of seconds. Exhale. "I think I'd like to go in now."

I enter the room ahead of Ryan. Mom meets us and puts her arms around me. She's been crying and has crumpled Kleenex clutched in her hand. We hold on to each other for a while, then move to the bed. Dad reaches out his hand for mine. I take it. Kate is stroking Seamus's shoulder. As soon as our eyes meet, she starts to cry. I reach over Seamus with my other hand. There's a big lump in my throat. My sister. My brother.

The only part of Seamus that really looks like him are the freckles on his cheeks. His red hair is stuck together with dried blood. The blond hair on his chest is stained with orange antiseptic. I see now, above the bedsheet, that his ribs are bandaged—he's wrapped around the middle like a mummy.

Everyone's here. It's like it's always been this way, like five years didn't go by while we were in hell. Nothing is the same inside me. I know I felt angry and hurt and alone. A few days ago, I felt hate and disgust. Now? Now, all I can think about is how close I was, maybe still am, to losing my big brother. I'm glad we're all here.

We stand and sit, hug each other, talk quietly about the weather, the Canadiens, Seamus when he was younger. Most of the time, there aren't any words for what we want to say.

As the day goes by, we watch. Watch Seamus's chest rise and fall. Watch the lines on his monitor make colorful zigzaggy patterns. Nurses and doctors come in and out, change things, record things, add things, take things away. We watch each other.

I lean over to Ryan. "I need to pee. I'm going to find a bathroom." We've been sitting together by the bed. I give a little wave to Mom and Dad and leave the room.

There are people in the hall. Nurses going about their business, other families, a food cart that smells like fake mashed potatoes and gravy. I push open the doors between the ICU and the rest of the hospital and start to scan for a bathroom.

Farther down the hall I spot a familiar figure. It takes a second for me to realize it's Leah. What the heck is she doing here? She's talking with a woman and a doctor in a white coat. The doctor puts the stethoscope she's been holding in her pocket and leaves. The woman enters the hospital room nearest to them, and Leah starts walking slowly in the same direction I'm going. She's texting.

I can't yell, so I try to get her to look back by hissing. "Pssst, pssst!"

She stops. She heard me. She's looking around.

"Pssst, pssst. Leah! Here!"

She turns around and puts the phone in the pocket of her jeans.

"Declan! What're you doing here?"

"I could ask you the same question. What is it with bumping into you in hallways?"

She looks down. Not even a small smile at my weak joke.

"Sorry. Is everything okay?"

"Bubby had another stroke. She's probably not going to make it this time." Her chin starts to tremble, and her eyes well up with tears. I put my arms around her and rub her back. She lets me hold her for a moment, and then we separate, and she blows her nose. "They're dissolving the clot, but there may be too much damage already. We're just waiting."

"Oh my god, Leah. I'm so sorry. How long have you been here?"

"Since about four thirty this morning. Mom heard something in the middle of the night and found her on the bathroom floor."

She shakes her head. I take her hand. Then she looks at me. "Why are you here?"

I feel like what I have to tell her isn't real. "My brother was in an accident. They called me out of my history test. Mr. Peters drove me."

"Oh, Declan! That was your brother? We were in Emergency when the ambulances came in. The police were there and everything. It looked bad. How...?"

I shrug. I don't know where to start. "He's alive. He and that friend were trying to outrun the police. They rolled the car. He's in pretty bad shape. We don't know yet."

"Oh, Declan!" She's still holding my hand. "What a horrible day."

"I know. I can't really feel anything. Kind of frozen."

She leans over and puts her other hand on my arm. "I can't believe this. I keep hoping I'll wake up and find out it's not real." Her voice is barely a whisper at the end, and her face melts into crying. She shakes her head. I put my arms around her, and we stand like that in the hallway for a minute. Little silent sobs echo in my body. She rubs my back with one hand, and I know she's about to pull away. "I have to go. I'll be in here." She points to the room her bubby is in.

"Okay."

She squeezes my hand.

"I hope Bubby's going to be all right," I say, but it feels useless to say it.

She nods and waves goodbye.

When I get back to the room, Mom and Kate are gone. Ryan's reading a magazine. Dad is standing next to Seamus. I stop at the foot of the bed. Stick my hands in my pockets. And look.

This mangled person is my brother. My big brother. I think about fishing for radio stations, about playing pitch and catch. He took me once, when I was about twelve, to play pool with his friends. It made me feel so special that he included me. Will we ever do things together again? I thought he was gone before. I was wrong.

I look up at Dad and run my hand through my hair and down the back of my head. He motions for me to come to him. As I walk toward him, tears burn my eyes. I can't stop them. Eventually my eyelashes fail, and the tears run down my face. Dad reaches with one arm and pulls me to him. With his other hand he holds my head against his shoulder. It feels hot inside my body where my heart is. I want my dad. I want Seamus. I want everything to be okay, like it used to be.

Kate and Mom come back into the room. I wipe my face on my sleeve, and Dad and I turn back to Seamus, his arm still around my shoulders. Kate puts her purse on the floor beside Ryan's chair. I hear them talking about Mandy.

I hope Mandy never has to see this.

Finally, about 8 PM, the nurse comes in and tells us we can keep a vigil— take turns staying with Seamus through the night. But from now on, there can only be one or two of us in the room at a time. There's a bed by the window and a family room down the hall with big leather sofas and blankets and pillows. She kicks us all out of the room and says to come back in an hour.

My parents and Kate and Ryan want to go to the cafeteria for coffee. Before they leave, we decide that Mom will take the first shift with Seamus, Dad the second, Kate the third, and then I'm on till morning. Ryan will pick up Mandy from daycare and spend the night at home with her. I feel weird leaving Seamus alone in the room, so I go back to his bed, but I don't know what to do. I put my hand on his shoulder. The nurse starts replacing bags of fluid, emptying the catheter, recording information on his chart, and I pull myself away.

TWENTY-SEVEN

The patient TV room is dark except for the bluish light coming from the screen. The sound is off as I click through the channels. Leah's sleeping on me, my arm around her shoulders, her head on my chest. I feel her ribs against mine as she breathes. We decided to come here to be alone instead of staying in the family room with Dad and Kate while Mom's with Seamus. Her parents are with Bubby.

Leah looks up at me with half-open eyes, and I kiss the top of her head.

"What time is it?"

I click to the weather channel and translate 23:23:07 in my head. "Eleven twenty-three. It's minus six outside."

She rolls her eyes. She asked me for the time, not the weather.

"Anything?" she asks.

"Nope. No one's been here."

We're both scared someone will come, because it'll most likely mean bad news for one of us.

I put the clicker on the table beside the sofa and put both arms around her. Our legs are resting on a wooden coffee table. She stretches out and drapes her leg over mine. I lay my cheek against her head, her soft, curly hair. She smells so good. I close my eyes and lose myself in feeling her body next to mine. Drift off to sleep.

I'm awakened by someone in the room. I sit up. Leah wakes up too, and we both turn toward the door. The fluorescent lights flick on above us, forcing us to squint and shade our eyes.

"Are you awake, Leah?" It's a woman I've never seen before, but I know immediately that it's Leah's mom. She has exactly the same curly brown hair.

My eyes aren't accustomed to the harsh white light. The TV's still tuned to the weather channel. We've been asleep for two hours. Leah focuses on her mom.

"Honey, she's gone."

Leah scrambles off the sofa and runs to her. "No!" They put their arms around each other and cry quietly. After a few moments Leah's mom lifts her eyes toward me, and Leah says, "Mom, this is Declan." I'm still standing by the sofa with my hands in my pockets.

"I'm so sorry," I say. I remember the conversation Leah and I had about meeting each other's parents. "I'm glad to finally meet you. I—I wish it wasn't like this."

Leah and her mom look at each other and shake their heads, like they know something I don't. I raise my eyebrows, wondering if I said something wrong, and Leah explains, "It's what Jews say at funerals, when they see each other because someone dies. *I wish we were meeting under better circumstances.* It's not wrong, it's right."

Leah's mom says, "Thank you, Declan. I wish it was a better time too." She smiles weakly, then puts her arm around Leah's shoulders, and they turn to leave the room.

"Leah—"

She turns back to face me.

"I'm sorry. I'll miss her too."

Leah nods, and they walk out the door. I watch them turn the corner to Bubby's ward, their arms around each other.

I turn off the fluorescent lights and return to the sofa. The weather channel still says −6. I lean back with my feet on the table. The screen blurs as I stare at it through tears.

TWENTY-EIGHT

Before I go into Seamus's room for my shift, I lean on the wide metal doorframe. The curtain is pulled around Seamus's bed. The rest of the room is dark. It reminds me of camping when we were little, with the lantern on inside the tent. Across the room, under the window, there's a padded bench you can sleep on.

I push back the curtain. A fluorescent light glows above the headboard. I fold my jacket and hang it over the back of a chair. "Hey." I'm alone with him for the first time.

Seamus's chest rises and falls to the steady whoosh and click of the respirator. I watch the accordion-like balloon go up and down in its chamber. Everything is exactly the same as it was before we left him except his arms are outside the covers, and I can see the cast on his wrist. I check my pocket to see if I still have that pencil stub. Maybe I'll write something on the cast later. On the other side of the bed, his left hand is connected to the heart-rate monitor with a clip that looks like one of Mom's clothespins.

I jam my hands in my pockets, take a step toward the bed. "How's it goin'?"

The beeping monitors mock me.

"Hey, shithead." I feel bad for a second, like maybe it's disrespectful to call him shithead.

I edge closer and smooth wrinkles out of the sheet with my fingertips. What would he think if he knew Mom and Dad had been here all day? Mom *and* Dad? And Kate and Ryan. And me. Me, here, keeping vigil. Me, taking care of him.

There's a green hospital jug full of water on the bedside table. Who's it there for? He certainly can't drink it. I pour some in a little plastic cup. "Fuck, Seamus. This really sucks." It's strange to stand beside him and not be nervous about what he's going to do. It would be just like him to sit up and roar at me right now, bandages and tubes and everything. Just fuckin' scare the shit outta me and laugh like it's the biggest joke ever. I'm used to him being my personal terrorist. Not this.

I take a drink of the water. It's lukewarm and tastes like bleach. This stuff could send you to the hospital.

It freaks me out how still he is. "This is fucking creepy, Seamus." I let my eyes wander over all the machines and poles and other crap around his bed. There's barely one part of him that's not hooked up to something or wired or bandaged. "Does it hurt?" It sure looks like it hurts. "Fuck, Seamus, just fuck!"

I stare at his sleeping face. His blond eyelashes are resting on his cheeks. I know underneath are Dad's blue eyes. *He has pneumonia,* Ryan said. I wonder if Seamus got the antibiotics he needed. I can't believe it was only two days ago. I'm glad I gave him the money. It was the right thing to do for my brother.

"It's been an interesting week. All in all, the highlight was you...was this." I toast him with my plastic glass. "You really know how to steal the show." I drink some more horrible water. As I watch him, everything that's happened—the police, Dad, Leah, Bubby—seems far away, almost like a dream, only this is the part I want to wake up from.

I don't want to watch him anymore. I push the curtain to the side on its track and walk over to the window, look out at the dark. A few lights wink back at me, and of course there's a Tim Horton's. Why is there always a Tim's?

I start thinking about Dad and some of the things he said, about starting from scratch—rebooting—and wanting to be part of our lives again, trying to create some sort of family. I'm getting used to the idea of him, of having *our dad* around. "We did always have one, you know," I say over my shoulder to Seamus. "Sorry. I was talking about Dad."

I shake my head and return to the side of the bed. "You probably don't want to hear this, but he's cool, Seamus. He's just a guy. You should see his truck. You'd love his truck." I start to feel good telling him about this, so I keep going. "Eight cylinders...four-wheel-drive...a fucking monster! He keeps the radio on CHOM, and the names of the songs scroll by in the little window…" I draw the outline of the truck with my hands and get so excited showing him how big and beautiful it is, I almost spill the glass of water. "Seamus, I want you to see that truck. It's a Chevy Silverado. Not a 1500, not even a 2500—it's a 3500HD! I've been in it twice now. You've got to fuckin' *ride* in that *truck!*"

I'm jacked up from adrenaline, and it's starting to turn to panic inside me. *What if he never sees the truck?* I'm breathing fast, and it feels like a tornado's building in my chest. *What if he fuckin' never sees that truck?*

We finally have a chance to reboot, or whatever, and he might have ruined it because he and that *moron* thought they were in a scene from *The Fast and the Furious*. Oh God, he might die! "What the *hell* were you thinking? I mean, how are we going to be a family if you—" I lunge at him, look him right in the face, words exploding out of me. "What the hell didya go and do that for? Can you hear me, Seamus? What the hell did you do that for? YOU STUPID FUCKING ASSHOLE! FUCK! *FUCK!!*" I pound the metal railing on the side of the bed with my fist. Plastic tubes, Seamus's body, the bed—everything jiggles and creaks and shakes.

The sound of my own voice bounces off the walls and brings me back to reality. *What the hell am I doing?* I straighten up. Seamus is still. I poke my head out to see if anyone heard. But the hall's deserted and dark and quiet except for the trouble lights buzzing near the stairwell. I tiptoe over to Seamus with my finger on my lips. "Shh—"

"HELLO? HELLO? IS EVERYTHING OKAY?" A mechanical voice blares at me through a little blue speaker above the bed, scaring the shit out of me. I freeze.

"HELLO? IS THERE SOMEONE IN MR. O'REILLY'S ROOM?"

"Uh, sorry. It's okay. I had something stuck in my throat." I spy the water jug. "Water—went down the wrong way."

"ALL RIGHT. PLEASE BUZZ IF YOU NEED ANY-THING." She sounds like one of those passive-aggressive salespeople who follow you around the store with a smile, afraid you're going to break something.

"Thank you." I salute the little blue speaker and flop down in the chair. Air escapes from the stuffing with a hiss. Miraculously, I'm still holding the water glass. Whatever water was left in it I've managed to empty all over the room.

I put it back down beside the jug and notice a little plant with purple flowers next to a get-well card. In Mom's hand-writing, it says, *Somthing to briten up your days. We all love you, my dear boy. Get better soon. Love, your family XXXXXX OOOOOO.* I count the spelling mistakes and the kisses and hugs. She always adds kisses and hugs from the people who should have signed the card. Mom, Kate, Ryan, Mandy, me...Dad. Six hugs, six kisses. I turn the card toward Seamus. "See? Not five." If he could, he'd make fun of her spelling.

As angry as I am at him, I really just want him to be okay. For Mom, for Dad, for everyone. *For me.* I know it might take a long time. I don't care about that. "Everybody's rootin' for you, Seamus. Mom and Dad, they love you so much. I don't know what it would do…just…just be okay, Seamus. Fuck! Just be okay."

I lean back in the chair and turn the card over and over in my fingers, listen to the machines, watch him until it freaks me out, because I can't believe it's him.

When I first got here, when we were all in the room, one of the nurses told us that maybe he can hear us. I wonder if it's true. If you ask me, the whole idea of him being *in there*, listening, is creepy. It's weird talking to a guy in a coma. Half the time I'm expecting him to say something, and half the time it's like he's not even here. I wonder if I said anything I shouldn't have. I'm not much of a talker, but I try to think of something else to say.

"So remember that tutor you were bugging me about before? Yeah, well, now I think she might actually be my girlfriend." I check for Seamus's reaction, expecting him to…I don't know, laugh at me. It's the first time I've said the word *girlfriend* out loud, and it makes me feel naked. "She's really cute."

I glance at the door to make sure we're alone, then lean in. "Actually, she's sexy as all hell, and I can't figure out what she's doing with me. Get this—she's an older woman. And smart! And she's with me! Actually, it hasn't been a great day for her either. Her grandmother just died, right down the hall."

Suddenly I feel like a real jerk. Leah went home from the hospital this morning without her bubby, forever.

And Seamus, he's lying in a hospital bed. He may never have a girlfriend, ride in Dad's truck, see Mandy again, have dinner with the family.

I realize how unbelievably stupid it is to wish someone was dead or, worse, act like they're dead when they're not. I admit there were lots of times I wished Seamus would drop off the face of the earth so I could have some peace. We all did it with Dad, pretended he wasn't there.

"Dad's *not* dead, Seamus. And...neither are you. That matters." I don't know why everything had to change so much. All the screaming and fighting. It was crazy for sure—unbearable even. But what's crazier is acting like people are dead, people you're supposed to love, when they live twenty minutes away.

"Don't you miss him?" I look at Seamus. What if he can hear me? What if he's thinking? "I do." I understand the difference now between gone and dead. Maybe that sounds stupid, like everyone knows the difference. "If he really was dead, Seamus, there'd be no more chances.

"And I want another chance, with you, with Dad, with all of us." Why does he have to be just lying there? "We've been setting the table for dinner at home now. There's a place at the table for you."

I take my pencil stub out of the pocket of my jacket, twist my body around to get a better angle and write *I miss you, shithead* on his cast. I put the pencil back in my pocket. Through the window it's gray now, not black. The sun is coming up. Seamus seems peaceful.

I want him back. What if I could get both my dad and my brother back? It'd be like in that Foo Fighters song that was playing is Dad's truck: *Down crooked stairs and sideways glances comes the king of second chances.*

Second chances.

Two fingers on his right hand are all I can find that's not taped or wired or clipped with clothespins or stuck with tubes. I grab them and squeeze as hard as I can. "Please, Seamus, please be okay. You gotta trust me on this. I'll show you. I need you to get better. We all need another chance."

ACKNOWLEDGMENTS

I often wondered why authors made such a fuss about thanking their editors first. Then I worked with Sarah Harvey. Now I know. This is my first novel. There would be no *Subject to Change* without her patience, wisdom, encouragement and love of Dave Grohl.

To my mom, Peggy, thank you for making me love stories and for insisting, when I got discouraged, that you have to be tough to be a writer. To my husband, Peter, and our children, Sarah and Eli, thank you for taking this journey with me and providing essential hugs and words of love along the way. This novel is as much yours as it is mine.

A loving thank-you goes to my friends Lina and Kathy— my writing group—for invaluable critiques and being with me from start to finish. Surrounding yourself with excellent writers makes you a better one.

Thank you to the Quebec Writers' Federation and children's author Raquel Rivera for initiating me into the editing process through the QWF Mentorship Program. Raquel, you are a jewel. I learned so much from you.

In 2010 I took a course at the QWF, where I met my first mentors, Monique Polak and Lori Weber, and started work on *Subject to Change*. The first chapter of this novel appears as the short story "Shift" in *Salut King Kong* (Véhicule Press, 2014), an anthology of short-listed works from the CBC/QWF Quebec Writing Competition.

Thank you also to the Lester B. Pearson School Board for enabling me to take a six-month writing sabbatical. Without organizations like the QWF being supported by grants from the federal and provincial arts councils, and leave options such as sabbaticals, novels would not get written.

I owe a ton of gratitude to the towns of Hudson and Rigaud for providing fertile ground to grow the story. But it is definitely fiction. While some names have remained the same, realities have been changed to indulge fancy and discourage too much direct comparison.

Thank you to my friends and colleagues who allowed me to riff off them as professionals in order to provide rich characterizations of school staff. You know who you are, and I love you.

Thank you to the original Declan for the kernel of inspiration that became *Subject to Change*. Sadly, you will never know who you are.

KAREN NESBITT holds a Master of Education in counseling and a Bachelor of Arts in psychology. She works as a school counselor at the senior campus of Westwood High School and at Horizon High School near Montreal, Quebec, and teaches creative writing at the Thomas More Institute in Montreal. Also the mother of two teenagers, Karen spends most of her days immersed in teen culture and has been writing since she was a teenager herself. She lives with her husband and children in Pierrefonds, Quebec. *Subject to Change* is Karen's debut novel.